"Ste

she demanded, aimii

He smiled again, this time to calm himself.

"You're a couple hours from Aspen. Just follow the river over that last mountain," he said, nodding his head west. "By horse, that is. Perhaps if you call…"

"Is that so? Guess I better commandeer a horse."

"Is that so?" he uttered through clenched teeth. He knew a challenge when he heard one. "How do you think you're going to do that?"

A brief, yet vexing smile crossed her face, as she eyed her revolver. "Guess."

He returned her smug grin with one of his own. "I can't imagine."

Her hands shook. "That's what the gun is for."

Jesse reached to loosen his already open collar. Lord, she was a hell of a spitfire. But no matter how much grit or how inviting her curves looked in what was left of that god-forsaken dress, she wasn't taking his horse.

Keeping her weapon trained on him, she advanced toward Rusty. "Look, mister, I'm sorry, really I am, but it's a matter of life and death."

"Your life and my death?" Sarcasm was never a smart tactic, but the lady's sudden apology was a little hard to swallow.

"You said this was your land."

"It is. So?"

"So, you can walk home. You don't need a horse."

Kudos for Kathryn E. Crawford

ROCKY MOUNTAIN RUNAWAY won the 2016 TARA contest in the historical category, the 2015 Melody of Love contest in the historical category, was a finalist in the 2016 Emily contest, and placed second in the 2015 Hook, Line, and Sinker contest.

Rocky Mountain Runaway

by

Kathryn E. Crawford

Rocky Mountain Runaway

Cover Art by *Debbie Taylor*

The Wild Rose Press, Inc.
PO Box 708
Adams Basin, NY 14410-0708
Visit us at www.thewildrosepress.com

Publishing History
First Cactus Rose Edition, 2018
Print ISBN 978-1-5092-2067-0
Digital ISBN 978-1-5092-2068-7

Published in the United States of America

Dedication

I am eternally grateful to the many friends and family
who have made this dream a reality.
Thank you to my Aunt Ursula, Sandy and Ed,
my siblings, and parents,
my beta readers who read and read and read,
my children,
and of course my husband
without whom this would never have been.

Chapter One

July 4, 1885, Aspen, Colorado

It was the smell, the unforgettable stench of burning horseflesh that turned Jesse Colburn's head. He didn't need to see what was on fire, in his gut he already knew—the barn. His stomach retched. Hungry red flames licked at the twilight sky just beyond the familiar treetops. Wiping sweaty waves of hair from his eyes, he leaned in low and gripped his mustang's worn reins. Without a word, Rusty, his horse and longtime companion, knew what to do, and together they raced down Independence Pass toward home.

"Andy!" Jesse called as he leaped off his horse and ran toward the barn. He grabbed the closest grooming bucket and tossed the brushes aside. Water splashed his boots as he filled the bucket from the trough and hurled it at the blaze. One bucket of water had no effect. He had to get to the horses.

"Where the hell are you?" he yelled.

A muffled cry came from the barn.

"*No.*" Sucking in his breath, he struggled to hear the noise again. Then he heard it, a shout from inside the inferno. Jesse battered the barn door with his boot. He kicked it open, emitting flames so hot he staggered and fell.

Smoke flooded his lungs. He coughed into the

crook of his arm attempting to suppress the invading odor of death. Forcing away rising panic, he shielded his face with his arm and braced himself. Against intense waves of heat, he plunged through the doorway. The crackle of splintering wood roared in his ears. Debris, charred remnants of a lifetime of sweat and hard work, surrounded him.

Violent coughing erupted at his side. "Andy, get out of here!"

"Get the damn horses," the foreman choked out.

"I will." Andy was too old for this. "Get out of here."

Timber sparked above. Jesse dove as part of the loft fell.

"Andy!"

No reply came. Jesse pushed himself to his knees and crawled to where his pa's oldest friend had stood moments before. "Where are you?" Clawing at the dirt, his fingers found a limp lifeless body. Fear clutched his chest. He threw off his hat, twisted a clump of the old man's shirt in his fist, and heaved him over his shoulder.

Jesse staggered, blinded by the flames and searing heat as he fumbled through the smoldering barn. Smoke singed his lungs. With his memory guiding him, he prayed he'd make it to the door. His knee struck something hard. Andy nearly toppled from his shoulder. He kicked at the object blocking his path. He gagged, realizing it was one of his stallions.

Jesse's lungs ached for air. Smoke and death encircled him, taunting him.

"Move!" He screamed helplessly at the dead horse. Pain shot through his arms and legs. His muscles cramped until he found another surge of strength. He regained his footing and stepped around the once-prized animal and through the burning doorframe.

Cool mountain air filled his chest, and he fell to his knees releasing his oldest friend.

"Andy?" he cried, shaking him. "Answer me, damn it." He shook him again and collapsed onto the old man's rigid chest.

"You're too stubborn to die." He begged for a reply. Andy had been running the ranch since Jesse's first pair of boots. He couldn't lose him too.

Suddenly, Andy gasped for breath and started coughing.

"You know I can't run this ranch without you," Jesse said, relieved.

The old man grabbed Jesse's shirt pulling him closer. "Did you get 'em?" The dry and rough sound to his voice was almost a plea. "Did you save the horses?"

Jesse couldn't look at him. Not when the man's lifetime of toil and sweat turned to an ashen grave right before his eyes. Sorrow caught his throat. "They're gone."

"Then you've come to it." He released his grip on Jesse's shirt and dropped his head to the dirt coughing. "Luke Tremain torched that fire."

"Don't talk. You need to drink." Jesse's fists clenched the water bucket's handle. His hands shook as he tried to pour water into the old man's mouth. Andy swatted the bucket away and coughed again.

Jesse squatted next to him. "You could have died." He splashed cool water onto their clothes. "You risked your life to save the stallions."

"To save the ranch." Andy spasmed with a cough.

"I was too late. That son-of-a-bitch stole your pa's blood and sweat right out from under ya."

"I said stop talking." Jesse trudged toward the barn. Yelling at Andy wasn't right, but the man had to save his breath and stop predicting the damn future.

The fire raged and ingested almost everything. He still had his land and cattle. Luke scared most Aspen ranchers into selling their land to the railroad for a pittance. Now, the only thing standing in Luke's way of railroad riches was Jesse's Enchantment Ranch.

After a few minutes he walked back. "I ain't done in."

"Your cattle ain't worth their feed." Andy labored to sit up. "Face it, Son, you can't pony up enough money in time to save your ranch with the crow bait you got left." Jesse hauled him to his feet. "You needed them horses."

Luke Tremain wasn't getting Enchantment Ranch—no one was. Within the past year, Jesse buried both Ma and Pa right here. Losing his ranch would be disgrace enough. Losing his folks' final resting place, at the hands of Luke Tremain? Never. He bit down hard and tasted the metallic mix of blood and sweat on his lips. He wiped it away with the back of his hand. This time it was his blood. Next time it would be Luke's.

Chapter Two

July 14, 1885, Boston, Massachusetts

With an exasperated sigh, Samantha Ward leaned out her second story bedroom window. "What are you doing here, J.W.? You agreed to visit the convent during the day and use the front door like a normal person." Her father never took a shine to being called anything remotely close to "Pa" so she, like everyone else, called him J.W., short for John Ward.

"And get a scolding from the 'Good Sisters'? Don't think so. Come down here."

"No," Samantha said as loudly as she dared. After living with the Sisters of St. Joseph for a few years, the nuns moved her room to the second floor thinking that would deter her father's sporadic and drunken visits. He still came, just yelled louder.

"Got a partin' gift for you," he called.

Samantha shook her head. "Pay off your debts, not me."

"I'm leaving for Aspen tonight."

"Running away again? Who's after you this time?" In her twenty years, she'd been talked into and fooled into so many dishonest endeavors she swore she'd never trust him again. No one did. Which is why on her twelfth birthday, the good citizens of Boston decided she'd be better off in the care of the Sisters.

"Just got a telegram from Aspen. I am getting my hands on some land out there."

"You need money to buy land." Believing him became too painful years ago. "I'm going back to bed."

"Sam!"

He'd never said it, but she knew that raising a daughter scared the hell out him. It was no coincidence that just when she started looking more like a girl than a boy, he shortened her name.

"If you don't come down here for your present, I'm going to climb up there."

"Sure," she scoffed. It was just another attempt to get money from her.

"Listen to me," he insisted.

"Sh!" she hissed, lowering the window.

"I'm off now. I'll send you a telegram when I get there. If anything happens to me, look up Luke Tremain."

"Luke Tremain?" She shoved the window open. "You said he was a no good son of a mudsill. You trust him?"

"Hell no, but he's gettin' me a deal on a ranch."

"A deal?" Sam yelled dangerously loud. "Are you swindling some rancher, J.W.?"

Muffled footsteps sounded in the hall. The glimmer of candlelight cast its sliver of a shadow on the floor below her bedroom door. It was probably just Sister Mary Ellen sneaking a snack again, but getting caught talking to J.W. could mean eviction or worse—disappointing the Sisters. She couldn't take that chance, so she quietly closed the window and dove into bed.

"You'll come when I'm settled. I'm going to make things right. You'll see."

6

"Ugh," she groaned, still able to hear him. He liked to remind her that she was a cowboy's daughter and belonged in the West. He would have been the father she deserved, he'd say, if they just lived in Aspen. But after all that had happened over the years, she wasn't sure where she, or he, belonged.

"The gift—it's what you always wanted."

Her heart pounded. Someone was going to hear him.

"Don't you worry about me," he said before his voice finally melted into silence.

Don't worry? It was his favorite thing to say. As a child, she had held onto his coat-sleeves with the strength of an ox each time he walked out the door. Too many nights had turned into mornings when she feared she would never see him again.

She replayed his words in her head. A gift she always wanted? What she always wanted was a father she could…wait. Was it Mother's bowie knife? She bolted across the room and flung open the window. She craned her neck into the night sky. The sound of crickets filled the crisp air. "I thought you…"

He was gone, but a pouch awash in the familiar scent of worn leather lay on the sill. He climbed up here? She clutched the soft bundle to her chest and held her breath. Huddled before a hastily lit candle, she unfolded the wrappings. The sparkle of silver danced in her hands. He remembered how much she wanted this piece of her mother.

A long-lost smile stretched across her face. What had Mother thought when she opened this on her wedding night? Mother was a Boston girl who fell for a cowboy. That's what J.W. said anyway, back in the days when he would talk about her. He promised her on her deathbed that their daughter would be raised back in her hometown. He'd kept that promise. The only one he ever did.

The sleek steel glided across her hand. Her fingers swept over a small ruby soldered in the hilt. J.W. had concealed the knife along with his memories of her mother. Sam had tried to reach the buried parts of him, but she'd failed and his demons took him away long before the nuns took her in.

The bowie knife was sacred to him so why was he giving it to her tonight? He was up to something, something that made him think he might never see her again.

She glanced at the window. The knot in her belly began to twist as it always did whenever he thought he was acting like a good parent. The ache in her stomach hadn't been this bad since the time he showed up at mass announcing his intentions to change and be a good father. Archbishop Williams, along with the rest of the congregation, pretended he wasn't even there. Drunk, he tripped and landed in the first pew. Instantly, his proclamations had turned to snoring for everyone to see and hear at communion. He was a swindler, a liar, and a drunk. He was also the only real family she had.

For him to team up with Luke Tremain meant he was in deep this time. She tore off her nightgown and threw on her dress. Rummaging through her sparse wardrobe, she unearthed her cowboy boots—contraband in her home for the improperly parented. Covering the bowie knife in soft leather wrapping, she slid her present under her pillow.

Years ago, she learned to accumulate only enough

belongings that could easily fit through her bedroom window. But tonight she'd be back, so she grabbed her usual rock along with her secret stash of money. The nuns forced her to give every penny she had earned, won, or swindled to the poor. But money was security, so she gave up enough to cleanse her sins and kept the rest.

"This is the last time I'm going to save your hide, J.W." With a deep breath, she slipped quietly down the stairs. The door on the main floor groaned open. Nudging the rock into place, she propped the door ajar for a safe return.

"J.W.," she called into the darkness.

No answer.

Nausea rolled in her belly. He wasn't really going to leave her again, was he? No, he wouldn't.

"J.W.?" The sound of her breathing was all that filled the night until the whistle of the Boston and Albany blew, announcing its imminent departure.

"No!" She spied the dim lights of the gas lamps at the train depot and ran for them.

Smoke and ash filled the air as the thunder of her boots pounded the wooden stairs. She rounded the train platform. "Wait!" It was too late. The caboose was already snaking its way toward Worcester.

He'd left. "Don't worry," he had said. They both knew better.

****

The tapping of Sam's boot kept time with the pounding of her heart as she surveyed the Boston Train Depot. Black smoke curled through the locomotive's cars and windows, engulfing the platform in its blinding ash. She had returned to the convent after J.W. left, she had no choice, but after two days of her pacing, the Sisters knew something was amiss. They also knew just what to say to get the truth out of her. If Boston had nuns enforcing the law instead of sheriffs, there'd be a lot fewer criminals on the streets. Confessing was the easy part. It was being cooped up in the convent, hovered over and watched day and night that Sam couldn't take anymore. Ten days had passed with no word from J.W. and with each passing hour the expressions on the Sisters' faces hardened, their smiles more forced their eyes downcast.

No one could replace a parent, but the Sisters came close. In the beginning she clung to the nuns for the stability she never had. Over time, the prostitutes and orphans who lived there too had become a surrogate family. Which made her resent J.W. even more for what she was about to do.

Sister Mary Ellen was the easiest to fool. Sam wasn't allowed out of her sight. So she simply told the Sister that she had to see a friend off at the train station. Not exactly a lie.

"The train is about to leave. Are you sure your friend is coming?" Sister Mary Ellen asked.

"Yes," she said searching the faces of the passengers. A close friend and reformed prostitute at the convent assured her that the nuns' lawyer was going to be on the train. "He's as bright as mineshaft. Afraid of women, won't try nothing. You'll be as safe as Reverend Mother at a whore house." Having met him before, Sam agreed that Wade Rush was the perfect man for her plan.

She took a deep breath as she spied the young lawyer boarding the train. When the last of the first-class coaches passed, she slid a note into the nun's hand.

"You are the friend. Please share this letter at home and tell them not to worry. I'll send a telegram when I get there."

"Not to worry? What are you...? Get where?"

"I'm sorry, but I can't risk losing him. I know you don't agree, but there is good in him." Wrapping her arms around the nun, she breathed in the fragrance of maple and molasses, the comforting scent of the woman who had wiped her tears and made her laugh over the past few years. "I'll miss you," Sam said. With sweaty fingers, she lifted her skirts and raced for the back of the train. She leapt onto the boarding crate and gripped the warm steel railing and climbed the stairs.

"Goodbye!" she cried to Sister Mary Ellen, who stood dumbfounded on the platform clutching the letter.

In the coach, plumes of smoke filled the cramped quarters. She spied Wade sitting alone peering through wire-rimmed glasses, his nose burrowed in a book as he chomped on a roll of beef jerky. She slid down on the bench next to him. Gusts of gray soot wafted through the air and the engine screamed as it began its steady chug west, sending her stomach fluttering as the train lurched forward.

Allowing herself one last look, she leaned over him and peered out the window. Sister Mary Ellen was still there staring at the letter.

Sam bowed her head. She was no nun, but she prayed they'd forgive her all the same.

"Tickets, please, sir," the conductor said to Wade. "And your wife's, sir?" he added patiently.

Wade coughed up his beef jerky and reddened

11

under his spectacles. "My wife?"

"Here it is." Sam handed her ticket to Wade. The man nodded and took her ticket. He frowned at Wade clearly disapproving of a wife handling her own ticket. She caught a glimpse of her reflection in the dusty window and smiled. He thought they were married. Just as she had planned.

****

Time dragged by as the train jolted its way through the countryside. By Albany, Sam finally convinced Wade to pretend to be her husband. Of course, it took scaring him into thinking the nuns would never forgive him otherwise. He was clearly jittery about either her plan or his trip, which one she wasn't quite sure. She didn't press him, even when he said that he had an important family matter in California and cryptically stated something about needing God on his side as much as possible.

She wiped the foggy remnants of her breath from the coach's window. As they left the cities behind them, the stench of the railcar grew more pungent. She buried her face in her lavender scented handkerchief hoping to mask the stale odor of her fellow passengers. Six days into their journey, they finally reached Colorado. Towns and streets had faded away long ago. Just past Denver, enormous mountains filled the windows. Her belly fluttered knowing that in a few hours Aspen would be just a stagecoach ride away.

Thin trees white as snow lined their path as they wound their way through boulders bigger than the railcar. Patches of land went on forever like a sloped green ocean. Tall grass decorated with purple and yellow flowers rode the wind's current like waves. The wilderness was as breathtaking as J.W.'s stories of Colorado; the stories that she'd clung to when he wasn't there to tuck her in at night.

He used to talk about showing Sam the place of his youth. Ever since she was knee high, she knew how to ride, shoot, and bluff. Everything a cowboy needed to know. She'd hung on every word. Not because of the stories themselves, but because of the man he became when he told them. He was happy, proud, and full of life. He never stopped planning their return; she just stopped listening. Realizing what he was capable of and hearing the wistful longing for a different life in his voice began to sting.

The thunder of gunshots echoed through the coach, and the musty stench of gunpowder invaded the air. The serenity of the landscape forgotten, eclipsed by the chaos of screams and fear.

"Wallets and jewels!" The demand was issued by a man clad in black, shoving a linen bag at the first row of passengers. A second bandit bolted through the coach wearing a bandana over his mouth and carrying a Colt .45.

The second bandit fixed his stare on Wade before his glare panned to Sam. His eyes caught fire as they landed on her bosom and lingered there. He approached wearing a devious grin. Studying Wade, the thief sneered, "Your money or your wife?" The emotionless tone of his voice turned her cold. A foreboding unease pulsed through her. His voice may have been calm and indifferent, but the scrutiny in his stare reflected the lust in his eyes.

The question ricocheted off the soot-stained walls. Her heart pounded as the question hung unanswered in the air.

The robber shoved the barrel of his revolver under Wade's chin. "What's it going to be, your money or your pretty little wife?" He grinned, revealing his few remaining teeth. "Tough choice?" he taunted. He regarded Sam and cupped her breast. "You must be a handful. 'Course, I can feel that for myself."

She slapped his hand away and looked frantically at Wade.

They weren't really married, but surely he'd part with his money to save her.

His eyes were wide. "Oh, um um," he stammered.

She elbowed him in the chest.

He fingered his glasses and pushed them above the bridge of his nose, "Sorry, ah, let me see." He felt his pocket and handed over his wallet.

She closed her eyes. The breath she'd been holding released. "Thank you."

Deep crevices formed at the sides of the robber's greased mustache as he smiled and leaned closer. In a low and sickening voice, he said, "Yeah, thank you." With a grin, he grabbed Sam's arm. "But Mama always called me the greedy one." The stench of booze seared her eyes. "Think I'll take both."

"No!" She kicked and struggled against him.

"Wait," Wade called as he rummaged through his pockets. "Don't take her. I ah, I have…"

The bandit stopped. He raised his chin like a dare, "What you got?"

"Boss." The gunman wearing the bandana reappeared from the back of the coach, "We got the payroll."

The bandit eyed Wade and his pockets, before

whacking him in the head with his gun. Wade slumped onto the floor, breathing, but not moving.

"Wade!" Sam screamed.

"Shut up," the bandit demanded and pinned her up against the wall, his beady black eyes inspecting his find. The train brakes screeched. She searched the bandit's face hoping for a sign of discomfort from the noise, but he just grinned and dragged her closer to the door. "Nothing like the sound of a train crying, hey, missy?"

She grabbed at her fellow passengers, tugging at their suit coats, but they pulled away.

"You didn't say nothing about no kidnapping," the second bandit said eyeing her.

"Improvising. Get the money and meet me at the fort in Aspen by nightfall."

Sweat pooled above Sam's collar and trickled down her neck.

"We'll be going now," the boss whispered in her ear, his breath parting her hair like drapes.

The train had slowed to a crawl. The robber yanked her toward the coach door. The locomotive made one last lurch before stopping completely. She fell to the floor. Her knees burned with pain. The bandit squeezed her arm, hauled her up, and kicked the door open. Bright sunlight hit her eyes, blinding her as she was tossed from the train.

Winded and unable to move, she lay still. Pain coursed down her back as she lifted her head and peered through the tall grass. Men were throwing luggage, wallets, and jewelry from the coaches as the train's black smoke swallowed the sky.

Fear gave way to desperation. She had not traveled

over a thousand miles to succumb to train robbers. Hollering and whistling filled the air. She eyed the tree line and slowly struggled to her feet.

"Where you going?" the bandit said as his calloused hands gripped her arm.

"You know the deal," he said to his men. "We bring Tremain the payroll. Then we get our cut. And no need to share nothin' with him about this lil' trinket, got it? You can get a piece of her at the fort."

Tremain? *Luke* Tremain?

He shoved her toward a horse. "Have you ever ridden, luv?" She shuddered as his calloused fingers stroked her knee and ripped the lower portion of her dress clean off.

"That'll make it easier…to mount," he said to the amusement of his men. "Well now, that puts an end to a hard mornin's work." He gripped the back of her neck and pulled her flush against him. "And the beginning of a pleasant afternoon."

She screamed for help, but the click of the gun hammer sounding in her ear was enough to silence her. "Shut your mouth and get on the horse." She closed her eyes as warm steel grazed her cheek.

Sweat trickled down her neck. She swung her leg over the horse and secured herself in the saddle.

He climbed up behind her, holstered his gun, and bound her hands. A thick arm coiled around her waist squeezing her against the man's massive form and fastening her in.

From the taste of bile in her mouth, she knew she was close to throwing up. Something she would welcome right about now.

"Be at the fort in Aspen by sundown," he ordered

his men. And with a kick to the horse's belly and the crack of the reins, Sam and the bandit rode off, leaving the lame train in their dust.

****

"You won't get away with this. The sheriff will hear about it," Sam said.

The bandit slowed the horse. "Holy hell, you have a wobblin' jaw, woman. Do you ever shut up?" He unbuttoned the neck of her dress and ripped the lace fringe from her shoulders. He pulled it taut gagging her with a part of her own dress.

She groaned. Her legs burned, her back ached, and her mouth was too dry to swallow. They had been riding for at least an hour. She wanted to cry just for the relief of one teardrop, but she refused. The only way out of this was to be calm.

Her bowie knife was still hidden in her boot. She still had a chance: stab the bandit and escape.

The horse descended the steep mountain trail. With her bound hands, she gripped the saddle horn. She waited for the right time to fight for her freedom. Neither the sound of horse hoofs scraping rock, nor the jolt of the horse's missteps, seemed to have any effect on the gunman, but her stomach rolled with every lurch forward. The trail was solid rock on one side and a sheer one hundred foot drop on the other.

They emerged into a valley. The bandit yanked the reins, directing the horse toward a loud and winding river. He quickly dismounted and hauled her off.

Though the current was quick, she was desperate for water. She elbowed her captor in the ribs and tore the gag from her mouth. She staggered toward the riverbed. He grabbed her arm and pulled her back.

Eyeing her, he raised his canteen to his lips and gulped brown liquid.

"I need water," she said.

"I'll be giving you what you need." He tossed the canteen next to her.

"Please, untie me. My wrists are raw."

"There ain't nowhere to go and no one to help you." He watched her closely as he untied her bindings. "Drink. I don't need no woman fainting on me. Wouldn't be the first time though, on account of my, ah, lady skills." He let out a loud laugh.

If the thought of sharing the canteen with him wasn't enough to make her vomit, the image of his lady skills certainly was. She grabbed the canteen and took a swig of whiskey. It was warm but managed to soothe her throat. The rancid odor of alcohol was a welcome relief to the rank smell emanating from him.

He laughed. "I knew you weren't no proper lady. Eat some jerky," he ordered, tossing a piece of dehydrated meat into the tall grass.

She clenched her fists. She couldn't get her knife in him fast enough.

"Eat," he demanded.

Hunger was not an issue right now, but escaping was. Carefully, she backed toward the food, bent low, and reached for it. Using what remained of her skirt as a shield; she pulled her blade from her boot and wrapped her fingers around its hilt. With the weapon hidden behind her, she faced her kidnapper and with one hand dutifully bit off a piece of jerky.

"You enjoying the good ol' Colorado hospitality?" He stepped closer. The bite of beef rose in her throat. Her sweat-slicked fingers tightened their grip on the knife.

A stream of whiskey trickled from his mouth. With a flick of his tongue, he licked it off his chin. He shoved her to the ground and hovered over her. His slobber practically crawled on her skin. "Now that you're comfortable, luv…"

The blade pricked her flesh as she landed in the grass. She concealed the knife within the remaining folds of her dress. Her breath staggered.

"Sorry to keep you waitin'," he said as he removed his gun belt.

His gun was within reach. She eyed it, measuring the distance.

Grinning, he kicked the belt away. "You really are a handful, aren't ya? Just the way I like 'em."

He lunged at her. Like an animal, his mouth attacked her flesh.

Lifting her back off the ground, she gripped her knife, raised the blade, and plunged it into his meaty thigh. He screamed and recoiled. With him writhing in pain, she dug the blade deeper into his impaled thigh. He grabbed her wrist and forced her hand away. She aimed her boot at the hilt and kicked it sideways. He cried out again and released her. She rolled toward the gun. Reaching it, she grabbed the Colt and leveled her aim at his chest. Her finger brushed against the trigger, stroking it. A little more pressure is all it would take. He would be dead. He was defenseless, crying like a baby. But she couldn't pull the trigger. It wasn't in her.

She staggered backward toward his horse. "How about those lady skills?" she said mounting his horse as he lay in a heap clutching his bloodied limb.

Without looking back, she gritted her teeth and

clung to the horse's neck. The reins were tight in her hands as if she were holding onto her sanity. She and her new horse were headed for Aspen. Her only regret was leaving her mother's cherished knife in the filthy scoundrel's leg.

She raced through the forest, narrowly missing clusters of thin white trees that blanketed the mountainside. River rapids white as snow pounded alongside her. The power and speed of the water pressed her onward. When her fingers were too chafed to clutch the reins and her heart didn't beat through her chest anymore, she stopped by the river.

Unfolding her cramped fingers, the blood flowed through her hands again. Soreness radiated through her back and legs. The midday sun peeked through the endless array of trees. Visions of the train robber flashed through her mind. She pushed the images away. Not until she was back in Boston begging the nuns' forgiveness would she think about what she had just been through.

The safety of the nuns, and Boston, was a thousand miles behind her. Time and time again J.W. told her that the West was a ruthless place. "In the East," he said, "men keep their word. Respect and honor come from education and family. In the West, a man will turn on his own brother for silver or women. Respect comes from guts, guns, and land."

The cramp of hunger beckoned her to the rogue's saddlebag. She dismounted and shoved her hand deep into his pack. The mere scent of beef jerky made her stomach jump with anticipation. She greedily bit off a piece and continued her search. Her fingertips brushed against stacks of paper. As she pulled them into daylight, a chill spread across her body. It wasn't just paper it was the payroll—the boss's money.

Her captor had told the men to meet at the fort in Aspen. "But first," he said, "the boss has to get his cut."

Tremain had arranged the train robbery. He'd be expecting the robber soon. Looking for him when he didn't show. And the robber would be looking for her.

Finding J.W. was all she could think of right now. What had he gotten himself into this time? He was no angel, but could he be part of robbing a train? She had to get to Aspen unseen by Tremain's men. Carrying the stolen money into town wasn't an option. She had to bury it and come back for it later. She fingered some bills. She hadn't stolen anything in eight years, her stomach rolled with nausea at the thought, but she needed money to survive. As J.W. used to say, "It ain't stealing if your life depends on it."

There were two guns. Her fingers trembled as she buried one with the money in the saddlebag and put the other in her boot. Her hands were speckled with blood, the kidnapper's blood. She had stabbed a man—to save herself, yes, but his blood stained her all the same.

She drifted back to the river. Splashing herself with the frigid mountain water, she did her best to wash away the feel of him. Salted tears rolled down her cheeks to her lips. Wrapping her arms around herself, she tried to control the overwhelming fear that shook her. She had escaped captivity, but she knew all too well that emotions were harder to run from.

Chapter Three

"Damn." Jesse's heart pounded. What in the hell was that roaring streak of horse and woman charging past him? His breath quieted, but his mind raced. If he were a gambler, he'd bet she never even saw him. She came close to landing him and his new hat in the Roaring Fork River. What the hell is going on? First Luke Tremain's low-life saddle bums were on his land, and now some crazed woman was running loose, too.

It wasn't hard to follow the woman or even get close to her. She was too concerned with washing her face and eating jerky to even be aware of him. At the river, he crouched behind a large rock and surveyed the surrounding tree line for a sign of Luke or one of his gang. There was no one else about; she was alone.

Sunlight glistened on her dark hair cascading around a delicate, but reddened neck. Tears seeped from a pair of sparkling green eyes. A pang of guilt crept across his conscious. He shouldn't look, but he needed to know what she was doing here.

Golden flecks shimmered on parts of her green dress, the parts that were still there. What would possess a woman to be alone in the wild? And what the hell happened to her? Her dress looked like she'd tussled with a mountain lion. Maybe this was Luke's doing. Maybe she got lost trying to make her way across the Great Divide, but why is she alone?

It was no secret how he felt about travelers in distress. He helped folks just as much as he cursed them for being fool enough to drive a wagon over Independence Pass.

Lately, everyone he came across made him suspicious. Luke would stop at nothing to get his hands on Enchantment Ranch. It wouldn't be beyond him to use a woman as a distraction. Time was running out to pay off the lien on the ranch. Burning down his barn was Luke's way of making sure the mortgage wouldn't be paid off in time. Question was where was the son-of-a-bitch getting the money to pay off his lien to take over the ranch?

"Okay, Rusty, let's see if this woman is working for Tremain." He fired a warning shot from his Winchester. The woman shrieked and dove toward the woods. She crouched behind a log and looked around. Her fingers were busy fiddling with something in her boot when suddenly her horse ran off into the forest. She started yelling after the gelding, but he was long gone.

"Damn," he said rethinking his theory of her working for Luke. The young woman's shoulders slumped, and she kicked at the dirt. He winced; she probably was just lost. On her hands and knees she crawled back to the river. What the hell was this woman doing? When she finally stood up and headed down river, he decided it was time to find out.

"Let's go," he said with some hesitation. He didn't want to frighten her. Lowering his rifle and holding Rusty's reins, he approached her from behind. Her back stiffened, and she raised her head quicker than a mama bear smelling a danger. Before he could even say a word, she reached into her boot and turned to him with a fiery blaze in her eyes. It wasn't her eyes that held his attention; however, it was the Colt double-action thunder revolver shaking in her hands.

Staring down the barrel of a gun wasn't a problem. The wrong end of a rifle had been shoved in his face more times than he cared to remember. He could size up a man in the time it took for his lips to break into a smile, but women were different. He'd rather predict the weather than face an angry or scared woman.

"Now hold on there, Annie Oakley," he said lifting his palms to the sky. "I ain't aiming to hurt you."

"Well, I fully intend to harm you if you take one step closer."

Her voice was steady, but it was the tremble in her trigger finger that stopped him in his tracks.

"What are you doing here?" she demanded.

"This is my land." He could offer more information, but since he didn't like being held at gunpoint, he was satisfied with his smug reply.

She dropped her chin and eyed him up and down as if he was as naked as head of beef. Her eyes scorched like flames in a fire pit, until she eyed Rusty.

"Throw the rifle into the river, mister, and back away from your horse."

"Tell Tremain I ain't falling for it."

"Tremain? Luke Tremain?" she asked. "You know him?"

He shook his head. "Yeah, I know him." Disgusted or surprised, he wasn't sure how he felt. She'd recognized the name, but he couldn't read her reaction and that didn't sit right with him. 'Course the gun pointed at him didn't help, either.

He tossed his Winchester just shy of the river. His fingers balled into fists. "Tell that snake I ain't fallin' for some sad lookin' woman on my land."

She squared her shoulders and lifted her chin. "Tell him yourself."

His jaw tightened. "I'm not the one working for him."

"I don't work for him," she drew out the words like she was talking to a child.

He met her glare. "Then how do you know him?" He stepped forward cautiously closing the space between them.

Her answer was a clenched jaw and a white knuckled grip on her revolver.

"You mind pointing your gun somewhere other than my chest?" With his luck some damn bird would chirp and she'd shoot a hole through his midsection.

"As a matter of fact, I do mind. You scared off my horse, and I need that horse."

"He'll be back. Any well-trained gelding will return to his master shortly after a scare."

An icy flash in her eyes sent a prickly sensation down the back of his neck.

"I don't need a lesson in horses. I'm not the one who shot off the Winchester." Her gaze bore through him like a runaway mining car barreling through a shaft. Jesse swallowed and waited, and waited, looking around optimistically for her frightened horse.

The woman was clearly distraught. Attempting to decrease the tension, he smiled, now not sure if she worked for Luke or perhaps had been wandering for days. "Please, put your weapon down. I told you I ain't going to hurt you."

"That's why you shot at me, mister?"

"Shot at you?" Jesse nearly choked. A blind man could've hit her with all the commotion she had been making, but he decided to keep that to himself. "Look, miss, put the gun down. I can help you."

Her lips parted and her chest heaved with a fortifying breath. "I can take care of myself."

Of course she could. "I can see that," he said. "My name is…"

"I do not see what your name has to do with my runaway horse."

The woman was scared but determined. It wasn't just the gun and fiery temper that piqued his curiosity. It was the flush of her cheeks and the dignified raise of her chin that caught his breath. She was keeping herself ace-high, for now anyway.

Her black hair spread across her reddened cheeks. "This is your land?" she asked, sweeping the gun around and pointing with it.

He instinctively ducked; fortunately, she hadn't shot the gun. When he looked up, his eyes fixed on her slim fingers wiping her hair from her face proving what his body was already telling him: although dirty and beyond sense, she was stunning. "Yes. And how did you get out here?"

"By horse," she said in a tone reminiscent of a schoolteacher scolding her class.

"Right." He swallowed the words he wanted to say. "Since we're clear about that, what are you doing out here, alone?" He changed his tone and spoke in his softest voice, the one he used when soothing a spooked horse.

"I am on my way to Aspen."

"To see Luke Tremain." He nodded encouraging her to continue.

"Tell me where to find him," she said ignoring the bait.

He sighed, "Probably in town. But I wouldn't..."

"Step across the river," she demanded, aiming her gun at his chest.

He smiled again, this time to calm himself.

"You're a couple hours from Aspen. Just follow the river over that last mountain," he said, nodding his head west. "By horse, that is. Perhaps if you call..."

"Is that so? Guess I better commandeer a horse."

"Is that so?" he uttered through clenched teeth. He knew a challenge when he heard one. "How do you think you're going to do that?"

A brief, yet vexing smile crossed her face, as she eyed her revolver. "Guess."

He returned her smug grin with one of his own. "I can't imagine."

Her hands shook. "That's what the gun is for."

Jesse reached to loosen his already open collar. Lord, she was a hell of a spitfire. But no matter how much grit or how inviting her curves looked in what was left of that god-forsaken dress, she wasn't taking his horse.

Keeping her weapon trained on him, she advanced toward Rusty. "Look, mister, I'm sorry, really I am, but it's a matter of life and death."

"Your life and my death?" Sarcasm was never a smart tactic, but the lady's sudden apology was a little hard to swallow.

"You said this was your land."

"It is. So?"

27

"So, you can walk home. You don't need a horse."

Walk home. Had she just dropped from the sky? "Lady, I don't know where you come from, but out here homes are not exactly close. My ranch is a three-mile walk over the most treacherous mountains you'll ever climb.

"Now, it's dangerous to be out here alone, so I'll bring you to Aspen," he offered. It wasn't the animal wildlife that worried him; it was Luke's roaming men. He wouldn't leave a woman stranded on Independence Pass.

She shook her head. Then, as if she suddenly remembered her manners, she declared, "No. Thank you." She waved her gun toward the opposite bank of the river. "Cross to the other side."

As he bit down hard to suppress his rising anger, he tasted blood seeping from his lip. He backed into the river steadying himself in the soft river bottom as the swiftly moving current nearly knocked his whole body into the frigid water.

"Come here," the woman beckoned, edging her way toward Rusty.

As she tugged on Rusty's bit, the horse let out a snort and pulled away. That's why he preferred horses to people. They're loyal. "Why don't you point your gun at him?" he taunted, but then ducked and cursed his rash tongue.

Cold river water filled his boots to the brim. "Damn," he swore under his breath as he readied himself for the opportunity to overtake her. The icy water crawled up his legs and leveled out at his thighs.

She nestled her face against the horse's neck.

He was thigh high in biting cold water, and she was

getting cozy with his horse? Hell, no. He eased his way closer to her while she whispered something to Rusty. Using her divided attention to his advantage, he lunged from the water and grabbed her wrist, easily forcing the gun from her hold. He held her slim figure at her waist with one hand.

"Miss, I..." Suddenly pain surged in his shin. She had kicked him.

He bit down on his lip again fighting to keep from losing his temper. She pushed him and pounded her fists on his chest. When that didn't work, she started kicking again. Instinctively he moved, causing him to lose his footing and fall backward into the raging waters. The current knocked the gun from his grip, but not the woman still bucking in his arms. Together they plunged into the cold water.

Jesse dug his heels into the river bottom. A surge of water poured over him loosening his grip on the woman. When he resurfaced, she was screaming and clawing for him. He reached for her. With the bottom half of her dress missing he had no choice but to grab one of her near naked thighs. With no other options, he gripped both soft thighs and lifted her above the current. Each step was excruciating as she clung to his neck choking and almost drowning him at the same time.

Finally, they reached the riverbed. He set her down carefully. "What the heck were you thinking?" He held her drenched and shivering body against his—not just because he liked the feel of her, but also because he wasn't about to risk another kick to his shin.

When she didn't answer, he gently lifted her chin, but she averted his gaze. Realizing the indecent restraint he held her in, he asked lightly, "What kind of boots are you wearing anyway?"

She turned to him but the defiance in her eyes registered too late. "This kind," she said, lifting her leg and stomping on his foot.

"Sweet vinegar!" Jesse hopped backwards, releasing her. About to unleash the series of swears forming in his mouth, he restrained his temper when he saw tears welling in her eyes.

She quickly looked down and smoothed what was left of her dress.

He looked away, too. A woman pointing a revolver at him was one thing, but a woman crying and fixing her pitiful dress while trying to look dignified, that was entirely different.

"Now what am I going to do?" she whispered.

Jesse wasn't sure if she was talking to him. Damn, how did this mysterious stranger hold him at gunpoint, try to steal his horse, get him all wet, and still make him feel sorry for her?

Mud seeped from her clenched fists.

"Look, no offense, miss, but you don't seem well." He felt her eyes on him immediately. He moved close to her, but not too close. It would be natural for her to be scared. She was lost and alone facing a stranger miles from help. At this moment she seemed vulnerable. "I...I mean you seem a little down on your luck is all. I'll take you to Aspen. Just tell me what you want with Tremain."

"I'll go alone."

"Let me take you." He shook his head. Now he was asking to do her a favor? "I know you have no reason to trust me," he said softly. "I swear, I am not going to hurt you."

She slid away from him, creeping closer to Rusty.

Jesse sighed and shook his head, "You're not taking my horse."

Suddenly, she flung a handful of mud in his face, stinging his eyes.

He spit out the taste of wet earth. "For the love of God!" The woman wouldn't give up.

When he opened his eyes, he could see why. She'd not only reached Rusty, but she was pointing his Winchester straight at his chest.

"I really am sorry," she said.

"I find that hard to believe." He was soaked, mud was crawling down his face, and this, this vixen was once again holding him at gunpoint. Only this time, it was with his gun.

He could understand her being afraid of him, but he sensed a different kind of urgency.

It wouldn't be hard to overtake her; he could easily disarm her in one beat of her sour heart. But she managed to spike his temper and arouse his curiosity. Her eyes were red and puffy. She was dripping wet, desperate, and, it seemed, more in need of his horse at this moment than he was.

"Throw me your hat," she ordered, interrupting his thoughts of forgiveness.

"My hat?" Why the heck did she want his hat?

"I need it."

"No." Hell no. He just bought it.

She raised her gun and eyebrow simultaneously.

"You're worried about your hair?" He threw her his wide brimmed hat, the one he just bought to replace the one he'd lost in the barn fire.

She caught it with one hand and put it on. "Back up into the river," she ordered, and assured him, "I'll leave your horse in Aspen."

"By the sheriff's office?"

"You'll get him back." She led Rusty in the opposite direction.

"And my hat?"

She cocked her head to the side and blew out a breath which sounded more like a restrained groan, "Yes, your hat, too."

Her frustration made him smile. "You're an accommodating thief."

"Thief? I'm not a thief. I told you, you'll get your horse and hat back. I'm not stealing them."

"Rusty."

"Rusty?"

"My horse, the one you're not stealing at gunpoint, with my gun. His name is Rusty."

He took pride in the scowl on her face, that was until she gripped the Winchester expertly in one hand, footed the stirrup, and proceeded to wiggle her body up the side of the horse in the tattered remains of her dress. It was impressive. Just as impressive as the creamy wet thigh and slightly exposed rear wiggling up the horse.

"Um…" she uttered, calling his eyes to hers. "I'll be needing your shirt, too." She scrunched up her nose as if she was sorry for asking.

"What?" he must have misheard her but he knew he hadn't. He shook his head. "No."

Her perfect red lips formed an apologetic smile. "I can't ride into Aspen dressed like this." She ran her fingers over her naked thigh.

Closing his eyes, he lifted his head toward the sky.

She was killing him. He let out a low growl. "Of course not. What would people think of a poorly dressed thief?"

"I told you I'm not a thief."

"Well, if you're not a thief, then I'm guessing you're not a murderer either," he said charging out of the river.

Sitting sidesaddle, she cocked the rifle and looked him straight in the eyes forcing him to root his feet to the mud.

"I'm not sure about that," she said faintly. The defiance in her eyes reemerged. "I am not a thief. This is an emergency, and I don't need your help." She scanned his body, and said, "Except, uh, your shirt."

Jesse reached for each button slower than molasses dripping from a spoon. She cocked her head to the side, giving him a look of annoyance. He couldn't help but give a brief smile of triumph. She raised her eyebrows in return reminding him that he wasn't exactly the triumphant one.

He took off his shirt and tossed it to her. He could've sworn her eyes were begging for more.

He spread his arms wide, "Anything else?" He fingered his belt buckle, "My dungarees, perhaps?" He tried to suppress a smirk.

Red bloomed on her cheeks. "I can assure you I have no interest in your pants." With one kick to the horse's belly, she and his horse sped toward Aspen.

Damn, was he just stripped close to naked, at gunpoint, by a woman? He had a feeling he'd get Rusty back, but the grin emerging on his face told him he cared more about seeing the fiery little thief again than his horse.

Chapter Four

The scent of sage and spruce emanated from every inch of the mountain pass. Grass, thicker and greener than anything Boston had to offer, brushed against Sam's boots.

"Wonderful, another man looking for me," she said to her new horse. With each step closer to Aspen, her stomach fluttered. Hopefully, Luke would be easy to find. She had to get to him before his men found her.

Fortunately, she had hidden the saddlebag before the man by the river showed up. Taking deep breaths had always worked to calm her nerves, but this time the scent of leather that lingered on the cowboy's damp shirt just made her more tense.

He was nothing like the stuffed suits parading around Boston. Those amber eyes were warm like his smile. His voice was soothing, yet fiercely masculine. Even though he hadn't believed her, his clothes really were a matter of life and death: the hat for one covered her face keeping her hidden from the bandit.

She could hear the lecture J.W. would give her if he knew she'd broken the "cowboy code," as he called it, twice. *"In the West riding another man's horse is as bad as riding his wife, but wearing his hat, that will make you swing."*

But he wasn't here, and she wasn't a cowboy. Besides, the man practically dared her to leave his horse by the sheriff's office in Aspen. She smiled. That's exactly what she would do. She gave a kick to the horse's belly and with any luck, she'd never see the man or his horse again. Or at least, he would never see her again.

The robbers were careless enough to mention Luke by name. Once she told the sheriff about it, she'd show him the stolen money and then Luke and his men would be arrested.

As for J.W., her hands were wrung dry from years of worrying about him. Usually she could depend on him to land on his feet. This time though, her gut was telling her he was in deep trouble, and when it came to her instincts, they were far more reliable than her father ever was.

The last of the sun's rays glistened in the leaves and no longer offered much warmth. Trees concealed the base of the mountains, and the hard rock was now framed by the colors of dusk. A slight breeze whistled as she descended the tallest mountain. The steep and winding path sent a flutter through her stomach. And then, beyond an immense and darkening sky was a valley home to cabins upon cabins: Aspen.

Reaching the foot of the mountain, the turbulent rhythm of the river quieted. Clanging dishes and laughter spilled from open windows as she passed through the lines of one and two story wooden buildings. Voices of differing volumes and accents greeted her ears. The scent of cabbage and stew wafted through the makeshift camp rousing her dormant appetite.

Ever since she could remember, J.W. talked about taking her back to Aspen. Now she was on its streets, within the boundaries of the place of her birth. It was the mysterious and mystical land where her parents met and fell in love. The images of the town blurred as her tears began to flow. She had made it here on her own, but she was still alone.

She didn't know much about the people of Aspen. J.W. would say that her mother thought the mountains were so high to guard the heavens from the miners. Her mother didn't like the West, he'd say, it wasn't so much the land she couldn't abide, as the townsfolk.

Thoughts of J.W. invaded her mind. She struggled to push aside her emerging fears. What if this was another ploy of his? Could she forgive him if she found him in one of the saloons drinking and gambling? She prayed he was safe, and, at the same time, that he really did need her.

Sam carefully holstered the rifle on Rusty's side for easy reach. Saloon music grew louder as she meandered through the streets. The town looked similar to J.W.'s legendary stories, but her imagination had added a layer of warmth and welcoming that clearly were not present.

She and her new horse trotted down the wide dirt road unnoticed. Through the dim lighting that hung on lines strung overhead, she spotted the sign for the sheriff. She spied a hitching post to which she tied the cowboy's horse, Rusty.

"Thank you." She nestled her head against Rusty's nose. "I don't want to let you go; you're the only friend I have out here. Although, I suppose you wouldn't consider me a friend." Hugging Rusty's neck, she attempted to bury her fear and plight for a moment. She was alone, half dressed, and had two very angry men searching for her.

The moon rose in the enormous sky. "Good bye," she said to Rusty, "and thank you for helping me," she whispered in his mane. The horse was her sole source of comfort after the terror she'd been through today. She wrapped her borrowed shirt tighter around herself. Safety was finally within reach. With one last glance back at Rusty and one deep breath, she proceeded across the street, careful to avoid the many ruts.

The ground began to shake and the sound of thunder rumbled behind her. A stagecoach headed straight for her. The driver yelled and waved his arms. She froze as a cloud of dust engulfed the carriage eating everything in its path. The sound of her own scream jolted her into action. She tugged at her boots but her feet were buried in mud. Finally, she managed to pull her feet loose just as sturdy hands gripped her arm and yanked her out of the path of the speeding carriage.

A voice echoed in her ears. "Damn stages. You got all your parts?"

Sam's eyes landed on a little woman. Her dress didn't cover her arms or shoulders and revealed a rather generous helping of creamy breasts.

"You pulled me out of the way?" Sam asked the woman who appeared to be only a few years older than she.

"The name's Julia." The petite woman brushed off her tasseled dress. "Pleased to meet ya."

"I don't know how to thank you. You...you saved my life," Sam replied, barely able to form words.

With the flick of her hand, Julia dismissed the notion. "Watch out around here. Those damn stage coaches race through here like they're the Hook and

Ladder boys."

"I…I guess I'd better be more careful."

Julia grabbed Sam's hat and studied her shirt. She cocked her head slightly, but asked warmly, "Where're ya from?"

"Boston."

"Well, welcome to Aspen." The stranger's gentle smile put her at ease.

"Oh, excuse me, I'm Sam Ward."

"Sam, huh, where ya headed, Sam?"

"I need to speak to the sheriff immediately."

Chapter Five

"Follow me." With a wave of a hand, her rescuer beckoned Sam down a dirt path. "So, ah, what ah, brings you out here to Aspen?"

Sam smiled in relief. Julia was acting like they were having a normal conversation maybe she didn't look as bad as she thought.

The woman raised an eyebrow, "Somethin' funny?" she asked and shared a warm smile.

Warmth flushed her cheeks. "I thought maybe I looked a bit disheveled. But you're not asking me about my clothes so I guess I don't look too bad," Sam said.

The woman snorted through a laugh. "You say what you're thinkin'. I like that. 'Course not many other folks will. So, I'll be straight with ya. You look like hell."

The corners of Julia's mouth turned up into a grin, and Sam laughed so hard she had to hold her stomach. She found someone honest and brave. The nuns must've said some prayers on her behalf.

She nodded for Julia to continue.

"Women gotta stick together out here. Only way we can survive these men including the sheriff. To me, women have good reasons for what they do, and I respect their privacy. But the sheriff's not especially fond of tenderfeet and Yankees and you, dear, are both. He might not ask ya what the hell you're doing out here at night alone and wearing a man's shirt that's three sizes too big. But then again, he might.

She swallowed the tinge of fear that crept up her throat. She pressed what was left of her dress against her thighs and pulled her borrowed shirt tight around her chest wrapping herself in it. "I am here to find my father." She tried to sound calm.

"He's lost?"

"Missing."

"Watch yourself on these damn holes in the street," Julia said taking ahold of Sam's arm. "We don't get many respectable folks from Boston out here."

J.W.'s not respectable. She kept that thought to herself. "Why not?" she asked trying to concentrate on the road and what Julia was saying. It was too dark to avoid every hole in the street. She'd be lucky not to have a broken ankle before she got to the sheriff.

Julia sighed. "Easterners aside from prospectors avoid Aspen. Not for any reason other than it being near impossible to get to and not worth the trouble of getting to unless you're hunting silver. Still, Aspen's filling up faster than a shot of whisky these days."

"So, lots of new people lately? Just not respectable ones?" Sam asked.

"There are more low-down miners round here now than ever before." They paused in front of well-kept building. "Anything else you want to tell me before you meet the sheriff?'

Nausea crawled through her belly. "Will the sheriff help me find my father?"

The bandit was looking for her, and she was making a complete spectacle of herself. A trickle of unease crept down her back until she raised her eyes to her escort. A comforting smile mixed with curiosity and encouragement greeted her eyes. "I had to make some quick choices on my way out here."

"Like I said, you speak your mind and do things your own way. I respect that." Her soft arm encircled Sam's shoulders and gently nudged her forward. "But Sheriff Brown has no patience for women, strangers, or silver-hunting prospectors."

"I'm not looking for silver. Just my father."

Julia looked her over from head to toe, again. "Your pa's a respectable man?" She patted her on the hand, "Then, the sheriff won't give you a hard time."

"Wait." She grabbed Julia's arm." What if he's not a respectable man?"

"Well then, he'll fit right in." She flashed a smiled. "Don't worry, I got ya." Together they climbed the steps to the law office and trudged right through the swinging doors.

"Miss Ward," the rotund sheriff said cutting Sam off and stretching his stubby legs onto his bare desk. "Men come here and enjoy themselves a little too much. Some even forget they're family men. Your father's probably over at Georgia's right now." He rubbed his eyes like she was giving him a headache. "Julia, escort Miss Ward to the Hotel Jerome," he said looking her over, "or wherever she is staying and see that she gets some rest...and a bath."

"Sheriff, you don't understand. My father is missing. My train was robbed, and I know Luke Tremain has something to do with it."

Sheriff Brown cleared his throat, slurped from a coffee-stained mug, and stared at her across his cramped office. The lawman's small brown eyes appeared overwhelmed by weight of his cheeks. His lips were flattened, crushed by enormous layers of red flesh. "Luke Tremain is an outstanding citizen of Aspen, as was his granddaddy. You, on the other hand, show up looking like you crawled your way over the Great Divide. Seems to me a crime wasn't even committed in Aspen."

"But Luke is responsible for the train robbery. The men mentioned him by name."

Sheriff Brown planted his hat on his head, slurped his coffee, and eyed her with disdain. Her mouth suddenly ran dry. She had entered an entirely different world. Back home folks knew she had a swindling father, but they also knew she lived with nuns and that bought her respect.

"You came here to find your pa?" The sheriff interrupted her thoughts. "Where was he planning on staying? The deputy will escort you."

"I don't know."

"You don't know? Why did he come out here, prospecting?

"He's...in the process of getting property here." She heard her voice, but it sounded foreign.

"Getting? How so?" He lifted his chin and shot a look at his deputy.

Damn J.W... She'd been through this whole interrogation a million times before with the Sisters whenever she tried to defend her father's actions. "I...I don't know."

He shifted his in chair. "You rich? Have rich relatives back east?"

"No, not at all." She felt the warmth of her cheeks. As soon as she found J.W., she was going to strangle him.

He sighed. "So you're saying that your father is out here to get land, but you don't know how. That he told you to look up Luke Tremain, the man you are now accusing of robbing a train? And you think—what, that Mr. Tremain kidnapped a man with no money?"

"Well, I don't—yes…I suppose," she stuttered.

Her words repeated back to her sounded a bit hysterical.

"Let's go," Julia said, gently taking her arm. "The poor woman has had a hell of a day and doesn't need to be treated like a damn fool."

The sheriff adjusted his seat again and put on what seemed to be his most patronizing smile yet. "The train already arrived in Leadville. You can be sure we'll be talking to every witness and getting a good description of these bandits."

"They work for Luke Tremain."

"Miss Ward," he said, setting his mug down and jaw tight, "trains occasionally get robbed, but penniless men seldom get kidnapped by respectable men."

"But—"

"This here's a clean camp, and you're making a serious accusation." He stood up and lifted his belt over his belly. She started to argue, but Julia tugged at her arm and guided her out the door.

"My cabin is just a ways back. Come on. We'll scrub ya real good."

"I have to make him listen to me." The words sounded weak.

Julia clicked her tongue. "Won't work. I know the man you're talking about, Luke Tremain. He's in real good with the sheriff."

"What about the mayor or someone else?"

"No one is gonna listen to an out-a-town woman, especially one wearing a man's clothes. Maybe where ya come from things are different, but here, when a woman's gotta get somethin' done, it's best to include men as seldom as possible."

****

"Yer wearin' out my only rug with all yer pacin'," Julia said as she pried open an old brown chest filling the room with the scent of cedar.

"Sorry." Anger, frustration, and plain old fear wrapped around Sam.

"Out here we take walks outside," Julia said with a wink.

Sam leapt toward Julia to help as she struggled to lift an enormous quilt. Grey, brown, and shades of green adorned the worn quilt's fabric. It's faded blues with white accents created the image of a powerful river snaking across the cramped cabin as Julia hung it from a rope to give Sam some privacy.

Julia pulled out a nightshift and shrugged. "My ol' granny passed this down to me thinkin' I'd have a wedding night." She handed it to her. "It's got the works."

"I can't wear your wedding nightshirt." Sam took a step back hitting her leg on the bed. There wasn't much room to maneuver around.

She waved her off. "Nightshirts are just a waste of time. If I ever have a wedding night, I'll be sleepin' in the raw just like every other night."

"But…" she called from behind the quilt. "Your granny gave it to you."

"Ah, it's about as useful to me as bull with teats."

Sam walked out from behind the quilt. A new scent, one warm and sweet welcomed her.

Julia held out a tea cup. "Chamomile? I save my tea for special occasions."

"This is a special occasion?"

"I don't dig into Granny's trunk for nothin'. You're one brave woman, Sam Ward."

"I haven't done anything," her voice cracked. She took a deep breath through her nose to keep the tears dangerously close to escaping at bay. "I couldn't even convince the sheriff about Luke." She bathed her face in the steam. "I need to find J.W. and get back to Boston."

"That's too bad. I think you'd make it out here."

"Me?"

"Sure, you got courage and a sweet nature. Both can get you dead real fast in this town. But you, you can hold your own. Not many women can do that out here."

Holding her own is what the nuns were all about. They taught the importance of helping one another but relying only on yourself.

"Now, about your pa. Is he the kind a man who keeps his word?"

There wasn't any real answer to that question. "Sometimes." She watched Julia's face for a reaction but couldn't quite read her.

"So, what makes you so sure Luke kidnapped him?"

She sighed. "I'm not. I don't know where he is—I only said that because the sheriff said it, and I thought he would do something about it."

The truth was that believing he was kidnapped was easier to swallow than thinking J.W. would abandon her.

"So you don't think he's kidnapped?"

"All I know is that Luke robbed the train. And J.W. said to find Luke if anything happened to him. I couldn't think of anything else to say to the sheriff."

"You did fine. You gotta trust your instincts and ya did."

"J.W. didn't send me a telegram." Sam looked at the matted rug in front of the fire. "Which, for J.W., actually means nothing."

"So it's easier than thinking he just forgot about ya?"

A wave of nausea rolled through her stomach. J.W. wouldn't forget. He'd trick her into coming out here by scaring her into looking for him.

"Luke may know where J.W. is, but J.W.'s disappearance is more likely due to whiskey or women rather than to Luke," Sam admitted. "I got caught up in thinking I had to rescue him like I've done all my life."

Julia took a long swig of tea. "Some folks suspect Luke's been up to somethin' for a while now."

"Like robbing a train?"

"Most folks don't say nothin' out of fear and all." Julia shuffled her feet. "You must be hungry. How about some bread with jelly?"

"That sounds good, thanks." The ache in her stomach wasn't apparent until now. While Julia made them a snack, Sam got lost gazing into the fire. The flames looked like they pushed each other down to climb higher and higher. "You live alone?" The cabin was clean and cozy with no signs of a man anywhere.

"I ain't alone much," she replied. "I rent the cabin, but everything in it's mine." She reached over the fire for the bread warming on a tin. "A woman livin' alone surprises ya?" she asked, spreading jelly on the toast.

"A little." She nodded. Boston and Aspen weren't just separated by land in miles, the landscape created a freedom too. For the first time in her life, she began to wonder if she truly could live without the nuns. Could she ever afford to live on her own? She looked around the cozy living space. The walls were covered with pictures. One was of a large family. "You support yourself?"

"Sure do. Not in a way I'd like." Julia nodded. "Whiskey?" She gestured a tin toward Sam's tea.

Sam dismissed the notion with a shake of her head. The woody vanilla scent reminded her of the bandit and made her shudder.

Pouring whiskey into her tea, Julia continued. "I grew up on a ranch. Someday I'm gonna get myself a piece of land and be beholden to no one."

"Have you lived here your whole life?" She watched Julia give herself a large helping of whiskey and wondered how a woman her size could drink so much and not fall over.

"Nah, I followed a damn fool from Leadville back in eighty-four. We didn't see eye-to-eye for long. Been working at Georgia's ever since."

"Georgia's?"

Julia took a large swig and made a guttural sound as she swallowed her whiskey and tea concoction. "It's a saloon in town."

"Oh," Sam said.

"Aspen is littered with men meaner than a cornered bear." Julia laughed. "A gal without family and money does what she's gotta do to survive."

Sam sipped her tea and nodded knowing how true those words were. A day hadn't gone by that she wasn't fed and dressed thanks to the Sisters of St. Joseph. Now, a thousand miles away she appreciated them even more.

"What happened to you? Give me the whole story not just what you told that mule's ass, Sheriff Brown," Julia said taking her seat in in the rocking chair by the fire.

Sam took a deep breath and recounted her story. She trusted Julia, but telling her about the payroll was a gamble so she kept that detail to herself. The money was all she had, and that was too much to trust anyone with.

Julia took a swig of her spirit-laced tea and leaned back in her chair. "What were you doing on that train alone?"

"I wasn't alone," Sam said. "I asked the Sisters' lawyer, Wade Rush, to pretend to be my husband on the train. He's a decent man." The look of fear in his eyes on the train was impossible to forget. "I hope he's okay."

"Not many men from the East have the stomach for the Rockies."

"I'm sure he's on his way to California to settle the family situation he was so worried about."

Julia clucked her tongue.

"What?" Sam asked.

Julia looked thoughtful for a minute. "Would he really just leave you to the bandits?"

Sam had been taking care of herself for so long that she didn't expect much from anyone else. The thought of Wade trying to rescue her never even occurred to her.

"I'm not Wade's responsibility."

"Suppose not." She gave her a faint smile. "I haven't noticed any new men at Georgia's. But there are more saloons in Aspen than stars in the sky. Your pa didn't send you a telegram, huh?"

"No, I sent a telegram to the nuns when I reached Colorado. As for J.W., he is more comfortable twisting or avoiding the truth than telling it. Truth is, he was probably double-crossing Luke."

"Sounds like one hell of a schemer."

"That he is," she sipped her tea, "but he's all I got and he needs me."

"Would ya have come anyway?"

"No, all I want is to root my feet somewhere deep where everything is safe, secure, and settled."

Julia took a long swig of her tea. "If that's the truth then ya best get on the next stagecoach back to Leadville."

"I will be once I know J.W. is safe."

Julia studied her as she took another sip of her tea. "If your pa doesn't have money, how was he planning on getting land? It don't wash."

"J.W. is complicated."

"Honey, men are never complicated. Just their way of doing things is."

"He tends to get himself into…situations."

Julia laughed. "There ain't a man alive who don't."

Sam smiled. Being with Julia was easy; just like being back home with the orphans and the "saved" girls.

"True," J.W. never did anything the simple way. "Somehow he always talked me into something."

"What's your plan?"

"I'm going to find Luke and ask him if he knows where J.W. is."

"Ah," Julia said with a wave of her hand. "You might as well walk over there carrying a white flag. What if his men recognize you, or told him what you look like?"

Sam rubbed her neck kneading her sore and tired muscles. "So, what should I do?"

"You need to find out if your pa is missing, kidnapped, or working with Tremain. The only person who knows that is Tremain, right?"

"Yes…"

"So, you ask him without making him suspicious."

"How?"

"You got to disguise yourself. Look nothin' like you did today."

"And then ask him?"

"Yeah, distractin' a man is the best way to go. Remember that." Julia refilled her mug with whiskey. "If you need to get information out of a man, get his mind on something else. In a man's head the possibility of getting what he wants is an elixir. Put on a pretty dress and a man assumes it's for him. Once Tremain is fixed on you," she said looking her up and down, "you can ask him anything without raising suspicion."

"Seduce Luke? I can't do that."

"Sure, you can. One look at you and his mind is going south. Right where we want him."

"But what if he thinks…"

Julia smiled. "Exactly." She raised her mug as if making a toast. Julia devised a plan using her expertise in seduction, and a red silk dress usually reserved for her wealthiest clients. Sam, on the other hand, decided she would have some whiskey after all. Julia's way of doing things was even more complicated than J.W.'s.

Chapter Six

"Take a swig. Good for the nerves." Julia insisted nudging her tin of whiskey under Sam's nose.

Sam turned away and peeked through the dusty office window. Specks of sunlight streaked through the glass revealing circles of cigar smoke hanging in the air.

"Luke's the land officer?"

"Yup." Julia waved the pewter flask as they huddled together on the boardwalk. "You sure you don't want some?"

The stench of alcohol usually turned her stomach, but she was tempted. As J.W. used to say, "A tin of Red Eye is better than a suit of armor. Takes away the nerves and doesn't weigh you down when you gotta run like hell."

What the heck, she was wearing a dress with less material than a pair of knickers. A little whiskey couldn't hurt. Her body shuddered as she forced herself to swallow a few sips of the "poison," as the Sisters called it.

"You gotta be discreet." Julia grabbed the tin, closed her eyes, sniffed the whiskey, but didn't drink any more. In a flash, the flask disappeared into the folds of her skirts.

Sam almost coughed up all her whiskey at the notion of Julia being discreet. She glanced around. "No sign of the train robber from yesterday," Sam breathed in a sigh of relief. "You promise you won't let anyone into Luke's?"

"Promise."

"I'm not sure about this," Sam said, peering through the window again.

"You're just introducing yourself while wearing an appealing dress is all."

"Right." Her "appealing" dress would shock even one of the soiled doves back home.

"What if he...?" Sam stammered at the thought.

"Wants something? 'Course he will. One look at you in that dress and his mind is mud. What he wants is his problem." she said barely suppressing a laugh.

"I don't know."

"If you lose control of the situation, do what any self-respecting woman would do," Julia said eyeing the door.

She shook her head trying to figure out what self-respecting woman would be in this situation.

"Faint. It sends men into a dither."

"Faint?"

"You need to find your pa. Here," her new friend said reaching into the folds of her skirt, "take another swig of whiskey."

Her lips pursed in silent protest.

"Just a little more to loosen your nerves." Julia said.

Does everyone out here drink whiskey in the middle of the day? She took a swig of the drink and wiped away the burn with the back of her hand. "Just make sure no one gets in."

"Especially an outlaw with a hole in his leg. Got

it."

Sam took one more sip and coughed up a little less than the first time.

"Julia? That you?"

A slight chill made its way up Sam's neck. The deep voice behind them was familiar. Her mind raced as she tried to place it. "I think I need a little more whiskey," Sam said.

"One of you ladies say something about whiskey?" It was the laugh that gave him away. The laugh that belonged to the man from the river.

She cast her eyes toward Luke's door, begging her feet to move, but they wouldn't budge.

"Morning." He spoke to Julia, but she could feel his eyes on her.

Coarse wood pricked her fingertips as she steadied her weight against the wooden wall of the building. Using the curls Julia created in her hair as a shield, she turned her gaze toward him.

Wavy brown hair fell to a set of broad shoulders. That smirk was there along with a muscular frame and a rugged strength that somehow eluded her yesterday. The feel of his hands lifting her by her inner thigh and carrying her across the river suddenly came back to her along with an unfamiliar sensation that prickled at her core.

"Gracing us with your presence?" Julia discreetly handed her the canteen.

The rancher gave her a sheepish grin beset by a morning's scruff of a beard. With shaky fingers, Sam slowly removed a hairpin releasing tendrils of hair to conceal more of her face.

"Never thought I'd see you in town again," Julia

chided.

"Needed to get myself a new hat."

Her stomach dropped. His hat was back at the cabin.

"And I thought I'd pay Luke a visit," he continued. He swirled a piece of straw in his mouth like a lollipop.

Sam faced Luke's office door and raised the warm tin to her lips coughing up a bit of the dark liquid.

Julia patted her on the back. "Poor girl suffers from coughing spasms." With a quizzical look, she returned to giving the rancher a hard time.

Curious about what other attributes of the rancher she may have missed yesterday, she returned her gaze to him. The top of his white shirt lay open allowing her to savor a bronzed and taut chest. Lowering her eyes, she admired his buckskin chaps wrapped snugly around his denim wranglers outlining a set of long, lean legs. He was relaxed yet powerful as he used his alluring brown eyes and captivating charm just like the cowboys described in Sister Mary Ellen's stash of dime novels. It wasn't working on Julia though; she was still needling him.

"What brings you and your friend here to Luke's?" He was talking to Julia, but his eyes were on her, all over her in fact.

"Jesus Mary and Joseph," she muttered and walked back and forth to the window.

Julia looked at her with a frown and then turned back to the man. With a lift of her chin Julia responded, "Business."

"Business with Tremain?"

"That's what I said." She narrowed her eyes silently scolding him.

Sam had to suppress a smile. Her new friend was unlike anyone she'd ever met. She said what she felt, free spirited and unfettered.

"Well, I've got some questions for him, too." A glint showed in the cowboy's eyes. He was having fun with this conversation.

"You're talkative today," Julia chided him.

"Guess I am," he agreed with a nod. The straw twirled in his mouth, and he started to move around Julia.

"About what?" Julia said standing tall and stepping in his path.

"Just checking out what he's up to. Word in town is that there was a train robbery yesterday."

"And you think Luke did it?" Julia stepped back into Sam's path, forcing her to stop pacing.

"His men were on my land yesterday, not too far from the site of the robbery."

She made a clucking sound with her tongue as if she was figuring out a mystery. "Is that so?"

"Yes, ma'am, stranger in town, too, that kind of thing." With one large step to the side, he made his way around Julia and closer to her.

"Stranger?" Julia asked forcing his attention back to her.

"A woman at the crook of the Roaring Fork looking to talk to Tremain."

Sam begged her heart to stop pounding so hard. She placed her hand on her chest before it gave her away.

"Well, this ain't her. She's from a convent, so quit staring at her like that," Julia scolded.

"Convent?" He nodded his head. "I like the new

look. Get a lot more folks to church with the nuns in that get-up. Better than those other clothes."

"Habit. They're called habits," Sam said out of the corner of her mouth without looking at the man.

"Isn't it a little early to be ministering to the sick?" he replied with a smirk. The tone in his voice felt like a slap on the bottom.

"Mind if I speak to Tremain before you, ah, conduct your holy business?" He took the straw from his mouth and made an obvious appraisal of her.

This dress was inviting more attention than it was worth. She should've gone with her instinct and just walked right into Luke's and demanded answers.

Carefully, so as not to show her face, she turned toward Julia, sliding her backside toward the rancher. "Yes, I do." The words came out deep and garbled. She was trying to disguise her voice, but she sounded as if she were a drunk old man.

"Miss," the ranch owner said, "you okay?"

"She's not herself right now," Julia answered, frowning and reaching over to relieve Sam of the canteen.

"Ah, coughing spasm again?" The man bent his head and peered over her bare shoulder. She shivered and instinctively leaned forward, inadvertently pushing her bottom into his legs. Realizing what she had done, she jerked her head up, nearly knocking into his shoulder.

"What order are you from, Sister?"

"Get on now," Julia interrupted, shoving him back. "She's on official business."

The rancher was having none of that. He positioned his sculpted chest between her and the door. Sam tilted her head down. She needed to go inside before the rancher figured out who she was and created a scene. The whiskey, or was it the cowboy, was making her mind hazy, but she attempted to speak anyway. "Be right out."

"Perhaps you need a little more to drink, Sister. Your throat sounds a bit dry."

"Ah," she let out an exasperated groan. The glint in his eyes and the curve of his lips said it all. He was laughing at her. She pivoted and gave him a rough elbow jab in the ribs.

"Whoa." He jerked backward.

Sam moved right in and wedged her body between the rancher and the door.

Julia looked as if she needed another drink of whiskey. "They're, ah, teaching the nuns how to defend themselves these days," Julia explained.

Jesse rubbed his ribs and nodded. "Well, if they're going to be drinking and dressing like that…"

"I'm going in." Enough with this man. She had to get in and out before losing her nerve or the whiskey wearing off.

"My business with Tremain won't take long," he replied. "Mind if I go in first, or is this a matter of life and death?"

She spun around. She was chin to chest with the man, but it was there in his eyes—the blaze of recognition. He tilted his head and leaned forward whispering into her ear. "Are you teaching Luke about those pesky ten commandments? I think there's one about," he paused resting his finger on his chin, "stealing, is it?"

She pursed her lips and gave him her best glare.

Then jammed her shoulder into his arm attempting to push him aside, but he was six feet of solid muscle and didn't budge.

Her fists curled ready to knock him out of the way. She took a deep calming breath and looked up at him with all the confidence she could muster. "Yes, I do mind." She motioned toward the door. He answered with his aggravating smile but stepped aside. "Thank you," she said reaching for the doorknob. "I will be out in ten minutes."

The heat of his hand covered her fingers. He held the door in place. "You're welcome, and, I'll be in, in five minutes." His voice, husky and firm sent a rush through her.

"Ten," Sam replied shoving her shoulder into him. Her mind was fuzzy, and her legs loose. Throwing all her weight into the door, she thrust it open and quickly closed it behind her.

Inside she steadied herself, checked her dress and pinned her hair back up. She breathed deep and prepared herself for the farce she was about to play. Too much whiskey, coupled with the scent of leather and the feel of the rancher's body rubbing against her, left her in a daze. The Sisters had mentioned something about men and bodies, but she couldn't recall the conversation at the moment.

Just get in and out before the rancher comes in. How did he recognize her? Yesterday she was a gun-toting horse thief. Today, she was a whiskey-drinking nun in a red silk dress.

Sam surveyed the scene inside concealing her trembling fingers behind her back.

"Don't make me regret my decision to bring you in

on this, Tremain, a crusty old man said from a crumpled couch nestled in the corner. Rangy cushions looked as if they might have once been a moss green color, but the absence of fresh air and any hint of cleaning had taken its toll. The couch was matted with a layer of brown grime and boot indentations on its worn, crooked arms. The wall above the plump man was adorned with commendations from the sheriff for assistance in apprehending several outlaws.

"Excuse me," she called over the loud, tense voices of the three men who filled the room.

She swallowed the last drop of moisture in her mouth and put on her best smile. The men quit talking, and each had his eyes on her. They made no effort to stand or greet her, only stared at her licking their lips as if her arrival announced feeding time.

Directly opposite her was a short unshaven man seated in a small chair. His grotesque belly hung over his belt. Dark hair carpeted the massive bulge in some places and was absent in others. The result made his stomach hair look like grass growing through a crack in a boardwalk. He, like the others, eyed her presence with a dangerous mixture of resentment and lust.

"Sorry to interrupt." Sam cleared her throat. Apparently, no introductions were coming her way. A man about J.W.'s age stood in the corner doorway. His arms were crossed. He was biting on a set of filthy fingernails. Beyond him was a smaller office with a candle burning on a desk. The candlestick seemed stuck to the desk from years of wax drippings.

"What can we do for you, miss?"

"I am looking for Mr. Tremain," Sam said, her mouth drier than the dirt on the floor.

The man straightened his wiry form and stood aside, waving her into the second dingy room. "Looks like this meeting will have to wait until later, gentlemen."

The smack of the door closing behind her reminded her of the heavy bang of a judge's gavel at one of J.W.'s court hearings. She eyed the closed door and wiped the sweat of her palms on her dress.

"Now, miss..."

Sam spun her head back around. The man, who she had to assume was Luke Tremain, was already seated behind a large mahogany desk littered with papers. He rubbed his forehead on the sleeve of his yellowed shirt.

A dimple divided his pointy chin. He steepled his fingers and looked over her shoulder at the door. Whatever he had been discussing with the men was not pleasant, that much was obvious.

"Sorry to disturb your meeting."

"You are much more pleasant to talk to," he said with a forced smile. Lighting a cigar, he leaned back in his chair and considered her as if she were mare for purchase.

"I understand you are the man in town to speak to about investing in the railway," Sam began.

"That was a private conversation," he said his gray eyes sharpening.

She forced herself to concentrate. Every word of the skit she and Julia had rehearsed was burned in her brain, but the whiskey fogged up her head. She heard Julia's voice, "Men listen with their eyes as much as their ears. You must use your womanly charms." Unaware that she possessed any womanly charms, Sam had laughed in nervous disbelief as Julia described the tactics she assured her would fool Luke. Then again, the dress certainly had an effect on the rancher—the one who would be barging in soon.

Clearing a space for herself on the edge of the broad desk, she sat down and leaned forward. "There is no need to be modest, Mr. Tremain." She almost choked on the words. "I can tell you're a very successful man. Who else in Aspen would have had the vision to think of a railroad through the Rocky Mountains?"

She glimpsed at the papers on his desk.

"Did you come here to talk about railroad expansion?" Luke asked, leaning forward and not very discreetly taking advantage of his view of her bosom.

Just as Julia had predicted, her red silk dress was working. Apparently, Luke's thoughts flew out the window when a better view came in the room. While part of the plan, his probing eyes and lip-licking tongue made her cringe. Her bust, larger than Julia's, overburdened the corset creating a waterfall of flesh to mesmerize him.

The whiskey warmed her body making her feel fluid like silk. She came back to the moment just as his bony fingers reached her face. She turned away concentrating her gaze on the aging floor clock in the corner—anything other than him. Like a nun slapping a ruler against her palm, the tick of the floor clock sounded in her ears. The last thing she wanted was the rancher to see her seducing Luke.

She didn't belong in this silly dress. She was not a woman who feigned demureness, but the alcohol swam through her body and made her woozy and weak. The hell with the plan, she couldn't pretend anymore.

"No, I am looking for my father," she purred.

Luke's eyes narrowed. He leaned back, releasing a growl from the chair's leather. A thin smile stretched his face as he nodded and took a long puff of his cigar. He stood and slowly circled the desk coming very close.

She held her breath waiting for him to say something.

He smiled. "Samantha Ward."

"How do you know who I am?"

"You have your mother's beauty and the grit of your father. A dangerous and intoxicating combination."

"Have you seen J.W.?"

"Maybe." He smiled, sucking on his cigar.

His smug demeanor made her sick. Was she on the verge of nausea or murder? Her fists tightened, and her heart pounded.

But something changed in his eyes just as a lump formed in her throat. The distinctive odor of cigar stung her nose. He shifted his weight and wrapped his arm around her waist pulling her into him. Her heart dropped. Luke's hands felt like the bandit's. She was back on the ground like yesterday fighting for her life. Paralyzed in fear, this time, she could only stare at him.

Suddenly the office door flew open. The rancher's body took up the entire doorway. "Sorry to interrupt your business meeting," he said in a voice drenched with cynicism.

Luke glared at him. "Get out."

But the rancher sauntered deeper into the room. "Save your breath. You're going to need it if your men take one more step on my property." The intensity of his anger sent a shudder down her spine.

"Your visits are becoming far too frequent and far too boring," Luke replied.

"Well, I can't compete with divine entertainment, now can I?" the rancher smirked.

The room began to sway, or was it her? She slid her fingers onto the desk gripping it to steady herself. His interruption saved her from mind-numbing fear, but she needed him to leave. Even nosey nuns were more tolerable than this. Her heart pounded; she was not about to lose all she gained; she had to do something. She was so close.

The rancher pushed his hat up against waves of hair. Above a perfectly sculpted nose were those deep brown eyes, this time flickering sparks of concern. "You don't belong in here." He leaned over her shoulder and whispered in her ear.

There was no hint of sarcasm in his voice. She wrung her hands and shook her head. She wasn't budging.

He tilted his head and looked down at her. "This is no place for you."

"This is no place for you," Luke replied glaring at him.

The pounding in her chest told her she needed to act. She took a deep breath and stepped in between the men. "Mr. Tremain and I are in the middle of a conversation."

"Conversation?"

"Yes," she said, raising her chin. Swallowing the aching desire to painfully stroke the stubble off the rancher's tanned cheeks, she gave him her best glare and aimed her foot at his boot.

But he slid his foot away just before she could reach her target. His eyes sought hers. Silent in his victory, the corners of his mouth lifted into a smile of triumph.

He lowered his mouth to her ear and with just a trace of whisper he said, "Not this time, Sister."

His body was so close. The scent of leather was intoxicating.

"What do you want?" Luke growled taking a step closer to her. Sam kept her eyes on the cowboy and slipped her hand onto his hip and felt for his holstered gun. But his steel grip folded over her fingers. She lifted her gaze to find the rancher watching her with what was becoming an ever-present grin.

Luke stepped closer, pinning her against the rancher and squeezing her in between the two men. She struggled to breathe against the rancher's rugged chest. Thankfully, he noticed her plight and pushed Luke backward, releasing her.

"You know what I want," the rancher said.

Luke crossed his arms. "I had nothing to do with your barn barbecue."

Pain flooded the rancher's brown eyes. His trigger finger flickered and crept toward the gun. Tomorrow a hole in Luke's head would be most welcome, but right now she needed him. There was no time to think, so she did what any self-respecting, desperate woman would do. She closed her eyes, sighed, and hoped one of the men would catch her before she landed on the filthy floor. She drew the line somewhere between desperation and dirt.

Strong arms seized her, and the scent of leather told her she landed in the arms of the rancher. Her stomach fluttered as large hands slid around her waist. The heat of his body and warmth of his breath on her neck sent shivers through her. He leaned into her, his hand brushing her backside momentarily. As if she weighed not more than a feather, he lifted her off her feet and carried her across the room. The feel of matted velvet pillows cushioned her descent onto the couch.

"Get some water," the rancher ordered Luke.

Through squinted eyes, Sam watched the man holding her. His strength and conviction were invigorating.

"Damn it!" Luke yelled.

"Get her water." the rancher yelled back.

"I don't have any water."

"Find some."

"Damn it!" Luke Tremain cursed again. Heavy footsteps pounded the wooden floor. The slam of the door told her that she and the rancher were alone, the opposite of what she had intended.

Chapter Seven

"Striking," Jesse Colburn decided as he watched the woman and hoped for a sign of her return to consciousness. Without a thought, he brushed his hand along her soft inviting cheek. It wasn't her face that he had recognized immediately. It was the feeling of being struck dumb for the second time in two days. Her face, oh, it had the same tall-hog-at-the-trough airs, but everything else about her was far different from yesterday. She'd gone through one hell of a transformation.

When he walked in the office her eyes, not their beauty this time, but the look of fear in them struck him. His stomach had clenched at the sight. She didn't let on that she was scared though. Not her, she acted like she had everything under control. How often did this woman get herself into these situations?

She was not from the West; that was clear. If she had run into the likes of the James brothers or Cole Younger yesterday, it would've been a whole different story. Sure it wouldn't have taken much to disarm her, but he chose not to. Other men weren't so forgiving. Especially Luke Tremain. Whatever she was up to, she was playing a dangerous game. She needed to learn not to mess with the men of the West. Hell, even the women of the West took aim before asking questions.

Two days in a row now he held the mysterious

beauty. Her soft body filled his arms perfectly.

Light streaked through the window and illuminated her cream-colored skin. Her figure was as inviting as her face. Her breasts rose and fell in a rhythm that made him ache. He pulled on his collar. "Where's that water?"

Whatever she and Julia were up to, he wasn't going to leave the defenseless woman alone with Luke. She couldn't even handle an argument without fainting.

But was she really defenseless? A frown edged its way across his face at the memory of her holding him at gunpoint the day before. The image of her milky soft thighs wiggling up her horse, no his horse, brought his eyes over her like butter on bread. The rhythm of her breasts rising and falling mesmerized him. He clenched his fists fighting his need to touch her. Yesterday the fighter in her intrigued him. Now, her softness, her vulnerability sparked his desire. He cast his glance down, pushing the image of her heaving chest from his mind. But he lost the struggle within.

His head shot up, and his shoulders flinched. Should she be breathing hard if she'd fainted? Heat flooded his face. She was faking. She fooled him again. It was time to teach her a lesson.

"I guess it's just you and me," he whispered. "I didn't recognize you out of my clothes." He caressed the silk that covered her body yet revealed every curve and inch of her mouth-watering figure. "It must be hard to breathe in this tight contraption," noting she had no trouble breathing. "Let me just reach over here and help you," he said releasing one of her lace straps.

"You really should take it easy on the whiskey, Sister. You can't handle a man's drink." No response.

He thought that would get a rise out of her.

"You said yesterday that you don't work for Luke. Yet here you are in his office, looking as if you're working for him." Still no reply.

"How can I make you more comfortable? Ah, I remember these boots from yesterday. They are dangerous, and besides, I'm sure your mama told you not to put your boots on the couch. He ran one hand down her body in order to relieve her of her boots. His fingers traveled where his conscious warned him not to. With a light stroke of his hand, he traced a circle around the soft part of her belly. The pounding of his chest stopped him long enough to gather his wits and set course down her legs. The feel of silk against his fingers soothed his inner turmoil.

Her lips pursed and turned white.

He had to give her credit. She was lasting a hell of a lot longer than he'd expected. He wasn't sure he could take much more of this. The softness of her body and that scent of flowers, or whatever it was, drove him mad.

Clearing his throat, he continued, "Your boots are buried under all kinds of fancy material here." He raised the hem of her dress. Her cheeks flushed, and her fingers formed tight little fists.

He smiled. Victory was within reach.

Holding the hem in his hand, he reached under her dress and pulled off her boot. He threw it recklessly over his shoulder. The woman winced when it hit the desk and landed with a thud. Jesse palmed her knee and started to make his way up her thigh.

Suddenly her hand came down on his with a sharp slap. She shot up stirring ringlets of black locks that fell to a graceful neck. Her dress hung low off one creamy white shoulder. A wave of desire burned through him. He swallowed all sense of decency as his gaze lifted from her delicate shoulder to the fiery green eyes glaring at him.

He was mesmerized. Fascinated by a woman whose name he didn't even know.

"How dare you! The audacity of taking advantage of a faint woman!"

He roared with laughter. She was a spitfire all right, one hell of mesmerizing fireball.

It felt good to laugh. Tension had been smoldering within him for months.

The office door flew open, and Luke bolted into the room, slamming a tin cup down and spraying water all over his desk. He scowled. "What the hell is going on?"

"Mr. Tremain," the woman cried, recovering quickly. She threw an elbow at Jesse and scooted off the couch. "I believe we were in the midst of an important discussion."

With one hand, she gripped her falling dress and flung her dark tendrils behind her. Her tongue circled her rose-colored lips. "Perhaps we could just take another minute to finish where we left off?"

Jesse felt his chin drop as she sauntered toward Luke. But with only one boot and too much liquor, she lost her balance and stumbled, knocking several hairpins loose and unleashing the remainder of her glistening midnight hair.

She was the best show in town. His eyes could not leave her. Nor could he contain his astonishment. She was no whore—that was clear. She flirted miserably, but that didn't keep his groin from feeling the heat of her seduction.

"I would like to continue our conversation, in private." She lowered her gaze, casting her eyes away, and swinging her head back to glance at Luke, blinking furiously.

"Got something in your eye, Sister?" Jesse prodded leaning toward her.

She grimaced, he noted with triumph. But forged ahead like a steam engine.

"All right, one more minute won't hurt." Luke turned his gaze back at Jesse. "See yourself out."

"Good day," the woman said, still holding her dress in one hand.

When he didn't move, she raised an eyebrow.

Lost in the moment, Jesse could only stare. His feet were molded to the floorboards. The bold and brazen woman was no match for the ruthlessness she was inviting. Contempt and apprehension brewed in his chest as he noticed Luke captivated as well. Jesse would never harm her or take advantage of her, but Luke would enjoy the hunt and the kill.

"Perhaps you should take a long walk, again," she said wrinkling her nose as she had done yesterday when she acted as if she was sorry for taking his hat and horse.

As a rancher, a kick or a toss from a steer was a daily occurrence. Knowing when to walk away and when to run from a battle kept him alive. Those eyes, that smile, even her raised eyebrow told him to run. Whoever she was, whatever she was doing, she had roped both men and it was headed for a tie-down.

He lowered his new hat and nodded at her,

"Pleasure to see you-—again, Sister."

"Don't call me, Sister."

"I don't know your name."

"That's right, and it's not 'Sister'."

"Fine." He raked his eyes up and down her body. "Goodbye, Red."

He smiled and strode toward the doorway.

At the door he turned to Luke. "Remember what I said. You will never get Enchantment. I will put a bullet through your eye if I as much as smell your putrid stench on my land again."

****

"That man is as ill-bred as they come," Sam cried in her best "surprised woman" voice as the rancher left the office. Finally, the tension settled, and she could get back to business.

Swallowing her pride and ignoring the nausea in her belly, she slid one finger up his arm and grazed his shoulder. The light caress conveyed a promise, an empty one, of what was to come. It worked and she won his full attention. "Now, you were telling me where my father is." She pressed her breasts against his chest just as Julia instructed. The contact forced the strap from her dress to fall off her shoulder.

Breathless and energized at the same time, she was relieved to finally be making progress. Usually men didn't have much effect on her. She'd encountered more than her fair share rescuing J.W. The rancher was different, though. He didn't feign respect for a woman just to get what he wanted. He called her out on her absurd scheme without giving her away to Luke.

The rancher was occupying too much of her mind right now. This needed to end. She took deep breaths to the point of hyperventilating while doing her solemn best to appear unfazed.

Luke reached for her strap and caressed the fabric between his fingers. Was it the reek of his cigar or the cologne he seemed to abuse that made her stomach lurch? Neither, it was the lick of his tongue across his lips that made her flinch.

He must have sensed her discomfort. "Miss Ward, it's been a pleasure, but I must be gettin' back to work."

"But you were about to tell me where J.W. is."

He sighed, or was it more of an exasperated gasp? He was studying her all the while shaking his head. "All right, I'll tell you where J.W. is."

"You will?" She almost screamed, before biting her lip.

"But I'm gonna need something in return."

Blood rushed from her face; her legs buckled and her palms grew moist. She knew what he was going to say. Hadn't she acted as if she would do anything? Now her worst fear was realized. She had never been with a man, never even been kissed, and now her stomach churned at the thought of Luke Tremain expecting her to...

"I need you to give me something."

"What?"

"Land."

"Land?" Her head jerked as shock, relief, and hopelessness flooded her mind.

"A deed to a ranch to be more specific."

"But how can I get someone to sell his property to me?"

"You can be quite persuasive when you want to be," he said as his gaze lingered on her bosom.

"But I don't know anyone here. Where is J.W.? Is he safe?"

"He will be once you give me the deed."

"How do you know I won't tell the sheriff?" Sam pressed him.

"If you want to see J.W. alive, you will not tell anyone of our arrangement."

"But…what land? How will I know who owns the property you want?"

A sinister smirk emerged on his cruel face. "I wouldn't do that to you, my dear. You've already met the landowner. His name is Jesse Colburn, and he just left."

Chapter Eight

Sam shoved the door open and stormed outside. Using her hand to protect her eyes from the blinding sun, she searched the area for Julia.

"Wouldn't mess with Luke Tremain if I were you."

She whirled around and glared into the enticing eyes of Jesse Colburn. He leaned against the wall, twirling a piece of straw between his lips.

"You are not me," she answered hotly. "Rest assured, if you were the last man in this forsaken filth of a town, I would not seek your advice."

He straightened and removed his hat while flashing what appeared to be a satisfied grin. "We have not been properly introduced, Miss...?"

"That is because, sir, you quite improperly introduced yourself."

His smile deepened. "Well now, it's not every day a woman falls into my arms. Next time, I'll be sure she has truly fainted before I catch her and carry her to safety."

"To safety? Seems to me I would have been safer on the floor."

"To be fair, miss, you stole my horse, my hat, my shirt..."

She shook her head and took a deep breath.

"I did find Rusty tied up outside the sheriff's office. My Winchester was missing though."

"I had a very good reason, Mr. Colburn."

"Ah, you know my name, but I don't know yours." He settled back against the building folding his arms across his chest as if preparing for an amusing battle. "Glad I could be of service to you, but," he said, his eyes twinkling, "I don't run a coach service."

"You are quite right. Your horse was of service to me. And if you were nearly as agreeable as your horse, you would take me at my word and excuse me." She turned and headed down the boardwalk.

"Well, of course, I mean as long as it was a good reason. Miss…"

"Samantha…Sam Ward." She yelled over her shoulder as she descended the boardwalk's steps. "No need to concern yourself with me, Mr. Colburn. I am quite capable of handling my own affairs."

"Is that what you call it?" His footsteps pounded behind her. He reached her and gently but firmly held her arm. "I warn you, I am a more forgiving man than Luke Tremain, but not by much." He held her still and stepped into her line of vision.

The grip of his fingers felt like a vice. She tried to pull away, but he shook his head. She winced from his clutch. "I am sorry you were inconvenienced yesterday." The bitter betrayal of warm tears surfacing. She was kidnapped and attacked, yet forced to apologize for stealing his horse, again.

How was she going to save J.W., if she needed this man's help? He just swore he would never give up his ranch. The tears forming in her eyes were dangerously close to releasing. Before her emotions gave her away, she tried yank her arm away, again.

His grip remained firm, but his voice turned soft. "I

accept your apology. Now, I need to know what you were doing with Luke."

"No, you don't." She winced hearing the tremble in her voice.

"Yes, I do."

"Why?" She forced the question through clenched teeth.

He shifted his head toward the door. "I need to know what he's up to."

"Then ask him. Now, let me go." She tried to knock him off with her shoulder, but his hold was unbreakable.

Instead of freeing her, he closed his arms around her. Holding her in an embrace, he lowered his face, his lips mere inches from her own. Her heart pounded as his chest melded with hers. Confusion and frustration pitted in her gut.

"You're playing a dangerous game with a dangerous man." The harsh drip of bitterness in his voice made her shudder.

"I can handle myself." Her chin jerked high and she held his gaze.

Strong fingers gripped her waist like a vice. His mouth brushed her ear. "So you've said." The coolness of his breath sent a shiver down her spine.

Fury welled in her chest. The whole town stood by and did nothing. She wasn't helpless, but fighting him right now would be useless. "I will be gone in a few days, and you can go on threatening him all you want."

The sternness in his gaze softened, and he relaxed his hold. "He will hurt you."

"Why do you care?" The smell of leather and the warmth of his arms were as intoxicating as Julia's whiskey.

He put one hand on her cheek and held her gaze. Confusion stirred within. It seemed as if he were contemplating kissing her. Her feet turned to lead and wouldn't move.

Seconds passed by like minutes. She let out a slow breath, and with all the courage and strength she could muster, she thrust her elbow into his ribs. With one last glance, she lifted the hem of her dress, stepped around him, and headed across the street.

He watched her, she could feel his stare, but she was intent on appearing to be a formidable force. She proudly marched across the street. Halfway there the pull of the mud wrestled her foot from her boot. Balancing on one foot, she dug her boot out of the mud and once again found herself covered with the Colorado earth. "Aspen, it pulls you down, covers you in dirt, and doesn't let go," she mumbled.

None of this was supposed to happen. She should be sitting safely back in Boston with the nuns, living a quiet and secluded life. Instead, she was across the country alone, in a new world, but doing the same old thing: saving J.W.'s hide. The Sisters told her to stop rescuing him a long time ago. Of course, she took advice just about as well as he did.

Sweat trickled down her neck, gathering on her bosom. She looked for Julia over the bewildered crowd that had gathered. "What's so damn special about Enchantment Ranch?" she muttered shoving her foot back into her boot and heading toward the boardwalk.

****

Jesse watched each excruciating step in awe. He couldn't help but grin at the slow and aching process.

What a woman. It was like watching a circus performer painfully self-destruct while acting as if it were part of the show. She wasn't fooling anyone, certainly not him.

Her struggle just to cross the road made him wince. It would have been easier to carry her across than watch her battle with her own boots. With her head held high, she continued right on marching. He'd never met anyone as stubborn or as breathtaking.

She was cream and gravy. Her outburst in Luke's office, demanding to be heard, had piqued his curiosity. And it wasn't just her figure or that sparkle of anger and daring that danced in her eyes. No, she was defiant to the point of disaster, and he could not stop watching.

He leaned against the wall, taking refuge from the midday sun while relishing in his current view of Miss Samantha Ward.

Her long black hair framed deep green eyes; her kissable lips belied her sharp tongue. The low neck of her dress revealed sumptuous breasts, full and inviting. His chest burned, and his fists clenched when she had caressed Luke; she had managed to turn his rage at Luke into jealousy.

Just now, he had wanted to kiss her. He had forced himself not to. The woman knew how to handle herself in certain situations, but when he pulled her into him, she had looked at him with panic and defiance all at once. Her small shoulders and tender skin felt perfect in his arms. What made him pull her close? He had no idea. Until he knew for sure who she was and what she was up to, he was going to have to control his impulses a whole lot better.

Last night he'd followed Luke to Georgia's. The crook was cursing and tossing furniture all over the saloon. Most likely he had gotten bad news from his boys. Luke was the one who masterminded the whole damn robbery; he knew it, although no one believed him. The two railroad men in his office this morning were angry, and Luke was nervous. That always put a smile on his face.

Tonight, like most lately, he'd be waiting outside Luke's office watching to see where the bastard went after Georgia's.

A smile crossed his face, and his eyes lingered a little longer on Sam Ward's captivating figure crossing the road. She had to be aware of the glances coming her way, but she appeared not to notice.

As soon as she was safely out of sight, he readied himself for the ride home. Suddenly he jerked forward, a shot of pain bolted from his shoulder, and he stumbled sideways.

"What the hell?" When he heard a groan, he silenced the remaining string of curses he wanted to levy on whomever knocked into him.

By his side a younger man lay sprawled out on the walkway. He was formally dressed and breathing hard.

"Damn it." Most folks took the time to walk the boardwalk, unless, of course, something was very wrong. From the size of the man, he doubted the stranger was seriously injured.

Hunched over, he uttered a garbled apology and peered up at Jesse. "Are you all right?" His disheveled and dirty clothing gave both the appearance of someone previously engaged in a business matter, as well as someone who had been dragged through hell recently.

"I'm fine," Jesse said, noting he wasn't the one on the ground. "Is something wrong, mister?" From his speech, the newcomer sounded like a Yankee. What was it with these Easterners banging into him or stealing from him and then making Jesse feel sorry for them?

"I need to find the law." The man motioned with his hands as he spoke. "Whereabouts is the sheriff?" His youthful hands were free of calluses and any sign of hard labor.

Jesse extended a hand and pulled the man up. "Down a little farther, around the corner by Johnson's Mercantile." Jesse nodded his head down the boardwalk. "What's the trouble?"

The stranger stood up straight but was breathing hard again. An expensive looking pair of wide-rimmed glasses lay on the sidewalk. Jesse reached over the gentleman's unscuffed dress shoes to retrieve them.

"Train bound for Aspen...robbed...bandits... yesterday." He took a breath and swallowed. "They robbed the train."

Jesse strained to understand the Yankee's words, but the anguish in his voice was clear as day.

"We heard. Carson's stage came in last night with passengers. What happened to you?"

"I stayed in Leadville hoping to find my wife." Red waves of thick hair fell across a set of wide eyes. He wasn't as young as he appeared, just a few years shy of Jesse's twenty-six years.

"Your wife?" Jesse pressed.

"Yes, she was taken from the train. I need to talk to the law immediately."

A chill ran down his spine. "Follow me. I'll take you."

The robberies and fires in the past year had to be

connected. He'd bet all the silver in the Roaring Fork Valley that Luke Tremain was behind all of it. But life in a mining town is rough and accidents happen, so no one pays much attention. If he could get the proof he needed, his family would finally have justice. Kidnapping women was a new low for Luke. He must be desperate, and that made him even more dangerous. Sam better stay away from him.

They quickly reached the sheriff's building. Jesse patted him on the back, trying to comfort the frantic husband.

The man stood shoulder to shoulder with him. Extending his hand, distress evident on his flushed face, the stranger replied, "I appreciate your help, sir."

"Sir? The name's Jesse Colburn."

"Thank you, Mr. Colburn. My name is Wade Rush."

Chapter Nine

"Eee yew, it's hotter than a whorehouse on nickel night out here," Julia said taking Sam by the arm and threading their way through the crowded boardwalk.

"Wait." Sam wiped away the wisps of sweaty hair strewn over her face.

"What's wrong?" Julia asked fanning herself with her hand.

"I ripped your dress."

"I ain't worried about the dress." Julia looked her over from head to toe. "What happened? You look like hell."

"Luke knows where J.W. is."

"That son-of-a-bitch," Julia yelled. "I knew he was in cahoots with that Big Bug railroader, but kidnapping, I didn't expect that.

"Sh." Sam glanced over her shoulder.

Julia scrunched her face as if she wasn't used to be shushed.

Sam took hold of Julia's arm and pulled her down the boardwalk. "Come on." She'd already created enough of a spectacle.

Julia pulled back causing them to stop again. "You gonna tell the sheriff?"

"No." She glanced around again. "Luke said if I told the sheriff I would never see J.W. alive again."

Julia whistled through her teeth and started walking

again. "We best get you out of here before your friend with a hole in his leg comes back."

"Comes back?" Her heart started to pound. She picked up her pace. "He was here?"

"Yup." Julia nodded. "I took care of him, for now."

They walked quickly around the side of a building and headed toward the edge of town.

Julia looked around. "I tried to keep Jesse out of Luke's, but when that saddle bum with the limp came by, I had to get rid of him quick. That's how Jesse got in."

"Hold on." Sam leaned against the nearest wall. Between the hot sun and the news that the bandit came close to finding her, she was about to be sick. "Are you sure it was the bandit?"

"Yup." Julia reached under her skirt and pulled out her flask. "Never seen him before, and he matched your description."

"How did you get rid of him?" Sam grabbed the tin from Julia and downed a swig.

"Accidently knocked into his bad leg." She grabbed the whiskey back. "He was as ornery as mama bear with a sore teat after that."

"You gotta way with words and men, don't you?" Sam said and despite the situation had to laugh. "We better get going."

"He deserved what he got. As my ol' granny used to say, 'If you don't got manners, you best have fast reflexes,' that saddle bum don't have neither."

"Well, at least I'm not a murderer," Sam said under her breath. She hadn't killed the man, but he was getting too close.

When they cleared the edge of town, Julia spoke

again, "Now, tell me what Luke said."

"Luke was angry when I arrived. The men in his office looked like they were putting pressure on him."

"I seen 'em. They're from the Denver and Rio Grande Railroad. They've been hangin' around for months. Aspen's been turning upside down on herself with all the railroad talk."

They reached the cabin just as the sun was at its peak. Stepping inside offered little relief from the heat. "I'll get you something to change into and a mug of water. This weather's gonna make you wither like a priest hearin' a harlot's confession."

Getting out of the dress was harder than getting in it. The silky material stuck to every part of her body. The more she struggled to get it off, the more entangled she became. A dull ache was starting to form in the back of her head. When the red dress was finally off, she downed the mug of water.

"Take this." Julia handed her a ripped old cloth and pointed toward a wooden bucket. Sam submerged the rag into the tepid water and doused herself enjoying the immediate relief.

"I don't have a lot of dresses to choose from," Julia said. "How about this one," she asked handing her a well-worn calico dress.

It was perfect: soft and comfortable. The nuns had strict rules about clothes. They supplied you with whatever they had left over or was donated, but they insisted it be proper apparel for a respectable young woman. That's how she learned to sew. The other girls would come to her and ask for help for anything other than having to wear one of Reverend Mother's cast offs. Sam smiled; those nuns were sneaky. Without even realizing it, she learned a trade just like most girls there.

"Thank you. It's exactly what I always wanted."

"The nuns have higher standards?" Julia asked knowingly.

"How'd you know?"

"I was raised Catholic too." Julia smirked. "That was a long time ago. Now, as I always say if you ain't comfortable in what you're wearing then you ain't comfortable." With that, Julia dipped Sam's mug into the water bucket again and handed it back to her. "What haven't you told me?"

One look at Julia's face and she knew she couldn't fool her new friend so she recounted what happened with Jesse.

Julia let out a long whistle. "Didn't know Jesse to be so...forward toward women. He comes to Georgia's every once in awhile, but he's only interested in eavesdropping. That man is hell bent on revenge. Nothing else interests him but getting Luke under the snakes."

"Well, he sure made himself comfortable with me."

Julia stood in the doorway looking out toward Aspen Mountain. "Jesse treats us with respect, a rare commodity to earn as a saloon girl. I'm sure he has his needs, just like all men." Julia turned to her with a smile. "I don't think just any woman will do, though."

"Why are you smiling?" Sam asked.

"He was teaching you a lesson. You stole his horse and such and left him stranded. He wasn't tryin' to hurt you none or take advantage of you." Julia took a long swig of her tea.

"Well, maybe I deserved it." Sam pulled the dress

over her head. "Jesse looked as if he was ready to kill Luke."

"I'm not surprised. Over the years Jesse Colburn and Luke Tremain have broken more furniture over each other's heads than all the goods in the Montgomery Ward catalog. It's a miracle no bones been broken," Julia said.

"Why?"

"Bad blood between their folks; been passed down like an old floor clock."

"Do you think Jesse would really kill Luke?"

"Nah, Jesse's no killer. He's worried about his land and dishonoring his family."

"His land?" Sam suddenly felt a chill run up her spine. "Why does Luke want it?"

"Railroading could make him a rich man. Jesse's pa refused to sell it and then about a year ago strange situations started happenin' at Enchantment. Jesse's pa mortgaged the place and then up and died six months later."

J.W. said Luke got him a land deal from some down on his luck rancher. It was sounding more and more like J.W. was probably after Jesse's land.

"How did his father die?"

"Don't know for sure. It was only a couple of months after Jesse's ma passed."

"Jesse really is a down on his luck rancher," Sam said softly.

"That's only the half of it. Jesse went up to Denver and bought himself a whole band of stallions. About two weeks ago now, his barn went up in smoke. Killed every last one of 'em."

"All his horses…died?" Losing horses was like

losing family. J.W. used to tell stories about ranchers sabotaging other ranchers by killing their livestock.

"Yup, and the railroads want the land. Big money for whichever railroad comes through here first."

It was two weeks ago when J.W. got the telegram from someone in Aspen. Sam's belly twisted with each thought. "So, Luke wants the deed to sell it to the Railroad?"

"Sounds about right."

"Pearl will be lookin' for a rub down and some fresh water," Julia said standing up.

"I'll do it." Sam headed out to a small area where Pearl, Julia's white mare stood. Yesterday, when she first saw Pearl, Sam could see the love that Julia had for her horse.

Julia handed Sam a wooden grooming bucket with two scraggly brushes inside of it.

"Someday, when I got enough saved and got me a piece of land all my own, I'm gonna get Pearl the best brush Dirk's got at the mercantile."

Sam smiled. Brushing horses put her at ease.

"You gotta follow Luke tonight. Knowin' you're in town, Luke will probably be goin' to wherever your pa is tonight."

"Follow him to J.W.?" It wasn't a bad plan.

"There's just one thing. You're goin' to need another disguise in case that bandit is still roaming around."

Sam nodded. "This time, I'd rather not get the attention of every man in town."

Julia was quiet. Sam stopped brushing and looked up at her. Julia started humming and kept on brushing, but she was nodding her head as if she'd decided on something.

"You're right about that. You gotta fit in so no one notices you."

"Maybe I should just ask Jesse for the deed." Sam kicked at the hay.

Julia clicked her tongue. "Jesse ain't givin' up his ranch; fortunately, I know just the disguise."

"Not even to save a man's life?" Her stomach churned at the idea of wearing another disguise.

Julia sighed. "Not for anyone." She shook her head. "I worry about Jesse. It's like my ol' granny used to say, 'Revenge is the dirt a man digs up to cover his own coffin.' He's gonna get himself killed one of these days."

Sam tried to concentrate on brushing Pearl, but Julia's words twisted her gut. She grabbed a pile of hay and threw it in front of Pearl. "Well, at least I don't have to try to seduce anyone," she said to lighten the mood. "We both know that didn't work."

"It may have worked, just on the wrong man." Julia smiled. "I'll get you some clothes from Ned Jackson. He works for Luke. He'll be at Georgia's tonight."

"You think he knows something that will help?"

"Hell no. Ned's got nothin' under his hat but hair. I'll liquor him up. You'll wear his clothes, and then you'll be able to follow Luke without anyone thinkin' nothin'."

Chapter Ten

Sneaking into saloons was nothing new for Sam; she was merely out of practice. Usually, she'd be dragging J.W.'s sorry self out of a bar. Tonight, she was sneaking off in a disguise; the second time in two days she'd be stealing the shirt right off a man's back.

At Georgia's she waited a few stools down the bar from Julia. As the hands on the clock struck ten, Julia nodded toward the man marching up to her. Sam studied the man and the clothes she would be taking from him. She winced and held her breath trying not to inhale the vapors from his rancid rags. Instead of watering down Ned's four shots of whiskey as Georgia usually did, Julia had asked the barmaid to give them to him straight. The idea was to get Ned even more drunk than usual, but Sam couldn't help but think she was the one who needed the extra alcohol.

Georgia did not seem to enjoy the plan. She threw her foul-smelling rag at Ned as he coughed and sprayed whiskey on the mahogany bar. He massaged his throat as he choked back tears. Whiskey didn't actually burn a hole in a man's throat, but it came close.

Julia had told her that men drank in fear of Georgia watching them a little too long, especially men like Ned who Georgia outweighed by at least fifty pounds. The woman would shoot a hole through a man without so much as a twitch. The saloon girls admired her. They said she took nothing from a man but his money. Not after years of abuse from her low-life, silver-hunting dog of a husband. One night when the drunk came home and raised his fist, Georgia surprised him by pulling out his Winchester. The jolt of the shot kicked her front teeth clean out. After that no one bothered her or the girls she kept watch over. She sat back, not waiting, not listening, just there if a girl ever needed her.

Back in Boston, J.W. had envied the barkeep. He always said serving drinks gave a man a place in society, like a preacher or a doctor. He wasn't God and he didn't save lives, but J.W. swore the barkeeper removed fears and took away pain. That was the problem. A few swallows of booze were the easiest, fastest antidote for most men's ailments, especially J.W.'s.

"What's the matter, Ned?" Georgia asked.

Ned finished his drink and rubbed his eyes like a baby. His eyes watered, and his mouth hung open as he searched her face. "Georgia, how many shots you done give me?"

"Didn't your mama teach you how to count?" Georgia taunted the man.

"Are you ready, Ned?" Julia interrupted. She looked down the bar to Sam, signaling her to follow. Sam snuck up the stairs behind them and hid behind the partition in the room.

Minutes later, Ned was sprawled out on the bed. Julia quickly helped him out of his dungarees and red shirt. Sam wasn't so sure this plan would work, but Julia assured her everyone in town knew what he wore day in and day out. If anyone saw her following Luke, they'd think she was Ned, and no one paid any attention to him. If the plan went as planned, Luke would lead her to J.W., and she would spring him once they were alone.

"Let me rub those tired muscles of yours; you had a long day," Julia said, as she rolled him onto his stomach. Drool pooled at the edge of his lips before streaming slowly down his dirt-covered chin clearing a white patch of skin. Between the stench rolling off the man in waves and the idea of breaking into Luke's tonight, Sam wasn't sure she could hold the contents of her stomach down much longer.

"I don't need no rub. You know what I want," Ned groaned.

Sam shivered, not from her nerves as much as her fear of what J.W.'s part was in all this.

She played with Jesse's hat, pulling it down as far as it would go. Knots raveled and unraveled in her stomach.

"How about a little something different?" Julia asked clearly suppressing a smile. She collected his clothes as she told him all about the techniques in the Orient.

"Orient?" Ned hollered over his shoulder. "What are you talkin' 'bout, woman?"

While Ned lay on the tattered mattress slurring his drunken protest, Julia tossed the heap of clothes. They landed behind the partition with a thud. Holding her breath, Sam pulled Ned's pungent apparel on. The shirt was soft and limp. The kind of soft one gets from too much wear and sweat and a serious neglect of washing. How could Julia stand that loathsome creature? She had a whole new appreciation for saloon girls.

From the sound of snoring coming from the other side of the screen, at least tonight her friend wouldn't have to worry about Ned. Instead, she was the one who had to get through the night with Ned's stink all over her.

****

Luke Tremain slipped through his fingers for the last time. Tonight, Jesse was going to follow that son-of-a-bitch and find out what he was up to. Someone was doing Luke's dirty work torching barns and robbing trains, and Jessie was going to find out who. Last night, Luke was real mad. Answers were within reach; he could feel it. With eyes fixed on the land office's front stoop, he relaxed. Suddenly his face broke into a broad smile.

"Would you look at that, Rusty? It's my lucky day," Jesse whispered, as Ned Jackson pranced in front of Luke's office. Jesse would know Ned Jackson anywhere—that slop-pot had been wearing the same shirt for a decade now.

His mama always told him to stick to his daily routine because he didn't have the brains to do anything different. Ned took this to mean he needed to wake at the same time every morning, eat the same food, and wear the same clothes every damn day. His mama was right; he didn't have the brains to do anything different.

Ned crouched and looked around before disappearing down the side of the building. There was a loud crash followed by a cry of pain.

Is he going through the window? Jesse shook his head. "Might as well wear a bell." Whatever Ned was doing, he didn't have the brains to get away with it. Sneaking around Luke's was something new for Ned, and that made Jesse's mouth water.

"Today's turning out to be a real beaut." Jesse smiled. His thoughts went back to this afternoon and one Miss Samantha Ward. The image of her crossing the street as she left Luke's warmed him more than the sun ever had. She had more fight in her than any mare he'd ever come across. The scent and feel of her warm body against his drove him wild and made him want to kiss her right then and there.

But with her head high and those defiant green eyes boring through him, he didn't dare try. He knew he'd been staring at a runaway train this afternoon; one he couldn't take his eyes off. Question was what was he going to do about it?

Ever since his barn was set ablaze and his prize horses destroyed, Jesse had no interest in anything or anyone other than Luke. Hate was all he felt; revenge his sole desire. Today, Sam Ward roused feelings in him he buried months ago.

Jesse promised his pa he'd keep the ranch going and never let one steel rail on Enchantment. He intended on keeping that promise. He couldn't afford to get distracted by a mysterious stranger, so he turned his attention back to Ned Jackson. The moon's glow set a clear path to Luke's door, as Jesse sat in wait as patiently as any man aiming for a fight could sit. A few minutes later, the tension in his jaw released as Jesse's present good fortune crept back alongside Luke's building.

It was a quiet night with a faint whisper of wind and the scent of spruce and fir drifting from the dense forest. An evening chill settled a few feet above the shadow speckled ground where Rusty waited tied to a post.

Jesse headed toward Ned. "Find anything interesting?" he called from a few feet behind him. Ned's shoulders tightened. He was no threat; he was too small and everybody knew it. He would always have a boss. He could never stand on his own.

Without answering, Ned lowered his hat and headed toward the cover of the trees.

"Where you going?" Jesse yelled watching Ned scurry away. Ned didn't answer which was no surprise, but he did tuck his shirt into his pants. In the ten years Jesse knew the man, Ned never wore his shirt tucked in his pants. "What you got there?" he yelled again. "Got something in your shirt, Ned?"

Easily catching up to him, Jesse grabbed his shoulders and pushed him to the ground. Jesse sighed as a whimper escaped from the small man. He took no pleasure in hurting people, but he needed answers. Kneeling next to him, he asked, "Stealing from Luke, Ned?"

Ned's hand shot up and shoved dirt in Jesse's face.

"What the hell?" He spit the soil from his mouth and grabbed Ned's arms restraining him with one hand while he rubbed the dirt from his eyes. "Damn it, that's the second time someone has thrown dirt at me in two days."

Ned began squirming and kicking. "Whoa, whoa, what are you doing? You know your stench is stronger than you are."

Jesse sat on the man's thighs keeping him immobile. "Whew." He twisted his head sideways and fanned the air. "Would it kill you to wash once in a while? You might even get a little muscle on these bones.

"Where's Tremain? Tell me, and I won't tell him you're stealing from him."

Ned didn't answer.

"No? Then I'll be taking whatever you shoved up your shirt." Ned squirmed so hard he could've sworn the ground was moving.

"Must be good, Ned. I'm impressed." And intrigued, the man wasn't smart enough to even know what to steal. He slid his free hand under Ned's shirt patting the skin on his surprisingly smooth belly and moving up toward his chest. "Where is...?" He froze. His palm cupped a mound of soft pliable flesh.

"What the devil?" His fingers were molded to warm rounded skin. "Ned?"

"Get off me and let go of my breast right now!" a female voice demanded.

Jesse fell back as he tried to register what was happening. Ned was small, but Jesse was certain he was male.

"Do you ever keep your hands to yourself?"

That was enough. Jesse knocked the hat from the person's head, grabbed an arm, and pulled "him" into the full glow of the moonlight.

He staggered backward as he stared into the glaring eyes of Miss Samantha Ward for the second time in one day.

"I...I'm sorry. Did...did I hurt you?"

"Hurt me? Why would it hurt to be thrown to the ground and prodded like a cow?"

"I thought you were someone else," Jesse said, flustered.

"Oh, so this is how you greet everyone, is it?

Sticking your despicable hands where they don't belong?"

"Maybe if you decided who you wanted to be instead of dressing up like everyone else in town, this wouldn't happen," Jesse countered.

"I see, you only accost people you know?"

"I didn't mean to accost you. I thought you were Ned. And exactly how did you get your hands on Ned's clothes anyway?" The crack in his voice registered in his ears. He removed his hat and rubbed his head in an effort to keep an emerging headache at bay.

She crossed her arms. "How do you know these are Ned's clothes?"

"I know they're Ned's. He's worn them every day for the past ten years. Are you borrowing them?"

"Yes." Her glare sent a shiver down his back.

"What a surprise." He gritted his teeth. He was angry, worse he was jealous that she stole Ned's clothes. Taking his clothes was a clever disguise, but it still annoyed him.

"Oh," Sam said shaking her head, "shut your mouth—you'll let the flies in."

"You mean the ones on your latest disguise?"

He stared at her, waiting for her to shift her eyes away. When she didn't he realized how childish he was being. "I'm sorry. I'm not usually like…this," Jesse apologized. "What…what are you doing?"

The thunder of horse hooves cut through the tense air. It was too dark to see into the cluster of trees bordering the edge of town, but he knew the horses were close and coming fast.

Sam started running toward a horse tied up a ways down the boardwalk.

Jesse grabbed Sam's arm and pulled her into him. "There's no time to run."

"I'm not running." Her elbow to his gut said she wasn't giving up either.

"Are you always this stubborn, or is it just me?" Did she intentionally frustrate him?

"Believe it or not this has nothing to do with you," she said with another elbow to the gut and shove with her shoulder for extra emphasis.

"Then what are you doing?" He held her arms to keep them both from getting hurt.

"If it's Luke I'm going to follow him."

"Follow him—are you out of your mind?" She changed from clever to crazy in a span of seconds.

"Good bye, Jesse," she said like he was just going to let her walk away.

He bit down on his lip trying to temper his response. "You're not following anyone in the middle of the night."

She looked him straight in the eyes as if she had a choice. "Yes, I am."

"Where do you get these ideas?" Without releasing his grip, he gently, but firmly, pulled her toward the cover of Luke's building. He held her securely out of view from where the riders were approaching.

He felt a kick to his boot. "Let me go," she hissed. Now she was getting her legs involved which meant trouble for him.

"Not until I know you're not going to get yourself killed."

The sound of the horses approaching grew louder. The rider's strides slowed around the corner from where they stood.

"Let go," Sam insisted.

"I will when they're gone."

Muffled voices became clear. "You better get that money before they come back to collect!" Luke's voice penetrated the air.

"I told you; I'll get it."

As soon as the second man spoke, Sam jerked backwards into Jesse's chest. He was sure he'd never heard that voice before and just as sure that she had. She wiggled and tried to run. Jesse held her firmly against his chest. "It's okay," he whispered trying to comfort her. This woman was as confusing as they come. She planned on following Luke but trembled when she heard him talking to someone.

"Let me go," she pleaded.

Jesse's heart nearly broke for her. She seemed terrified, but if she ran, Luke would see her and think she was Ned. "Now's not the time." The only thing Jesse knew about the woman he held in his arms was that she was suddenly frightened and always unpredictable.

Luke's voice cut through the darkness. "How can you be sure? He stabbed you and stole your horse. Seems to me he out-smarted and out-fought you."

"The crook is in town. I'm working on it," the stranger said.

"In Aspen? Damn it. Who is he?"

"I said I'm working on it."

"Colburn's got to be behind it," Luke said. "His land is right there. You shouldn't have separated from your men."

"Luke is calling me a crook?" Jesse muttered under his breath.

"You'll get your money," the unfamiliar voice said.

"It's not my money!" Luke said in a rage. "You got that? Get the payroll—all of it and soon, or it'll be both our necks."

Jesse smiled. The pieces were coming together. First, Luke owes money. Second, the money his man robbed was stolen from him. And, unfortunately for Luke, his life was in danger if he didn't get the money back.

The second man groaned. "Here's the crook's blade. It looks valuable; there's a ruby in the hilt."

Sam suddenly sprang forward. "My," she blurted before Jesse's hand clamped over her mouth and secured her taut against him. The softness of her body gelled into his. Slim fingers pulled on his wrists.

"Shh, it's okay," Jesse whispered.

"Ruby in the hilt? Let me see that," Luke responded to the robber.

"It's real," the man replied.

"Good. We might need it as collateral until you get the payroll back," Luke said. "I am not losing this land deal. Handle Colburn; I know he's behind this."

"It ain't Colburn."

"How do you know? He could save his ranch with that money."

"He didn't know we were hitting the train."

"Nobody did."

"Except J.W."

Sam squirmed again and tried to break from his embrace, but he wasn't budging.

"J.W.? You think he robbed us?"

"Has he come through on his part?"

"Not until tomorrow. You find the payroll. I'll deal

with J.W."

The whip of a crop hitting horseflesh resonated through the air followed by the pounding of hooves racing away. Jesse craned his neck around the corner attempting to catch a glimpse of the men, but he was too late. Jesse could only see their backs as they rode off.

Holding Sam's now silent and trembling form, Jesse tried to digest the turn of events. Luke was definitely behind the robbery. It made sense now. Luke was angry last night because the train robber was robbed.

It was the first time he learned anything useful from staking out Luke's office. Luke suspected him or someone named J.W. of the robbery. Even more interesting—Luke had to answer to someone else— railroad men no doubt, the ones in his office today.

The thought of Luke being scared made Jesse smile, but being lost in thought is dangerous when you're with Sam Ward. Something he should have remembered. A sharp pain shot up his leg from his ankle.

"For the love of God!" She had kicked his instep. If he wasn't wearing his boots, her kick would have laid him out.

"Let me go," she demanded.

Jesse spun her around. He held her shoulders firmly, but at a safe distance from his feet.

"Who's that man with Luke?"

She didn't answer.

When he was a boy, Pa told him to count stars when he needed to cool off. So he took a deep breath and did just that. When he was ready, he softened his voice and asked, "Why does he scare you so much?"

"He's a train robber."

"You seemed very interested in their conversation. Thought you were going to join in."

"I…" She stopped and looked away.

He studied the stars again. "Sam, I know you're scared. I want to help you."

"No, you don't. You just want to get Luke." She tried to break free of his hold. "Let me go." This time her voice was weaker.

Jesse wanted to comply, but he couldn't. He had hope, an emotion he'd buried long ago. Luke didn't have the stolen payroll. That's how he planned to get the deed, but now he didn't have the money. Someone else in Aspen had it. He had to find out who and get it first. The train robber knew who had the money, and he had a connection to Sam. She could help him.

"You're not afraid of Luke," he studied her expression, "and you're not afraid of me," he said in a throaty whisper. "So why him?"

She didn't reply.

"How do you know him?" He followed the movement of her head. "Tell me," his voice cracked. Suddenly he needed to know who the man with Luke was, not just because of his connection to Luke and the payroll, but because of his effect on Sam.

She lifted her head and pushed hard against his chest. "Hmm, I don't know, maybe because he's not the gentleman that you are." Her words were harsh, but there was no venom, no fight in them.

She was right. His behavior had been far from admirable, and she had no reason to trust him.

He brushed away the dark hair that shielded her

features. The desire to touch her became too hard to ignore. He stepped closer, bringing his body against hers. But the look in her eyes told him the only thing she wanted from him was to be let go.

So he did. He took a step back, out of the patch of moonlight and into the darkness. "The train robber was robbed," he mused hoping the change of subject would distract her. "Both men are in town." He shook his head and started pacing.

"It doesn't make sense. Why would the second robber stay in town when there's a gang of outlaws looking for him?" He walked back toward her. "He's got to know he's a dead man when they find him."

"I need to go," Sam said.

His experience with women's moods was limited. The anger in her eyes had softened into an emotion he couldn't read. His fists clenched as he struggled to contain his desire to hold her again.

The knot that twisted in his gut telling him something wasn't right was there again. Her demeanor had changed when she had heard the stranger's voice. First her fear turned to defiance before it melted into resignation, and that was dangerous.

She stepped around him and headed for the front of the building.

Sweet Vinegar! He straightened his hat and kicked at the dirt. He didn't know what was more maddening, his desire to protect her or her stubborn disregard for his help. Just yesterday, he knew his enemies and enjoyed his isolation. Today, his small world had suddenly become unfamiliar and unpredictable.

This beautiful, confusing woman shows up out of nowhere. He had no reason to trust her, but he did.

There was something about her that drew him in like the heat of a campfire.

Since Pa died, Jesse had wrapped himself in loneliness so cold only the lies he told himself warmed him. He blamed Luke for his parents' deaths, but deep inside where even a whisper of the truth could not be uttered, he wondered if he was to blame.

That was too hard to think about, so he concentrated on other people: their problems, their pains, and especially their crimes.

Jesse followed Sam to the front of the land office. He picked up the hat he had knocked from her head and handed it to her.

"It's your hat," she replied.

"I got a new one."

"I told you I would return it."

"I needed a new one anyway," he lied. It had only been two weeks since he'd bought the one Sam wore to replace his favorite one lost in the barn fire.

She tilted her head to the side. "This is a new hat."

"Didn't fit right. Too small."

"I thought it looked perfect on you."

"Oh?" he said with a smile. "Is that so?"

"You're right. You do need a bigger hat to cover that huge head of yours."

He laughed. "You deserve to have something of your own anyway."

For the first time, she smiled back. "I need to return Ned's clothes."

"Georgia's is no place for a woman from a convent," he said attempting to get another smile from her. "I'll take you."

The moon's warm glow lit the sky with beauty

reserved solely for Colorado as the two made their way toward Georgia's.

Chapter Eleven

The wind whistled through the swaying tree branches. How did the bandit know she was in Aspen? It wouldn't take long for him to track her down now. The rest of his gang was probably looking for her too. She knew enough about men to know that few would admit to being out-fought by a woman. If the men recognized her, they'd ask questions and most likely more than that.

How was she going to evade the bandit? More questions nagged. Why would Luke suspect J.W. of robbing him if he had kidnapped him?

And what about Julia? Had she put her in danger? Should she head out on her own?

Evading dangerous men was nothing new. To J.W., it was an art, a talent he considered necessary so he passed it on to her.

She did learn something very important tonight. Luke's life depended on the payroll. Once she found it, she would control the situation.

Saloon music serenaded their walk through the streets. The town was mostly made of short framed wooden fronts. From the buildings to the people, Boston was a world apart from Aspen. Aside from the beauty of the mountains and the clean air, she couldn't figure out why her father was so drawn to the place. The uneven boardwalk, the muddy streets, there was no structure, no guarantees, no way to even guess what you were going to find around the next corner, except for a saloon of course. Perhaps that's what he liked the uncertainty, the risk, and the saloons. As they approached Georgia's, the shimmer of light through open windows illuminated their way, and the whooping sound of rowdy men rattled the night.

"Thank you," she said breaking the silence between them.

"You're thanking me for, what was it, prodding you like a cow?"

That crooked smile never seemed to leave his face. "You were right." Sam tilted her head up to look at him.

One brow arched and there was that twinkle in his eyes again. "I was right about what?" He leaned closer. "I mean, what exactly are you admitting I'm right about?"

"It wasn't the time to confront Luke."

"Oh?"

"Sometimes I can be a little…rash," Sam said, with her right hand over her heart in feigned confession.

He shook his head. "Really, and here I thought you always thought things through." He grinned, his eyes as warm and welcoming as morning's first mug of coffee.

"Sam?" Jesse stood so close. She felt something, a thread of emotion pulling her to him. He looked down at her with concern.

"Not that you asked my advice, but I don't think you should go into Georgia's."

She'd probably been in more saloons than he had. As a child, dragging J.W. out of a pub was almost a nightly ritual. Jesse was right though, but not for the

107

reason he thought. She couldn't be seen.

"What about Ned?"

"Do the whole town a favor and don't return them. He needs new clothes."

"No, I could never steal a man's clothes." She let out a girlish giggle before hiding her face in her hands.

He shook his head and laughed. Until, that is, she started to unbutton the shirt. She laughed again when his eyes widened, and his mouth fell open. His gaze met hers, and he walked closer stalking toward her like he was going to shield her from view. When he realized she had a shirt under Ned's, he took a deep breath and swallowed before looking away.

When he glanced back at her, she couldn't help but grin. His face reddened, and his eyes beamed with a smirk. No words exchanged, but a heavy presence, a weight seemed to hang over them.

She wondered if he felt it too. "Why are you looking at me like that?" With a shake, she shimmied from the trousers.

He shoved his hands deep in his pockets. "How was I looking at you?"

As if he was trying to picture what underclothes she was wearing, but she would never say that.

"Give me the pants." He held his hand out. "They're going to think there's dead bear out here. He tossed the clothes in a pile by the door. His voice thickened. "He'll find them eventually."

She avoided his question just as he avoided hers. "I can find my way from here."

He cleared his throat. "To Julia's cabin?"

"You know where I'm staying?" Fear laced up her spine. How many other people knew where she was staying?

He smirked like a child getting caught stealing a cookie. "You have managed to catch some people's attention."

She felt herself blush, and her gut twisted again. That's what she was afraid of.

"Let me take you back to Julia's."

"And you think I'm stubborn."

The Sisters taught her that most men fell somewhere between the pitied and the pious. Growing up in saloons, she learned there was another side to men. By nature, some were predators, some were protectors, and some were a little of both. Jesse wanted information from her, but it also seemed that he genuinely wanted to help her. Truth was, she could use his protection, but she wasn't giving up any secrets.

"Okay, thank you."

An eyebrow rose. "You're agreeing to let me take you home?"

"Yes." Her skin warmed, and she felt herself blush again.

Confusion flashed on Jesse's face before his expression quickly changed to curious. "Okay, good."

He took Rusty by the reins. "Come on," he said and mounted Rusty. "Leave Julia the horse." In one swift move, he reached for her arm and lifted her behind him.

"But…"

Before she could finish, he reached around behind him and took her arms wrapping them around his waist. With the click of his tongue, he signaled his horse, and they took off.

The methodic rhythm of the clop of Rusty's

hooves, together with Jesse's hips rocking back and forth in the saddle, soothed her nerves. With the exception of the taverns they passed, the town seemed settled.

Tonight, her arms held a man she had met only yesterday, and tomorrow she would rescue J.W. while evading a train-robbing kidnapper. From a modern city to a camp town in only one week, she had ventured into a different world. A land and a lifestyle she may never have discovered if she hadn't risked her life of security with the nuns.

Growing up with J.W., she had learned never to ask for help. Never to rely on anyone. That, she had slowly realized, was why he was so unreliable.

The Sisters taught her differently. In time, she had accepted their help and enjoyed the safety that life with them offered. The thought of losing them or leaving them had kept her awake at night. For the first time in her life, she accomplished something for herself by relying on herself. Tomorrow, she would test herself once again.

When they reached the cabin, Jesse extended his arm to her. For a moment, she didn't want to get down. Jesse obviously knew she didn't readily accept the offer, but he didn't say anything. When she finally accepted his arm, he gently lowered her to the ground.

"Thank you," she said looking up at him. The wind picked up and began to play with the bottom of her shirt. As she headed for the cabin, she felt Jesse's gaze follow her.

The sound of boots hitting dirt made her stomach flutter and her head turn. He tipped his hat and put his hands up. "Don't worry, I just want to make sure you get in safely. I will keep my despicable hands to myself." There was that devious grin again. He headed toward the cabin and stopped just short of the door where a lantern hung. He lit it and turned to her.

Brown wisps of hair slid across his eyes. "I didn't say I was leaving though."

A stir of nerves raced through her heart. She wasn't about to say she didn't mind.

"Sam, I know you don't trust me. You're smart not to," he started. "I've lived here my whole life and only trust two people."

Of course, he had questions. Ones she couldn't answer. She closed her eyes and took a deep breath. No one asked more questions than the good Sisters. She had mastered evading their inquisitions years ago. Jesse's questions would probably be about Luke. As long as they weren't about her, she wouldn't have much trouble lying. There were times when the ease of lie, scared her, but not tonight. Telling him anything would endanger J.W.

"I'm home—well here, safe, thank you." She turned to go.

"Sam, wait." He held her arm. "There's something I've got to say."

Even though his words were direct, his demeanor seemed hesitant, reluctant. He lifted his hat spilling thick brown hair. Another shot of nerves sped through her. The men in Boston were so confined in their dress, mannerisms, speech, everything. Jesse was free from all that.

His arms filled the sleeves they encapsulated; muscles taut against fabric. The men in Sister Mary Ellen's dime store novels and photographs couldn't compare to Jesse. She swallowed and waited for thoughts to form and words to come, but none did.

"Sam?"

He was smiling again. Amused was the word. That was the look in his eyes.

"Sorry," she said. "I'm listening."

"Really, it didn't look like you were."

Darn it. He caught her admiring him again.

"You were saying I'm smart not to trust you."

He held up his hand as if it were a peace offering, "I'll say my piece, and then I'll go and never bother you again."

Never bother her again. The thought of not seeing him again stung.

His hands were the only ones that had ever touched her. Here they were in the darkness; it was the most intimate moment she'd ever had. Yes, he was trying to get information, but she could feel the weight, the heaviness between them again. He desired more than information.

"Yesterday…"

"Jesse—"

"Let me finish. I want to say this." He shifted and looked away from her.

Her heart started to pound. Please don't ask about yesterday.

"I never asked if you." He pursed his lips like he had to say something he didn't want to say.

Before he asked something, she couldn't answer she interrupted him. "Jesse, I really am sorry about stealing your horse. I understand you are upset. I…I can pay you for it…" The money needed to stay a secret, but he was heading in a direction she was even more afraid of.

"No, that's not it. Please let me say this."

She took a deep breath and retreated toward the cabin.

In two quick steps, he reached her. His fingers cupped her shoulders gently. The scent of leather released a warmth through her body.

"When we met in the woods, yesterday..." He swallowed. "I saw you, and I didn't even ask if you were okay." His eyes softened, pooling with warmth. "I'm sorry."

Her knees felt weak. She looked away suddenly embarrassed.

"Sam?"

She fought to suppress her rising emotions, but they persevered.

"I just wanted to say I should have asked if you were all right."

For years J.W. woke up from his drunken stupors without a thought as to her well-being. He risked his life time and again, and she saved him time and again, but not once did he ever ask if she was okay. Tonight, was the first time she'd been asked, and it was by Jesse.

"If you want to tell me what happened, I'll listen." His voice sounded tight.

"You must think I'm crazy."

He smiled with a nod. "I like your kind of crazy."

She smiled back at him. It was only a guess, but it seemed the feelings emerging from her, were similar for him.

"Thanks for asking and thanks for the hat," she managed to choke out.

"You're welcome, Red," he said with that now

familiar gleam in his eye.

"Red?"

"I can't call you 'Sister' now that I've..." He couldn't finish his sentence and just gave her a sheepish grin.

She knew what he was thinking. Now, that he'd felt her breasts. She blushed and was grateful for the darkness that hid her face. She started to walk away but turned. "About yesterday, I was fine. You saw me. I held my own."

Jesse shifted his feet and averted his gaze. "What I saw was a woman who looked as if she was wandering the wilderness for days. Your dress was torn..." He shook his head suddenly angry with himself. "I should've been more concerned about you than about my horse."

"I had you at gunpoint."

He shook his head and stepped closer. He reached his hand toward her face but let it drop. The man who usually appeared so confident seemed unsure. He swallowed and looked at her; his reluctance was obvious. "I could've disarmed you, Sam, easily."

"You have no idea what I can do." Her voice betrayed her. Shock, anger, and fear rose in her throat and choked her words.

"You're right." He smiled wryly. "I don't even know who you are."

Sam shifted. He had a way about him that clouded her thoughts. She had no intention of letting him see the effect his words had on her.

"Why are you backing away from me?" His voice was gentle. "You ride around mountains, break into Luke's..." He stepped closer. His hands tentatively held her arms. "And now you're afraid of me?"

Her fingers reached to her neck playing with a necklace that wasn't there. The shame of being accosted was something she would never share with anyone. Pity was the only four-letter word she never used. Fear though, that was familiar to her. She was afraid, but not of him. She was afraid of the man searching for her. She was afraid of losing J.W. and of being alone. Her whole life was spent being afraid, and now, in this moment, she was afraid of what her face, her voice would reveal.

"I..."

"Are you scared of me?" He cleared his throat. "Because I touched you?" He looked at her, straight at her. "I really thought you were Ned."

Her chest rose and fell with each word. A shiver ran down her neck beneath her windblown, unruly hair.

"I would never intentionally hurt you."

She bit her lip and swallowed the words she wanted to yell. The emotions that welled within her scared her. "I...have to go," she blurted.

He tilted his head, "I know you were scared tonight." He took a step closer. "And I know you were scared in Luke's office this afternoon. I saw it in your eyes when I walked in."

She wiped her sweaty palm on her shirt but didn't dare speak.

"I'm not going to hurt you."

She stood silent, glancing toward the cabin. Her heart pounded but she wouldn't let him see the effect he had on her.

He sighed and shook his head. "And I'm sure as hell not going to let Tremain hurt you either."

Tremain. He was digging for answers about Luke again.

"What were you doing at Luke's?" His voice was low and thick.

"Hoping to find him."

"And then what? What were you going to do?"

"Follow him." She swallowed knowing how foolish she sounded.

"Follow him, in the middle of the night?"

"Yes," she said raising her eyes to his. She didn't answer to him.

He leaned his head to the side. "Luke's not a good man."

"I know."

"Yet you would try to find him, alone?"

Why did he keep pushing? Was he ever going to stop? "I had to."

"Whatever he said to you," he cupped her chin gently, "it was a lie."

She held his gaze and pursed her lips.

"What has he got on you?"

She shook her head. "Nothing."

"You show up here from God knows where to find Luke. You try to seduce him and follow him?"

"Jesse—"

"Sam, the more you are afraid to tell me, the more I know Luke is somehow hurting you." Answers and honesty: were they so much to ask from people? Folks in town were too afraid to tell the truth. No one faced it. Hell, he didn't even face it when it came to questions he'd buried, but he wanted it from her.

She said nothing just stared at him with defiance in her eyes. He had to move, had to do something before his anger frightened her. It made no sense, he'd only known her for two days, but it still felt as if Luke were taking her from him.

He had no desire to be in the rescuing business. But he couldn't let Sam face Luke alone; it would be a slaughter.

"Then I'll find out for myself." He turned and headed for Rusty.

"Where—where are you going?" Sam shouted.

"To get some answers."

"No, no!" She grabbed his arm and tried to stop him. The force of her was miniscule.

He turned to her and caught her as she ran into him. "If you're not going to tell me, then Tremain is." He gripped her shoulders to steady her.

Her head snapped back as if she had been hit. "Why can't you leave me alone?" She pounded his shoulder. "This isn't your concern."

"Sam…" He swallowed. Horses and cattle were easy to calm. It was all in the tone of voice; the words didn't matter. With her, words did matter, and he had no idea what to say.

"Okay." He pulled her to his chest. It was a gut reaction. The right words never came easy to him. Everything he did seemed to be wrong. Holding her was all he could think of at the moment. He wrapped his arms around her. "I won't do anything. I promise."

He didn't want to leave her alone. But if he stayed he'd just keep asking questions.

"You swear you won't ask Luke about me?"

He nodded. "I promise."

She didn't want his help or anything from him and yet, it felt like what she was asking for was akin to betrayal.

The click of the lock brought his thoughts back to the present. He hadn't even heard her go into the cabin. He watched the light dancing under the door and the flicker of a candle in the small window. Within seconds the glow of the lamp vanished.

"Good night, Red."

Chapter Twelve

"Somethin' happen at Luke's last night? You were tossing and turning like two miners fightin' over a ten-dollar nugget," Julia asked as she poured steaming coffee into two mugs and handed one to Sam.

The chicory aroma brought her out of her sleepy haze and put a smile on her face. She wrapped fingers around the tin cup. Even in the nearly oppressive morning heat, the warmth of the coffee soothed her nerves. Rest had eluded her last night as thoughts of Jesse kept her awake. When she finally fell asleep, images of the bandit haunted her dreams.

"Jesse Colburn happened."

"Ah." She nodded with a smile of her own.

"He was watching Luke's place, I think."

Julia shook her head disapprovingly. "Every man is entitled to scratch his own itch, but that man has got to let it go."

Sam savored her coffee. The scent reminded her of mornings with J.W. before she lived with the nuns who drank tea.

"The bandit was there too." Warm steam bathed her face.

Julia sat in her rocking chair cupping her coffee. "No surprise he came back."

"He gave Luke my mother's bowie knife."

Julia cocked an eyebrow. "The one you stabbed

him with?"

She mindlessly traced the rim of the mug with her finger, "I just hope J.W. doesn't see it. He knows I'd never give it up without a fight."

"And he'd know you're here fighting for him."

"Maybe," she said with a sigh. "Luke is using it as collateral. He owes money to someone, and he sounded scared last night."

"Figures, he's probably in a heap of trouble and has to pony up more money than he'll ever see."

Sam swallowed. "Yeah, because he doesn't have the money from the train robbery." They needed to use her knife to replace the money she took from them.

"The train robber didn't steal the payroll?" Julia narrowed her eyes.

"He did; but he…lost it."

"Train robbers don't lose their loot."

"I know," Sam said solemnly wrapping her hands around on her mug.

She felt Julia studying her. "What happened to the money?"

"I happened."

"You?"

"Yup."

"Didn't see that comin'," Julia said with a smile.

She smiled back. "When I escaped from the bandit, I took his horse."

"I thought you took Jesse's."

"Jesse's was the second horse I stole."

Julia let out a whistle. "You stole two horses from two men and the payroll?"

She felt a huge smile break out across her face. She nodded to her new friend who stared at her with her eyes wide and incredulous.

"You, the one raised by nuns?" She laughed. "That's a real beaut."

"Don't forget, I was with J.W. until I was twelve."

"Guess it paid off. You've had the loot from the train robbery this whole time?" Julia asked. "I'll be damned; you ain't no soft-horn. What the hell are you sitting around here listening to me fer?" Julia started laughing so hard she almost spilled both their coffees.

"Except now the robber is looking for me…for the payroll."

"'Course he is. You got the best hand at the table. You tell Luke if he wants to see his money, he better give up your pa right now."

"Tell Luke I have the money?"

"Hell, you don't have to wait on that crook. Go demand your pa back. Luke's life depends on that money and that means you."

Sam swallowed and took those words in. "I'm sorry I didn't tell you sooner."

"Don't be." Julia patted her on the knee. "You gotta be real careful who you trust."

Sam nodded in agreement as she scanned the cabin. "If the bandit figures out I'm here, you'll be in danger."

Julia grinned. "Let that robber come here lookin' fer ya. I'll take care of him."

"He's dangerous."

"Dangerous? Nah, stupid is what he is. I ain't afraid of no shoddy thief dumb enough to kidnap a woman in the middle of a train robbery. And lose his horse and his loot in the process." She snorted a laugh and put her feet up on an old chest. "It's like I told you, men can't handle more than one thing at a time.

"They're greedy," she clicked her tongue, "and they just can't do it." Her eyes twinkled. "As my ol' Granny would say, "Bless 'em.' Makes our lives a whole lot more entertainin.'

"It won't be long before Jesse confronts Luke about what you two heard."

"You think he will?"

"'Course. It's what he's been waiting for. He knows Luke's running scared, and he'll serve him up good."

"Just as long as he doesn't mention me to Luke."

"If he said he wouldn't than he won't. You can trust Jesse. But you don't need to be scared, you're holding the cards."

"Julia," she said taking a long deep breath. "I could give Jesse money to pay off his mortgage."

"Jesse wouldn't take money from you. No, you came out here to save your pa, and that's what you're gonna do."

"But he could save his ranch."

"He won't do it."

"Taking money is beneath him, but being homeless isn't?"

"If men had brains, they'd be riding side saddle." Julia laughed and continued, "What did I just tell you about men and their decisions? Trade the money for your pa."

Sam nodded absently as she sipped her coffee. Last night Luke said that J.W. was doing his part today. What did that mean?

"This is Aspen. Most folks care more about spit than people and more about pride than spit. Get the money, then you tell those crooks what you want."

Sam let a long sigh.

"What's that look on ya face fer?"

Sam put her coffee on the wooden table. "I care about people and…"

"And what?"

"What if J.W. brought this upon himself?"

A wrinkle appeared between Julia's brows before her skin settled back to its usually relaxed state.

"Get that money and then figure out your next move." She opened the door. "There's a storm coming. You best get goin'."

"What about the robber?"

"What about him?"

Julia acted as if the bandit was of no consequence. The man had kidnapped her, attacked her, and was hunting her down.

"What if he comes here?"

"Ah, in the words of my ole Granny, "'twould be grand'." Julia's eyes sparkled as she sipped her coffee and eyed her pistol.

Chapter Thirteen

Jesse rose before dawn cast its first hint of morning. Sunrise in the Roaring Fork Valley was as welcoming as a wool blanket on a winter's night. The sun crept overhead knowing ranchers moved fast before the sun showed her full face.

With little sleep, his body was marching on without his mind. The mirror reflected a face in need of a shave. He hadn't indulged in one for a while. His hair was getting long, too. Waves of hair blew in the wind when he rode and fell like a shadow in his eyes. There would be plenty of time to hit the barber's in a couple more days. Right now, he had something, someone else, on his mind and for the first time in months it wasn't just Luke Tremain.

Last night left him with even more questions about Sam Ward. Was the mystery woman a master manipulator or victim of Luke's like Pa?

The photograph of Pa on his dresser captured the image of a proud man; a man practically born in a barn. But business was a different story. Being a businessman meant making tough decisions, heartless ones even. Letting go of deadbeat ranch hands or killing livestock just wasn't something Pa was cut out for. Jesse never said it, but he would've run things differently.

Ma and Pa didn't keep up with the new facets of modern life. Just like other old timers, they struggled to keep up with the changing landscape. They wanted to keep life the way it always was. Cattle drives and life on the trail. Life moves on though, and those who don't keep up, well, they didn't just fall behind, they were targeted by men like Luke.

Jesse grabbed his new hat and pulled it down over his waves of hair. He admired the new hat in the mirror and pictured Sam wearing his other one. The hat and the red dress yesterday would make one hell of combination. He made his way to the door. A long ride was in order just to get that image out of his mind.

Across the horizon, clouds were thickening. A storm was making its way down valley; which meant he had to prepare the remaining livestock.

There was a time when ranch hands would've done it, but now no one could be trusted. Help had become too costly over the years. That is, except for Andy and Mrs. Maple, the housekeeper. There was no doubting the loyalty of those two; anyone else was a risk.

Hard work had always been the answer to any problem. For others stealing paid the bills, but it just wasn't in Jesse's bones.

All that was behind him now, anyway. Andy was meeting up with a cattle rustler from Leadville in a few hours. With a good price for the livestock, the three of them would at least have enough money to eat and put roof over Mrs. Maple's head. He and Andy could sleep under the sky again, like on the trail. When Jesse was back on his feet, he'd take care of them again.

After the cattle were secure, Jesse would head to town by way of Castle Creek. The pounding water always helped him think straight. It was also close to where he'd met Sam, but nothing was helping him to think straight about her. Then he'd see Dirk Johnson at the mercantile about selling off his furniture.

The thoughts of revenge that usually occupied his thoughts were getting stronger thanks to whoever stole the money from the train robber. But his hatred for Luke, deep and dark, had dulled a bit. Sam Ward brought new feelings to mind and stirred emotions he'd long ago extinguished. His body was gathering heat and heading for a storm.

That was a problem, though. What was he thinking assuring Sam he wouldn't harm Luke? He'd been after that rat far too long to make that promise, but he made it, which meant he'd keep it.

The little thief was frightened when they'd overheard Luke talking to the train robber. The feel of Sam trembling in his arms had pulled at him. Her fear wasn't because the man was a train robber like she said; there was more to it. There was no use asking her though. She was as tight lipped as a preacher. He laughed; she sure as hell was no preacher.

Chapter Fourteen

The expanse of the swaying green grass brought to mind visions Sam had seen a thousand times, but never like this. Photographs don't capture the color and life of their focus. For the first time, her imagination paled in comparison to her surroundings. Fragrant flowers mixed with the scent of layer upon layer of thick pine and fir trees, and rows of white trees standing sentinel around her.

Beside her, clear water slid down rocks and raced toward Aspen. The open space of the land and sky captivated her.

The calico dress she borrowed fit snuggly around her bosom. She pulled on the cotton to stretch the material, but there wasn't much give. Thoughts of Jesse's hands touching her yesterday sent a tingle fluttering through her. She closed her eyes enjoying the memory.

When he chased her, thinking she was Ned, she had panicked. Now she relived his touch moment by moment. A thrill coursed through every inch of her body. His weathered hands cupped the softness of her skin. Instinctually she pushed her breasts forward as if his hands were still there, willing him to continue.

He had brought her back to the cabin and held her face in those hands. His lips were mere inches from her and lured her in. She closed her eyes and willed the sensation of his fingers back to her.

Like rays of the sun after sunset, the heat of his embrace still warmed her. The strength of his body and the intensity of his gaze posed no danger, no threat. Men had looked at her like that before, but most left her cold and rigid. Not Jesse, he made her feel warm and soft: feminine.

Gray clouds slid effortlessly through the immense sky and mountaintops disappeared replaced by a menacing army of impending darkness. Her fingers clenched Pearl's leather reins with a white-knuckle grip. J.W.'s life hinged on her and a saddlebag buried in between rocks and dirt. If the rain dislodged the bag, she'd have nothing. She kicked the horse's belly urging her on, "Come on," she said to Pearl, "we have to beat the rain."

Her heart pounded along with the rhythm of the horse hooves. Soon her surroundings became familiar. Thoughts of what she had endured two days prior invaded her mind, but she pushed them away, again.

Waves of wind swept over her body and the sprinkle of raindrops patted her cheeks. "We are almost there, Pearl, I think," Sam yelled over the pounding of the water surging downstream.

Pulling the reins to the right on the horse's neck, she edged Pearl closer to the river. She looked up and down the riverbed hoping to recognize something more. Farther downstream, she came upon rock ledge. It seemed familiar, but too treacherous to ride a horse.

"This could be it." She lifted her leg over the saddle. Her skirts whipped against her legs as she attempted to dismount. She braced herself against the wild wind. A strong gust lifted her hat and whisked it across the rock ledge.

"No!" she cried as the hat tumbled toward the river. She left Pearl and chased the hat when she noticed the rocks where she stashed the bag off to her left.

Thunder rumbled in the distance. Trees parted, branches bent and heaved sideways. Leaves fought the wind, broke free and spiraled to earth. She had never been in a storm like this before. In Boston, she'd run outside into thunderstorms. They were an escape from boredom. If it were raining hard enough, she'd think of herself as hidden in plain sight; a reprieve from the rules and structure of the Sisters.

Pure happiness coursed through her. This was it, soon Luke would have the money, and she and J.W. would head home.

The wind jostled her about forcing her to crawl toward the satchel. On her hands and knees, she stretched her arm and felt in between the rocks for the strap. Her hand swept over the leather saddlebag, and her finger brushed against it. The money wouldn't float away, which solved one problem, but now she needed some kind of stick to hook the strap and release it from the muddy grip.

As she backed away a downpour unleashed on her like a cold slap. She waded through the rain. Suddenly the feeling of being watched crept over her. Every muscle tightened. The bandit's Colt .45 lay buried under the cash in the bag. She lunged toward the money's hiding spot, throwing her body on it. A shadow loomed behind her. Hastily she dug her hand into the pack rooting for steel. She found it, gripped the handle, and rolled over onto her back with arms extended and aimed above her.

A man stood over her. The tilt of his hat hid his face, but there was no mistaking who he was. With his head cocked to the side, he lifted his hands, revealing Pearl's reins. "Lose another horse?"

Sam let out a deep breath. Jesse took the gun and tossed it aside. She accepted his hand, and he pulled her to her feet.

"What the devil are you doing here?" he asked.

Even with the chill of the rain, she felt her face burn. Droplets fell in her eyes, down her neck and soaked her dress flat against her skin.

Jesse lowered his hat over his eyes clearly not sure where to look.

"I…was looking for my horse."

He glanced down at where she had been rooting around. "You were looking for your horse?"

"Yes, the one from the other day, remember? When you shot the gun…"

"I remember." He looked from her to the water. "And you think he fell into the river?"

"No."

He shook his head in obvious confusion. "Do you have any idea how dangerous it is up here? And I am not just talking about the weather or the wildlife. Luke's men were on my land the other day."

"I can't abandon my horse."

"That was two days ago."

"I know." With a quick glance at the saddlebag, she confirmed that it was still suctioned in by the river. She needed to get him away from here and quickly. "You're right. I should go."

He nodded slowly, measuring her, clearly not

believing her.

Jesse glanced at the clouds. "We're in for a good one. I'll take you back."

"I can make it on my own." She took Pearl's reins from him.

"Like I said, I'd never leave a woman stranded on Independence Pass. I will go with you."

"I'm not stranded."

"You will be soon," he said pointing at the clouds.

Thunder rumbled again, closer this time. and a flash of lightning broke through the sky.

"We'd better wait it out," Jesse yelled and pointed down river. "There's a cave over there." He headed for a small landing.

She swallowed hard and glanced back at the hiding spot. She just wanted to get the money and get back to Julia's.

"Come on," he called.

"In a cave?"

"You're safe with me." He tipped his hat. "Promise."

"I like the feel of rain on my face," she said. Her stomach twisted at the thought of being alone again with Jesse.

"I once had a steer who ran out into a lightning storm, never was the same after that." Jesse shook his head. "Nope, his head contorted, and he trudged around drooling all the time." His attempt to make her laugh worked, somewhat. She felt a little lighter for a moment, but the weight of his stare sent a shiver through her. His eyebrows fixed in a line. He picked up the cowboy hat. "After last night," he said, and placed it on her head, "don't you trust me?"

A pleasant shade of red bloomed on his face causing her to blush. She guessed, he too, was thinking of him touching her.

The storm rumbled in the distance like a band of soldiers marching forward. What she needed was time to think.

"I'm coming. Wouldn't want to walk around drooling like your dumb cows," Sam said.

"It was a steer," Jesse corrected her.

Sam took a small step toward the cave. She'd never even been in a cave before. Rain cascaded down the side of the rock walls like a waterfall. There was a light woody smell from inside.

Although the cave provided a dry escape, the air was cold and damp, and with her wet dress flush to her body, she started shivering. It wasn't just the chilly air her body was responding to; it was the thick air of tension emanating from Jesse.

He was different today. His gaze lingered a little longer and followed her more closely. Men had looked at her before, but when it was welcomed and the feeling mutual, as it was with Jesse, it made her heart race.

"I've never seen snow on mountains before," she said, hoping to cut the tension. Her body was telling her she wanted his attention, but her head told her she was here to get the money to buy her father's freedom. How could she be physical with Jesse and then hurt him?

Conflicting feelings were nothing new. For many years they had been an everyday occurrence. She tried to help J.W. and hoped that he would return to being the father he once was. At the same time, she resented him for making her feel like she was hard to love. Feelings were complicated, which was why living with nuns was safe. They cultivated unquestioned, untested obedience and faith, which protected them against the menace of emotions.

"Winter is always close," he said.

"The mountains in the East are hills compared to these."

Jesse gripped his copper belt buckle with both hands and surveyed the area. "I hear the ocean breeze and the sound of waves is something to behold. That's what Andy says anyway."

"Andy?"

"My foreman, really my pa's old foreman. He and Mrs. Maple, my housekeeper, are the only family I've ever had beside my folks."

The idea of feeling related to people you shared no blood ties with was familiar to her. Having a home, or even any kind of an attachment to any place like Jesse did, was unfamiliar though.

"Andy's right. The ocean is breathtaking," she said. "There's no end to it. Just like these mountains."

"I can't imagine being anywhere but here."

The nuns used to say that her head was always in the clouds. J.W. would say they were wrong though, her head was in the mountains, where she belonged.

She found herself babbling, "In Boston, they've been filling in Back Bay since before I was born. Water to mortar, brick by brick, men have changed the course of a river and built a hill."

"Miners scrape entire sides of mountains. But right here," he kicked the cave's dirt floor, "it's unspoiled and that's the way I want to keep it."

"I know," she said in barely a whisper. The way his hair swept up under his hat and over those intense brown eyes made him look so seductive she could barely concentrate. She turned with heat burning in her cheeks when he caught her staring at him.

Most men weren't hard to read, their thoughts were obvious by the direction their eyes roamed. This time, she was the one wondering what lay beneath his clothes and wanting to see more.

"What are you thinking, Red?" he asked with a smirk.

"Ah, nothing, why?"

"Your eyes are making that little fold."

"What little fold?"

"The one you make when you're thinking things you don't want to think about," he said raising his hat off his eyes. As expected, there was a glint shining through.

"You're making that up."

He gazed into her eyes and raised an eyebrow.

"I was thinking that I hope the storm stops soon and that Pearl's okay." She shook off the skeptic look in his eyes.

"Really?" His eyes narrowed. "I'd say it was more of an admiring look than one of worry."

"Well I guess you can't read the 'fold' in my eyes after all."

"Maybe." He shrugged. "Don't worry about Pearl. She's fine."

Sam nodded, yet still strained her neck to see out of the cave.

"Are you eager to get back to Julia's cabin or just away from me?"

She glanced sideways at him. He could be so blunt yet hold just as many secrets.

He fingered a red rock that looked like clay and tossed it outside into a puddle much in the way one would skip a pebble across a pond. "Seeing as how you just said how beautiful it is up here, I'm guessing it's me." He answered his own question.

She bit down on her lip to suppress a smile, but it didn't work. Being with him frazzled her nerves, and yet she enjoyed it. That was the problem. She needed to get the money, the money that would cost Jesse his ranch, before her feelings for him grew.

"Why do you look at me like that?" Jesse asked.

"I'm not even looking at you."

"Yes, you were. You look like you want to run away. I told you, I'm not going to hurt you."

"I know," she assured him nodding her head.

"No, you don't. You take risks, incredible risks. That's what makes you different."

"I'm not different."

"Yeah, Red, you are." He lifted his chin and with a tilt of his head, he concentrated his gaze on her completely. "You look as if you can't make up your mind about me, yet you're alone in here with me."

He was right; she hadn't made up her mind about him. But she had made up her mind about what to do with the stolen payroll. It was getting harder to be with him knowing what she had to do.

"And?" He stepped forward.

Holy Reverend Mother he was just an eyelash distance away. He set her heart pounding and her mouth running dry.

"I want to know what you want?" he asked softly.

A thrill ran through her. What did she want? That was changing rapidly. Since the time she was eight she wanted her father back. The J.W. who cared for her, read her bedtime stories, taught her how to shoot and ride.

In church, at Mass, she had watched the families pile in together. They sat close to each other practically sitting on one another and nobody minded. They wished each other peace and walked out the doors knowing that they would be back the next day in the same pew.

Her adopted family of reformed prostitutes and orphans wasn't enough. When she looked at one of them, she wished they were someone else, someone who loved her. And she felt the same from them. They looked at each other wishing they were looking at someone else.

That was why she was here, why she had travelled a thousand miles, because this time J.W. would realize what he had in her: a dedicated daughter, a family, and that would be enough for him.

Now, those feelings of love were expanding. Her growing attraction to Jesse was distracting her and she wasn't so sure what she wanted from him or at all. A secure and planned life sounded sane before, when all she knew was from her youth. Yet, being on her own, making her own decisions and crazy mistakes, and feeling the power and the response she got from Jesse was opening a door she wasn't sure she wanted shut.

"You're cold." Jesse shook off his duster. "Here." He draped it over her shoulders and blanketed her chilled frame. Weight and warmth suddenly called her attention back to the present.

The white shirt he wore remained dry, but judging from the way his chaps hugged his thighs, his legs were damp.

"Is that better?" he asked. He reached under the duster and began rubbing her shoulders.

Sam bit down on her quivering lip and nodded. There was a message in his eyes, an expression of curiosity.

"Yes," she said in a little more than a whisper. His hands were warm, but his touch sent shivers through her body. She felt her face flush as he studied her. He slid her hair off her face and wiped the water from her cheeks.

"Jesse," Sam managed to utter much calmer than she felt.

"Sam," he replied as he lowered his head and leaned his forehead to hers.

The mist of his breath caressed her cheek. His lips were so close she took a staggered breath and brought her eyes to his. He was searching her face looking for a sign of approval.

That was the problem. She wanted him to kiss her, but then she would only hurt him more when he knew the truth of why she was here.

"I'm sorry." Sam stepped back. He gave way but held her arm.

"No, I'm sorry. I said you'd be safe with me, and I meant it. Just, don't go out there."

"I don't mind the rain," she spoke quickly feeling the heat in her cheeks. "I kind of like it and besides the Sisters always said water washes away sins."

"You commit a lot of sins?" He laughed.

"They think my soul needs a lot of rain."

"The nuns wouldn't approve of you stealing men's clothing?"

She couldn't help but laugh. "They would not approve of anything I've been doing."

"Do you need their approval?" he asked suddenly serious.

Outside the cave, lightning struck, lifting a shade from the dimness.

"I don't know. I always thought so."

He nodded and picked up another stone. "If you're so worried about your soul, what were you doing in that red dress yesterday?"

His eyes lit up like the ocean sparkling minutes before sunset. His easy smile was the clincher. It never left his face, for him, laughter was always within reach.

Thunder roared and lightning flashed in rapid succession, illuminating their surroundings. The guilt she had momentarily escaped was beginning to build its way around her again, imprisoning her. He was seeking answers. Answers she couldn't give him.

Rain pounded the ground outside the cave. Little rivers formed and water whisked in circles. She looked outside the cave. "Maybe I should go wash some sins away."

Jesse turned his gaze toward the sky, hopeful this torture would soon end. His duster was so big on her she didn't even bother to button it. He stared intently as she caught the sprinkle of raindrops in her mouth. Droplets slid off her chin, down her delicate neck falling out of view under the cotton clinging to every curve of her body.

The tension in her body was evident when he had touched her. He felt it too. A knot had formed in his stomach that had not been there before—not ever. His desire to hold her turned into a struggle for him when she had rustled from his embrace. He could've kept her in his arms, he wanted to, but she wanted him to let her go.

Her name was the only thing he knew about her; the rest was a mystery. She rode through an unknown wilderness seemingly without a care, climbed mountains hundreds of feet high not even knowing where she was going.

"Damn!" Jesse cursed, as his eyes lingered on her saturated dress mercilessly revealing the curve of her breasts. Rain spared no part of her body soaking her rounded hips and those shapely pink thighs.

He swallowed hard as she laughed. She affected him like no woman ever had. He stood entranced as she languished in the downpour unaware of the storm she stirred within him.

"The rain will stop soon, but the lightning is still dangerous." He approached her doing his damndest to keep his eyes trained on the trees behind her.

"What do you care if I walk around with my head contorted, drooling all the time?"

"That's not what I'm worried about."

"What are you worried about?"

He didn't know how to answer that or what to do with her. Being with her in the cave or watching her stand in the rain—neither offered any relief. "Getting struck by lightning," he replied.

She looked up at him slowly. Without a word, she conveyed that she knew he was breathing in every part of her. She walked toward him forcing him to take a deep breath. The way she eyed him straight through the center like that drove him wild.

With his hand on her lower back, he led her into

the cave. "Once the storm passes, you can be on your way."

"Okay," she agreed through rattling teeth. The cool air of the cave, together with her wet dress, made it impossible for her to be warm even under his duster. "Here, take my shirt," he said reaching for the collar button.

"You're offering me your shirt?" She raised her eyebrows, "Thank you."

He shook his head. "Yes, I can be gentleman."

As he unbuttoned his shirt, it was his turn to watch the expressions on her face change. Her fingers swept back and forth over her throat as he slowly lowered his hands from button to button. Her dark eyelashes revealed her gaze lingering near his chest and then lowering to his stomach. His desire grew as she bit her bottom lip in anticipation. She watched intently. With a tilt of her chin, she raised her gaze and with a deep breath her face brightened. Her eyes acknowledged the feelings between them.

He was ready to explode right there. Without thinking, just reacting, he eased his arm around her waist. She shivered at his touch as he swept his fingers across her body. His mind was numb, but his skin was on fire. With his shirt open, he pulled her into his bare chest. With a tilt of his head, he lowered his lips to hers. She hesitated at first but returned his kiss with equal fervor.

Suddenly, he felt her squirming. He released her waist and started to tilt his head away, but she twisted his collar in her fingers and yanked him even tighter against her. Sweet Jesus she wasn't trying to stop him. She had thrown off his duster and was now pressing her full wet breasts and ripened nipples into his skin. He tightened his hold on her savoring the taste of her, caressing her body from her waist to the nape of her neck.

Her fingers slid down his neck and brushed against his chest. The slight pressure of her fingertips brought his body back under control.

She dropped her gaze. "Are you going to give it to me?" she asked tentatively.

Sweet Jesus, was she sent from God? "What?" The word caught in his throat.

"I'm wet."

He groaned. Could this really be happening? "Are you sure?"

"Yes." She laughed. "You offered it to me, remember?" She looked up at him searching his face questioningly. "Your shirt, remember?"

Damn. If she kept talking like that and asking for his clothes, he'd need all the cold water in the Roaring Fork River just to sit in the saddle. "If the Sisters knew what I was thinking…"

"They'd dunk you in the river?" she asked with that innocence in her voice that drove him wild.

"No," he said, her lips still just below his, "they'd throw me out to sea."

He edged the shirt from his back and handed it to her. His jaw dropped as her eyes lingered on his chest. Her gaze pierced his skin as if her eyes were her fingers tracing the contours of his muscle. Sweet, sweet Lord, he couldn't take much more.

"Turn around," she ordered.

"I know," he said struggling to control the strain in his voice. She was about to wiggle her way out of her clothes just inches from him. The thought of what lie beneath the wet dress just about did him in.

He tipped his hat and gave her a grin, but he wasn't smiling on the inside. The images in his mind weren't fair to any man. If she would just say the word, he would treat her to pleasure he had a strong feeling she didn't even know existed. There was something about a woman from a convent; wet and naked wearing cowboy boots that made him lose his mind.

Soft little groans came from behind him. Out of the corner of his eye, he saw her twisting and squirming.

"You need help?"

She yelled something unintelligible which clearly meant no.

Next came a sigh and the thud of her wet clothes hitting rock. Good God the dress was off. The seconds ticked by as he waited for her to slide on his shirt.

"What's taking so long?"

"Your shirt is hard to button."

"Then don't button it. Unless you want me to button it for you?" he asked pretending to turn around.

"No," she shrieked and pushed him.

"I'm counting to ten and if you aren't finished…"

"Done," she interrupted him. "You can turn around now."

He turned. Slick black hair was draped across her bare neck and down one creamy shoulder. The sight of her made him grit his teeth and draw a breath.

There was a slight tremble in her fingers as she smoothed the bottom of his shirt to her thigh. The rise of her breasts peeked out of the top of the shirt where it was too long in the neck. Hidden beneath the shirt he wore day in and day out was a set of soft breasts. One knee was bent, probably out of an attempt at modesty; it didn't work though. The curve of her hips and the contour of her thighs brought on an ache he was all too happy to bear.

When he looked up to her face, her eyes were making their way up his chest.

"Ahem," Jesse cleared his throat and raised his eyebrows.

Her cheeks turned the color of the reddest leaf in autumn. She lowered her gaze quickly and, once again, swept her fingers across her sumptuous throat. It was a habit of hers that was driving him wild.

"I'm sorry." A coy grin escaped her lips.

"You are a lot of things right now." He stepped closer, "and sorry ain't one of them." Good God in Heaven, that gut-clenching smile spread across her face and her eyes lit up with mischief.

"You shred my insides when you look at me like that." Damn, his mouth watered. In his mind, his hands were already exploring the valley between her thighs.

If she'd let him, he'd make his way down her body tasting every inch of her. He'd lay her down on his duster and drive in deep and dig and dig until he unearthed the buried parts of her.

She must have seen the desire in his eyes. She stepped back.

"I'm sorry, Sam." He raised his hands in a sign of surrender. "I didn't mean to make you feel uncomfortable."

"I don't know what I'm feeling." She lowered her gaze. Her eyelashes were long and dark against her soft cheeks.

He took her hand and held it to his chest. "Do you

feel my heart pounding? That is what you make me feel."

"I think the storm is ending," she said glancing at the mouth of the cave.

"I want to kiss you again." He heard the hunger in his voice.

She took her hand from him and wiped a strand of hair toying with her mouth. She returned her eyes to his. "I want to kiss you too."

The tenderness in her voice hardened his desire. She edged closer bringing her body firmly against his. Her nipples were still hard and the thin layer of his shirt did nothing to hide that fact.

His fingers slid through the swell of hair at the nape of her neck. Encircling her waist, he relished in the response of her body. The quivering of her mouth and the fluttering of her gentle breaths against his throat brought him to the brink.

She stood on her tiptoes and delicately drew her lips to his. The trust and curiosity in her touch roused every ounce of him. He closed his eyes and enjoyed the tender touch of her exploring him. Her small fingers made their way up his shoulders and neck. He leaned into her. He wanted every bit of her: her scent, her gentle moans, and the softness of her arms against his neck. He lost himself in her. Her fingers twisted his hair and pulled his head down to her as she kissed him harder and wilder.

She knocked the hat from his head and donned it herself. "Ah," he groaned. She was killing him. He brushed the hollow of her back and traced the contour of her flat belly.

The sensation of her warm fingertips across his

chest ceased. In that time, his mind returned to his body. Even though her eyes were full of want, his gut was telling him to slow down.

He looked over her head struggling to keep his eyes and mind where they belonged. With one last look at her, he saw the confusion on her face become understanding. She smiled as the blush of her cheeks returned in full bloom.

"Ahem," Jesse cleared his throat, "I'll take you back now." Jesse headed out of the cave toward the horses. The clouds were beginning to clear and the sky was somewhere between gray and the darkest blue. Birds chattered and sang. The storm was over, but she didn't want to leave. She closed her eyes burning this moment into her memory.

At the convent, she'd discovered the sisters' secret stash of dime novels. By candlelight, she'd devour the books until dawn. Imagining a man yearning for her, craving her as he pulled her taut against his firm chest, holding her in his strong arms. She'd lay awake itching for a man's touch, for the time when he would be real and not just a figment of her mind.

Through it all, what she longed for was someone to understand her, to know what she was thinking just by the look on her face.

As Jesse made his way back toward the cave, the intimacy between them warmed and saddened her simultaneously.

He rolled a long piece of straw between his teeth. The confidence in his stance and the steadiness of his gaze drew her in. She had to stop it. Find the money. Find Luke. Save J.W. She'd never felt these sensations before. They'd been through so much together in so little time.

"I can make it back to Julia's on my own." Pretending she was heading back before doubling back to the river was her best option.

"Not this again. It's dangerous." He sighed. "How about I take you down the mountain, just to the path?"

"Deal," she agreed. Goosebumps formed on her flesh, and it wasn't from the weather. Just like the flutter in her stomach, his gaze, his strong fingers filled her with want and a nervous excitement.

She secured her dress to the saddle. Jesse did the same with his duster and handed Pearl's reins to her with a devious smile stretching across his face.

She took the reins and narrowed her eyes. He was acting suspicious.

Without a word he mounted Rusty and with amusement in his eyes, he tilted his head and raised an eyebrow as if to say, "Your turn."

That's when it became clear she had to mount Pearl in just his shirt. Never having turned down a dare in her life, she wasn't about to let Jesse think she was afraid of showing a little leg and perhaps even more.

With one foot in the stirrup, she pulled herself up and held the saddle horn. Narrowing her eyes, she squinted at a tree behind Jesse's shoulder and gasped in surprise.

As expected, he jerked his head sideways and drew his pistol ready to shoot.

When he turned his gaze back to her, confusion covered his face. She was seated in the saddle gently smoothing the shirt onto her thighs.

His mouth narrowed in a line.

Trying not to laugh, she lifted her chin and strained

her neck to see behind him.

He holstered his gun and bit the inside of his cheek, clearly fighting the urge to say something.

She shrugged. "Oh, I'm sorry. I thought I saw a steer drooling and contorting off in the distance. Guess it was nothing."

And there it was—the easy smile. With the tilt of his hat he acknowledged his defeat. His eyes however, conveyed admiration.

"Ready?" he asked.

As the sun peeked through the thinning clouds, she took in his tanned smooth skin. He leaned back, barely holding the reins. The pleaded muscles in his chest and gut hardened.

"Yes." She tightened her grip on the reins as she relived the feel of her body pressing into his chest. It was the tingle of his kiss and the excitement that fluttered from her belly to her toes in the cave. It wasn't meant to be, though. Nestling in the intimacy of wearing his shirt, she resolved that one kiss was all they would ever have.

"Tsk, tsk." He maneuvered his horse in front of her on the narrow path. She swore she saw another smile cross his face. Did he intentionally ride in front so she would stare at his muscular back?

"Enjoying the view back there, Red?" he asked, confirming her suspicion.

"Eh," she said, suppressing a laugh.

He laughed out loud and said, "You are a hard woman to impress."

She was more than impressed; she was captivated. His deliciously sculpted arms and shoulders revealed beauty in his strength. He worked hard on his land; his physique vouched for that. Admiring his broad shoulders and back was not enough. She craved to see more. Her eyes had made their way down the length of his body. Unfortunately, his chaps blocked a more extensive view. The contour they outlined was more than enough to make her swallow her thoughts, however.

The West had changed her. She'd never been so brazen, so free to do what felt good rather than right. The familiar knots in her stomach loosened. Perhaps it was the beauty, the openness, the lack of structure and containment that made her feel as if she had no bounds. She was doing whatever she wanted, whatever felt good without the strings of fear, called "sins," controlling her.

"What are you thinking?" he asked.

About sinning. But she couldn't tell him that. She dipped her chin suppressing a smile. Right now she was coveting Rusty as Jesse's hips rocked back and forth on him. "Ah," she stammered, "I guess I was thinking about the view after all." The view, like Jesse, was rugged, complicated, and dangerous.

"And what are you thinking?" she asked as the path widened allowing them to ride astride.

He tilted his head, his gaze lingering on her eyes, "The beauty up here."

She looked away, afraid the blush of her cheeks would give her thoughts away.

He leaned his shoulders closer to her using his leg he nudged hers then mercifully he changed the subject. "My folks loved this land as soon as they saw it. They dedicated their lives to it. I think that's the secret to Enchantment."

"The secret to Enchantment?"

"Yeah." He laughed. "Everyday Ma would say, 'that's the secret to Enchantment.' I think she meant that they were happy because they didn't answer to anyone else, though I can't be sure. She never actually said what the secret was."

"Maybe she wanted you to figure it out."

"Maybe," he replied looking across the horizon. "Sounds like something my ma would do," he said with a smile.

"You miss your folks." Sam envied Jesse's description of his upbringing: two parents working together for something and someone they loved.

"I wish they lived to enjoy what they had."

She understood that better than most. Her mother had suffered that same fate.

"What's over there?" She pointed up the mountain behind them.

"Independence."

"Independence?"

"Yeah, the town of Independence. Folks live just below the summit of the Continental Divide. Come here digging for silver—might as well be digging their own graves, if you ask me."

"Why do you say that?"

"Folks put themselves and their little ones in harm's way, starving in winter 'cause there ain't no food and nobody dumb enough to climb up there and sell 'em any."

His brown eyes scrutinized the mountain. "Women clutching babies as their fool husbands drive a piece of wood on four wheels down an eleven thousand foot mountain.

"All for the hope of finding silver," he continued, shaking his head in disgust.

Silver or land—that's how it was for J.W., too. There was something always greater to be had and someone always standing in his way.

Jesse rode close to her, pointing to his left. "See over there, beyond this mountain, that was Ashcroft. That town lasted three years. Now just about everybody's gone. When the silver runs out, so do the miners."

"Aspen is changing," Sam said.

"Yeah, sometimes I wish those fancy barbed wire fences would keep folk out rather than cattle in. Talk of locomotives coming through here got coin in everybody's eyes. Folks don't work anymore—just invest, or steal, or mine."

He bowed his head. "I'm sorry," the line of his jaw hardened, "you don't need to hear me complaining."

"I understand," Sam said. She kept quiet. There were no words to comfort him and even if she could think of them, they would be lies. Saving a man's life is more important than another man's home, but being deceitful was wrong, nonetheless.

"I'm not going to let my folks' graves be trampled over by the railroad."

"I can't believe a railroad will come through here. That seems too incredible."

"Midland and the Denver and Rio Grande are racing to get here first."

He clicked his tongue and moved his horse along the path in front of her as it narrowed again. When they came to the bottom of the mountain, the path widened. They were getting close to the cabin. She needed to make her way back to the river before dark, so they had to separate soon.

"How did you end up with the Sisters?"

He was easy to read this time. He was trying to distract her so she wouldn't notice he was bringing her farther than agreed. "I lived with my father for most of my life." Her eyes shifted to his, "He's a good man with bad habits."

"Hmm." He nodded.

"What do you mean, 'hmm'?"

"It makes sense that he was a good man. You're a good woman. And the fact that he had bad habits explains why you have a hard time trusting people I think, anyway." He shrugged. "And you've got a few bad habits of your own," he said with a smile.

"Oh, such as?" She smirked knowing he was baiting her.

"Today, at the river, you pulled a gun on me for the second time."

"You have some bad habits too, like sneaking up on me."

"Actually," he said straightening his hat, "I have a habit of finding you in...unusual situations."

"That is true." She had to agree.

A good woman? She didn't agree with that. She was lying to him. She'd been deceitful most of her early childhood. But lying to Jesse was different. Suddenly, she yearned to confide in him and stop pretending she wasn't scared and worried.

Luke said he would kill J.W. if she told anyone. His life depended on that money and, therefore, on Sam.

"Where's your pa now?"

The exhaustion of it all caused the tears to fall and her body to shake. Worrying was wringing her dry. Days of fighting and scheming took their toll just as the outlying land to Julia's cabin came into view.

"Does he know you're out here, alone?" he asked.

She took a deep breath to settle her nerves. She didn't want him to see the kaleidoscope of emotions that were most likely all over her face.

"Sam, what is it?"

"I'm just tired. I can make it from here on my own."

It must've been the catch in her voice or the slump of her shoulders that gave her away. He sped up and blocked her path. "I didn't mean to upset you."

She looked away, but she couldn't stop her tears.

Jesse jumped from his horse, reached for her waist, and hauled her into his arms.

His firm muscles grazed her cheeks as he pulled her into his chest. His fingertips were rough, but his caress was soft. As he wiped her tears, his gaze softened and concern lit his eyes.

Her breathtaking beauty mesmerized him. Her soft and pliable body fit perfectly in his arms. She was a mystery he yearned to solve. She curled herself into him and he stroked her hair. Soon the shower of tears on his chest dried and her body relaxed.

An hour ago, she was brave and brazen riding through the mountains unescorted. Not afraid to be alone with him, she was open and willing to allow him to touch and explore her. His body hardened at the memory. Now her smooth legs rubbed against him. His mouth watered, craving the supple mounds of flesh beneath her shirt. His teeth cut at his lips as he tried to mask the pain of his desire pressing against his pants. He wanted to soothe his ache between her lush and creamy thighs. Gently, he lowered her to the grass-bed, his chest snug against her body. Could he slide her legs apart and drown himself in her warm wet pleasure?

The answer was no.

She wiggled and squirmed under his weight. He shot up immediately releasing her. He wanted her to trust him and now he let his lust take over.

Scrambling to her feet, she backed away.

"Sam." He sighed, keeping the distance between them so as not to scare her even more.

"Jesse." She raised her arm flexing her palms as if she could hold him off.

"I'm sorry, Sam. I would never force." His words broke off. He bowed his head. He hoped he hadn't ruined what was building between them. He knew better than most that trust is hard to part with and even harder to earn.

"You don't understand." Her voice was thick with breath. She slid next to him, her face just below his. "I am not afraid of you. I...felt it too." She shook her head. Confusion flooded her eyes. "What you were doing to me...I wanted it. But I can't."

He felt his mouth drop open. He shook the desire and surprise from his thoughts.

"No, I never should have." He brushed her cheek, "You're so soft... I can't stop thinking about you." If he said anymore, it would scare her no matter what she said.

Her delicate body tormented his thoughts. He had never hungered for a woman like this before. Why now? Why her? He didn't even know who she was.

"Why are you here, Sam?"

Her eyes widened. She bent her head and twisted the bottom of her shirt in her fingers. With a deep breath and looked up at him.

"I want to trust you," she said.

His heart pounded. He didn't move or even breathe. Had he finally earned her trust?

"So, I will tell you," she continued.

He nodded his head ever so slightly.

"My father left for Aspen three weeks ago." She bit her lip. "He's missing."

"Missing from Boston?"

She shook her head. "No, Aspen."

"You came here to find your father?"

"Yes. He said he had a deal with someone to get land out here—a ranch. He said that if he didn't send me a telegram when he arrived that I should find…" she took a deep breath and exhaled, "Luke Tremain."

"Luke?" Jesse's shoulder went rigid. "Your father knows Luke?"

"Yes, from when he lived in Aspen twenty years ago."

"Your father lived here?"

She looked at him and swallowed. "I was born here."

Jesse took a deep breath. She could tell from the expression on his face, he was trying to make sense of what he was hearing, "You're from Aspen?"

She nodded. "Before my mother died, she asked my father to raise me in Boston."

"Aspen was a small camp twenty years ago." He stared at her as if searching his mind for a memory of her. A puzzled look shadowed his features. "Your pa knew Luke twenty years ago, and you came here looking for him?"

"Yes," she twisted her fingers.

"They're friends?"

"I don't know what they are. After you left his office yesterday, Luke said he had my father." She stepped back and hid her face in her hands. Tears streamed off her cheeks; her body shook as she sobbed.

Bring on the strongest man, the quickest six-shooter, or the wildest stallion. Jesse could take them all. But he was no match for a woman's tears. He couldn't stop them, and he couldn't handle being helpless.

Taking a shaky breath, he reached for her and cradled her in his arms.

"Luke said he had your father?"

She had finally opened up to him, and all he wanted to do was to beat the hell out of Luke Tremain.

Luke stood right in front of the whole town profiting and scheming all while hurting innocent people and now the son-of-a-bitch was doing it to Sam.

"This is your secret? This is why you're sneaking all over Aspen?" Jesse didn't want to breathe let alone speak. It was close—the answer he needed to make sense of the mystery that was Sam Ward.

It just didn't add up, though. What could her father, a man who lived a thousand miles away, have that Luke wanted?

He watched her taking deep breaths. The strength in her shoulders returned. It was only a second of pain in her eyes before she reclaimed herself.

His questions could roll out like barrels on a river if he wasn't careful.

He spoke softly, "Who was the man Luke was talking to last night? Why did he scare you so much?"

"His voice reminded me of someone."

Jesse watched her, but he did not believe her; she was still holding back. A moment, a breath was all he had before she shut him out again.

"Luke told me that if I told anyone he'd kidnapped my father; he would kill him."

"What does he want?"

"Land." She looked straight in his eyes, "Your land."

"Enchantment? That's what this is about?" Jesse exhaled, disgusted with how far Luke could slither. His fists clenched at the thought of Luke frightening Sam into getting his land. Feelings, emotions, those couldn't be broken, but Luke's neck could be.

The emerald gaze that pierced him defiantly so many times in the past two days was fixed on the ground.

"What are you going to do?" Knowing her, she had plan.

"I don't know yet."

The hell she didn't. "You're up to something."

"You wanted to know what I'm doing here, well that's it." She twisted out of his embrace.

The knot in his stomach tightened. Kidnapping just wasn't Luke's style. Stealing and diversion were, though. It was too much of a coincidence—she needs the deed to Enchantment to save her father. A man no one even knew was missing. This story didn't wash. "Why would Luke think you could get the deed?"

"I don't know, I swear."

"So you were alone in the woods the other day

because you were looking for your pa? Is that why you are out here now?"

"Yes."

"If Luke has him, why would he be out here?" He wanted to trust her, but he wasn't getting the full story.

"How did you get out here the day of the robbery?"

"You saw me, by horse."

"That wasn't your horse."

"How...?"

"Your horse wouldn't have abandoned you. Even startled, he would've come back."

Her fingers clenched into fists but he continued anyway. "The sheriff needs to know about this. Luke's time of putting fear in everyone around is over."

"No, Jesse, I thought I could trust you. Please promise me you won't do anything."

Jesse searched the sky. She had no idea what she was asking. He had waited for so long to have something to hold over Luke. Now he had another witness, someone else who could put Luke behind bars. Without Sam, it was nothing, he had nothing just another taste of something with nothing to tear into.

"He sent you out here to ask me for the deed because he doesn't have the money from the train robbery."

"I'm not asking you for your deed." She stepped back, away from him. "I will figure this out on my own."

"Don't you get it? He kidnapped your father." She wasn't running way this time. He needed her. "He's dangerous."

"I know." She was looking at him, but her thoughts were elsewhere.

"Then come with me and tell the sheriff." His tone was sharp. He wanted to hide his frustration, but it was becoming harder to mask his feelings.

"No." She clenched her teeth. She was digging in, preparing for a fight.

"Damn it, Sam. You're still holding back." He stepped into her, grabbing her, seizing her roughly, binding her against him. She needed to be scared. She needed to know he wasn't letting this go.

"Jesse! Jesse!" The sound of Andy's voice and the pounding of horse hooves made Jesse's gut wrench.

"Andy, what's wrong?"

The foreman's face was red. He pulled up on the reins. "It's the cattle."

"What about them?"

"They're sick. Looks like white snakeroot."

"They've been poisoned?"

Jesse turned to Sam. He started to speak.

"Go," she interrupted him. "I'm fine on my own."

Chapter Fifteen

Jesse and Andy sped past the river toward the buzz of swarming flies and the low moans of dying cattle. Most of the heifers and their calves lay still. One calf died right there on his mother's udder, drinking in the poison. The heifers were unaware they were killing their own babes with every suck of milk they supplied. His foreman was right. It was milk poisoning from white snakeroot—all the signs were there. Problem was there was no root around there. Hadn't been any there in thirty years. Pa got rid of the stuff when word first came round about the poisonous plant decades ago.

Someone tried to make it look as if the cows ate it in the meadow. But the cattle were in a tight circle, next to each other, which meant they weren't grazing. The culprit herded them up and fed them their final meal.

Blackness penetrated his mind as the carnage before him became too much to bear. First his horses were murdered, and now his cattle were slaughtered. The pain in his hands barely registered as his fingers curled into fists and pierced his palms.

Helpless animals used as pawns. Whoever did this not only made sure he couldn't sell or eat them, he made him feel like it was his fault they were dead.

"Luke was in town this morning. Laid eyes on him myself," Andy said, reading his thoughts.

Luke being in town didn't mean anything. "He may

not have fed them the white snakeroot, but he put up the swamper who did. Just like the barn fire."

The old timer shrugged. "Didn't see nobody out here today except for you."

He knelt next to a heifer. The smell of the rotting carcasses turned his stomach and so did his thoughts. There was one person around today. Did Sam fool him? Was she a part of this?

"What is it?" Andy asked.

"Nothing. Forget it."

"It's time to cut and run, Son." He collected tinder for a fire.

"You'd never say that to Pa," Jesse argued.

"I did say it to your pa. He was just as stubborn as you."

He got to his feet eyeing his foreman, his father's oldest friend. "What do you mean, you said it to him?"

"Your pa would tell you himself. His pride got in his way. He died with regret, Son. That's no way for a good man to go."

"What did he regret?"

"That he left you nothin'. He gambled Enchantment takin' out that mortgage. He cinched his own noose with it. And you're just digging him deeper in his grave by doing the same damn thing."

"You expect me to just walk away and accept this? To forget the ranch?"

"There's nothing left." The old man's tone was calm. He never raised his voice or lost his cool.

"There's justice," Jesse spat back.

"Not in this town there ain't."

Fury boiled in his bones. How could his pa's best friend stand there amidst their dead cattle and give up?

Did he even care about himself? "What about you and Mrs. Maple?"

Andy turned away heading toward the tree line. "Don't be puttin' your pride on us," he called over his shoulder.

Jesse had no horses, no cattle, no hope of paying off the lien, but he'd be damned if the only family he had left had to suffer for it, too. Anger and frustration washed over him and festered in his chest heavy and twisting so hard he could scarcely breathe.

"I have to know who did this." Jesse stalked after him. He could track any horse and its rider better than any man in these mountains, any man except Andy.

Andy turned to face him. "Six months is long enough."

"Long enough for what?"

"To quit living." He reached down collecting twigs.

"I've been living," Jesse said through gritted teeth. He took the wood from Andy's hands and threw them across the grass.

Without emotion visible in his face. No anger in his eyes. Not even pity Andy replied, "Breathing and hating ain't living."

"What am I supposed to do?" Jesse fell to his knees. Using his hat, he cradled his head and buried his face. He let his pa down, his cattle down, his stallions, everyone.

Andy gathered up more kindling. "We gotta burn the herd before every animal round here tries to feed on 'em."

"I am not letting this go," Jesse said.

Andy chewed the tobacco and spit it out. "Quit

feeling sorry for yourself and being stupid."

Damn, the old man knew how to get to him. "I have to know."

The old man sighed. "You're gonna end up under the snakes over this ranch."

"I don't have anything else."

Andy glared at him. "You got things backward. You can't eat revenge; it eats you. You gotta move on."

Andy tossed moss and pine needles, sticks, and branches into a pile. He took out his flint and steel and masterfully lit the kindling. The fire popped and the heat grew.

"Pa would've expected me to get justice."

"Don't be puttin' this on your pa neither. He'd want you to move on. He learned too late. Doesn't have to be that way for you."

Their only source of income was burning. May as well have starved them. Luke and his band systematically destroyed his ranch and his only hope of reclaiming it. In one morning, it went from weeks to days of them being able to survive.

The barn fire was more than enough. He had no intention of letting the stench of smoldering cattle claw at his eyes and nose again.

He circled the area hunting for a clue. He found a set of hoof prints behind a cluster of trees. Within minutes he left Andy behind and was at the river. He looked around for additional prints. They would tell him if Sam was the lookout, the distraction, or the killer.

He found more along the opposite bank. They were fresh, made after the rain. She was the distraction. The trail was clear—like reading the night sky if you knew what you were looking for.

"Tsk, tsk." Jesse signaled to Rusty and they took off.

The prints went along the water and cut in toward the path to town and to Julia's. If they led to Julia's cabin then Sam could be with whoever killed the cattle right now. He quickened his pace, the answers to his questions within reach.

****

Mud flew at Sam as Jesse raced after Andy to his cattle. With only a few hours of sunlight left, the knot in her gut tightened. Jesse was occupied, which hopefully would give her enough time to get back to the buried money.

The schemes she employed: seducing Luke, dressing like Ned—that was easy. Searching for the money that will ensure the loss of Jesse's ranch while he's trying to save his poisoned cattle was lower than she thought she could ever go. The guilt encircled her and squeezed her like a vice.

In the cave she was drawn to him. Her body physically reacted to him in every way Sister Mary Ellen's novels had described. His kiss and the feel of his body against her made her want more. He gently pulled her body to his, his lips brushed hers and his tongue demanded a response that she readily, greedily, returned.

She waited awhile after Jesse and Andy were out of sight before she and Pearl trotted back up the path toward the river. When she entered the clearing by the cave, she saw smoke rising above the tree line in the distance.

Her stomach dropped realizing there was a fire.

She doubled back a ways and crossed where the river narrowed. She urged Pearl onward toward the fire. The horse battled her not wanting to go closer.

She dismounted behind an Aspen grove. Through the thin white line of trees, she saw the herd, moaning in pain. Maybe it was her imagination or maybe it was real, but she felt as if they were scared and confused. Most of the calves, if not all, were dead. They were on their mother's bellies in a tight circle. It didn't look natural. She'd seen cows in the farms around Boston, even helped a blind widower farmer once in a while. Cows grazed. Some may stay together, but not the whole herd.

It wasn't the smell or the sight that sickened her the most. It was the uneasiness, the irrational dread that J.W. was somehow involved in this.

Over the past six years, Sam had sat through lectures and homilies for hours. What she listened to most, though, was her gut. J.W. had been going on about snakeroot for years. The poison killed his granny back in the late '40s.

When he was drunk, he would talk about her death and how it changed his ma. After Granny died, there wasn't much left of his ma or his family.

Of course other ranchers would know about snakeroot, too. Sam bit her bottom lip and tried to keep her fears at bay. Last night Luke told the bandit that J.W. was doing his part tomorrow, meaning today. Would Luke kidnap J.W. to make him kill the cattle with snakeroot?

A one-thousand-mile trip ending with J.W. killing a man's cattle was too grim to imagine, so she did her best to push it out of her mind.

The crunch of tree limbs crackled under foot as she climbed through the woods and thick grass to see what happened. That's when she saw Jesse. His pain, even at a distance, was palpable. He leaned over one of the heifers and patted her. He covered his face with his hat. His shoulders slumped for a few seconds and he stood tall again.

Whatever Andy was saying, which wasn't much; Jesse didn't appear to be listening.

She pulled Jesse's hat low over her face. She couldn't watch anymore.

She mounted Pearl and headed back. The trail divided. She knew the way to the money was to her right and the way to Julia's was to the left. The image of Jesse, his sorrow, caught her throat.

Pearl snorted and shifted her weight. The horse lifted her legs and shook her neck waiting for the feel of the rein to tell her where to go. But Sam couldn't do it. She couldn't give the money to Luke—even to save J.W. Not tonight, anyway, not after what she just saw. She was supposed to help people. Even before the nuns taught her charity, she'd been a savior.

"Samantha, my savior." She hadn't heard those words in ten years. That was when everything changed. Until then, J.W. would get down on his knees and pull her in close. Each night before he went out or she went to bed, he squeezed her tight as if his life depended on it. "Sleep tight, Samantha, my savior," he would say.

Every night as she lay in bed waiting for him to come home, she searched her mind for what she had done wrong. Then she found it—the telegram from Aspen rolled in a ball in his pocket. Someone had died, someone J.W. had never mentioned, but it changed him nonetheless. She did everything a ten-year-old could think of to win him back.

She did everything she could think of to survive. The only thing she would never do was to beg. Pity was for the pitiful, that's what J.W. said, anyway. When she was twelve, she was caught stealing. She had to steal; they had to eat. That's when she was taken away from J.W. and put in the care of strangers.

Her new life was with the Sisters of St. Joseph at the Home for the Friendless. Apparently, she'd become pitiful. They took her in during the summer. It wasn't until the fall, when J.W. was hungry and out of Red Eye, money, and options, that he came looking for her.

She was his savior no more, not until that night three weeks ago when he called to her from beneath her bedroom window. That's when she knew she was needed again. She would save J.W. from Luke. But not tonight. There wasn't time to get to the river. The moon and stars would soon replace the sunlight.

She meandered her way back to the cabin. Pearl was tired and deserved a good rub down so once she realized Julia wasn't home she headed straight for the grooming area. With brush in hand, she thought about her new friend. Life was tough out here especially for women. For the first time she realized just how much she had taken the Sisters for granted. She concentrated so much on J.W. that she hadn't realized how fortunate she was to have the nuns on which to rely. She put some hay out for Pearl and was more than ready for a rest too.

One foot in the door the smell of apple pomade stopped her like a wall. Uneasiness rippled through her from the familiar scent. It was a man's cologne. J.W.

had always reeked of it after he visited the barber.

"Hello, Sam," said a voice from behind her.

She screamed. She knew that voice. It was one she would never forget. From the corner of the cabin his form appeared.

It couldn't be—but it was. "J.W.?" She leapt toward him. "It's you. You're safe!" They could leave Aspen and go back to Boston.

"Are you hurt?" She patted his arms and chest searching for a sign of injury. He looked well rested and well fed, much better than he did in Boston. "You're not hurt?" She said relieved. There was no distress in his face only surprise.

"No, I'm not hurt. Why would I be?" She flinched from the anger in his voice. Shaking her head, she backed away, right into the corner that she had put herself in time and time again. Her gut had known all along. He hadn't escaped from anywhere. He didn't fear for his life. He had all the time in the world, which made her stomach twist even tighter. She had been duped by her own father, again.

"What the hell happened to your dress?" J.W. asked.

"I got caught in the rain. This is Jessie Colburn's shirt. I'll explain later." She felt the heat burn in her cheeks at the thought of explaining to her father why she was half dressed in a man's shirt. "We can go back now."

"Back? To Boston? Hell, no, why would we do that?"

She wanted him to admit to it. To say out loud that he never intended to send her a telegram. But then there was the part of her that hoped she was wrong. That he really had been taken prisoner.

She knew when to wage a battle and when to wait him out. "How did you escape?" Her fingers fisted. She held her breath and closed her eyes silently pleading and preparing for the disappointment that would destroy their relationship. She couldn't let him control her emotions any longer. The Roaring Fork River—one river that became two. That was them, united now, but on the verge of separation. The flow of water was too powerful; the sickening truth was coming barreling toward her. Her own way was the only path.

"Escape?"

"From Luke."

"What?" he said with a laugh.

"Luke." She felt the nausea like the first raindrop before the torrent. "He said he'd kidnapped you."

J.W. straightened and stood rock solid. "Luke kidnap me?" He squinted.

"That's what he said."

He laughed again and shook his head. "You got it wrong…" he trailed off and turned his back.

"No, I don't," she said walking around to face him. "He said that if I didn't give him the deed to Enchantment Ranch, I would never see you again."

"The deed to Enchantment? No, Sam, you got it wrong. He didn't kidnap me. I was laying low until our plan was done."

"Your plan?" Her heart started to pound. The pit in her stomach ached as it grew larger, heavier.

"Yeah, I told you. I was working to get land." He sat down and pulled out his canteen.

Sam grabbed the canteen and threw it across the room. "Working? You mean stealing."

J.W. shook his head. "It's not stealing when it belongs to you in the first place. Them Colburns are a bunch of squatters."

Her stomach dropped. "Belongs to you? You're ranting again." It all came back to her. Soon after the telegram from Aspen arrived, J.W. would come back from the saloons hollering about someone owing him land. "I came out here because I thought you were in trouble."

He stood and moved toward the canteen lying on the floor. "We're close, just a few more days." He raised the canteen as if he were toasting the mayor.

"Close to Enchantment Ranch?"

"'Course." He looked at her as if she were crazy. "You were great today."

"You saw me?"

"Yup, saw you get Jesse to take you into that cave." He sipped his Red Eye. "I told Luke we could depend on you."

She was trying to listen, but her mind was suddenly foggy. "Depend on me?"

"Never been so proud of you." He toasted her this time.

"You're only proud of me when I am doing something for you."

"I had to wait for the rain to cover my tracks. Thanks to you, Jesse never saw me." He raised his drink again. "Luke was right; you were the perfect distraction."

It was true—he'd used her. Luke knew she would spend time with Jesse to try to get the deed, which would distract him from whatever their plan was. She had fallen for it.

"Look at you, all grown up and in the family business."

Her fingers balled into fists. "I am not working with you. Luke didn't tell me to be a distraction. He told me he'd kidnapped you and the only way to get you back was to get the deed to Jesse's ranch."

His eyes narrowed. "Deed?" He stalked across the cabin rubbing his hands through his hair. "He told you to get the deed, huh?"

She couldn't look at him. She bit her lip suppressing the rising anger, the boiling dread. She wanted to scream at him. At the look on his face. The one she despised, the one that said he suddenly realized that the swindlers he conspired with were capable of deceiving him, too.

"Yes. I was out there." She pointed toward Aspen Mountain, the tremble in her voice impossible to calm. "In that storm, in the forest, alone, because I thought you needed me."

"Why would you be out there in the storm if you thought I was kidnapped?"

She had said too much. He would pounce on her like a cat on a ball of yarn if she weren't more careful. "To get the deed from Jesse. I was afraid Luke was going to kill you. I came all the way out here for you."

"Sam…"

"Are you listening?" She threw her arms up in the air. "I thought your life was in my hands."

J.W. lowered his drink. "I thought you knew. I don't know why that bastard would tell you that." J.W.'s eyes turned soft. "I thought you were in on the plan when I saw you at the river. Luke said he saw you yesterday and that he told you I was lying low for a spell."

She sat in the rocking chair sick to her stomach, tears on the verge of consuming her. She would never matter as much as his pride or land.

She closed her eyes and wrapped her arms around herself. "You said you were going to send me a telegram."

He shrugged. "Like I said, I needed to stay out of sight."

"You could've sent one when you arrived at the coach station in Leadville." The region behind her eyes ached. Why was she even trying? There wasn't even a point to asking, but she had to, she couldn't let him get away with his excuses anymore. "Why didn't you send word to me? You knew I would worry."

"'Cause it was the only way to get you away from those…" he raised his voice and turned to her anger and resentment in his eyes.

"Nuns?" Sam asked, her stomach clenching with each word he spoke.

He had plenty of opportunities to get her away from the nuns. He could've stopped drinking or gambling, but no—he decided when she was grown up that's when he would get her away from them.

"Remember when you were little? You were always my second-hand man, my savior. You'd come running and grab my sleeve." He smiled. "No one was going fight me then. I knew you'd come out here if you thought I was in trouble."

"You wanted me to worry?" She leaned into the rocking chair. "So I would come out here?" The truth crushed her. Fell on her and squeezed every last hope from her. She shook her head, every shred of childhood joy, every ounce of faith she had in him collapsed around her as the truth wrung her dry.

"I did this for you. We're going to have a ranch house soon and a bit of land. Luke will have most of the land, but the house will be all ours."

"Luke is planning to sell the land to the railroads. Did you know that?"

"Makes our land more valuable."

He looked toward the door. "Aspen has changed, not the same as it used to be. Everybody's squaring off land and keeping you in."

That's how she felt, squared off and kept in. This was the real J.W. He was a rake; the kind of person you look away from on the street because you know he'd look right into you sizing you up for what he could steal. Invading you. He wasn't going to change. Her stomach turned at the truth. She had deluded herself long enough. He was just going to drag her down into a life he couldn't and wouldn't leave.

"What about Jesse?"

"His pa never was cut out to be a rancher."

"You knew his pa?" She shook her head in disgust, "How can you do this to him?"

"There is more to Jesse and Enchantment than you know. Enchantment should be mine. It should be yours."

"I don't want any part of this."

"You're feeling sorry for him?" The veins in his neck bulged like a leather hose filling with water. He stood up and started pacing, "You don't know half of it."

"I don't know any of it because you never told me anything."

He was shaking his head as he paced. "How could you even think I'd been kidnapped?"

"This is my fault?"

J.W. cocked his head. "Well, I just told ya, Luke is working with me. I ain't been kidnapped."

"Jesse will lose his home."

"Yeah, to us."

J.W. was greedy, but this was beyond anything he'd ever done before. "You put my life in danger so I could live with you in a ranch you swindled?"

"How were you in danger? Colburn would never hurt you. I know that much about him." He shifted his feet and pursed his lips. "I watched the stagecoach depot every day for you." The pitch of his voice deepened. "I never saw you."

He turned around; suddenly his eyes looked like they could pierce glass. "How did you get into town?"

She caught her breath. He was on to her like a dog smelling prey. Bringing up the bandit right now would be a mistake. No matter how angry she was she had to keep quiet. He'd press until he wore her down.

"By coach, you just didn't see me."

"No." He shook his head.

"Did you poison Jesse's cattle?"

He grinned. "You changing the subject? Getting rid of the cattle was necessary."

"Andy found the cattle and followed your tracks to Jesse and me."

"So?"

"Jesse probably thinks that I killed his cattle."

He glanced out the window. "Get your things. It's time to go. Keep your mother's bowie knife close."

"That's why you gave it to me. So, I could protect

myself when I came out here because you knew I would have to."

"She'd want you to have it anyway."

"I'm not going anywhere with you." She ignored his last statement and hoped to hell he didn't ask to see the knife.

"You ain't staying here."

"Why not?"

"'Cause Julia's a whore, and you don't belong here."

"At least she's not a killer."

"Cattle die. Happens all the time." He softened his tone. "We are going to live together on the ranch. Like we should have years ago."

The guilt wasn't going to work, not this time.

He turned to her and took a step closer. That's when she saw it. The rage, the ire in his eyes. She always knew it was there. Once in a while after drinking or visiting her at the nuns' it would come unleashed, and just as quickly as it appeared, he'd store it away again. Well, he could be as angry as he wanted. She was angry too.

"I wasn't much of a father. Boston hated me. I never could get a respectable job. This is my chance to make it up to you. Don't take that away from me."

She felt the blood run from her face. He was doing it again. Closing in on all sides. Shutting down every escape route.

"Tremain shouldn't have lied to you." He took another swig from his canteen. "I've got business to take care of," he said.

The change in him was lightning fast.

"Business?"

"Yeah."

"Why did you kill Jesse's cattle?"

"You think Jesse is such a good man, don't you? Truth is he's a desperate man. He stole money from Luke. He ran his ranch into the ground and has debts to pay, so he robbed a man workin' for Luke to pay it off."

She lifted her chin and leaned toward him. "Stole it how?"

"From the train." Reaching into his pocket, he took out a tin of tobacco and swished the contents around with his dirt covered finger.

"You think Jesse robbed the...train?" She had to shake the words from her head. Is that what the train robber told Luke?

"Jesse robbed one of Luke's men. Shot at him and stabbed him."

Her foot slipped; she fell backwards. Her mind turned muted and fuzzy. "So you killed his cattle?" She recognized the crack in her voice. It was bitterness, grief, and anguish bundled together.

"He needed to understand that he's not keeping what doesn't belong to him."

A chill trickled up her spine at his justification. J.W. killed the cattle because he thought Jesse stole the money from the train robber.

"Be ready to leave Julia's at sunup," J.W. said screwing on the top of his canteen.

"I am not—"

"Shh."

Horse hooves pounded the ground not far from the cabin. J.W. bolted to the front window. "Damn it. You gotta visitor." Pulling out his pistol, he said calmly, "Stay here."

"No." she lunged at him.

He stared at her. "You don't need to worry about me anymore." He cocked the hammer and reached for the door.

"J.W., wait. Who is it?" It could be Julia.

"It's Jesse."

"Jesse. I'll handle him. You stay here." She ran out of the cabin before J.W. could stop her.

Jesse leapt from his horse.

"Are they dead?" she asked immediately backing toward the cabin.

Jesse ignored her. He stalked around the side of the cabin.

"Your cattle are they…dead?" she repeated.

"Not all." He walked straight at her, the anger and pain radiating from him. "The calves and heifers are the sickest." His voice was strained. "It looks like white snakeroot."

"So…what are you doing here?"

"Tracking the killer." As he walked around, his eyes were pinned to the ground.

"Tracks, but the rain…?"

"Yeah, tracks. You know anything about white snakeroot?" he asked.

"I know people died from eating sick cattle years ago. Not so much since."

"Andy and my pa cleared the grazing area of snakeroot before I was even born." He turned and was making his way around to the front of the cabin.

"So the cattle strayed?"

His eyes were trained on a set of footprints starting at the edge of the woods leading straight into the cabin.

"No. Someone brought the poison to the cattle."

"Who would do that?"

"I'm guessing the man in your cabin," Jesse said kicking the cabin door in with his boot. Sam rushed in behind him expecting a gunshot, but they were met with silence.

The back window was open. In two steps, Jesse was looking out of it.

She craned her neck over Jesse's shoulder praying J.W. was gone. But he was barely out. She took a deep breath and a step back.

Jesse turned to her. "Who is he?" The anger in his voice and the look in his eyes were almost pleading, pleading for her not to lie again.

When she didn't answer, Jesse stepped around her and took off as fast as he'd come.

Chapter Sixteen

Jesse ran to Rusty, heaved himself up into the saddle, and took off. The man he was after was older, his gray hair bounced up and down under an old styled hat as he ran for a cluster of Aspen trees. Jesse leaned in low as he and Rusty threaded their way through the grove. The man was about to reach his horse. Jesse pulled up on the reins changing his strategy. He would pursue the stranger from a distance letting the man lead him right to whoever was behind this—probably Luke. Maybe he'd even find out where Luke was keeping Sam's father.

What was left of the sun hung behind a patch of thick clouds. The pit twisting in his stomach was the same as the ache he had a few weeks ago. The old man slowed as he entered town. Jesse's heart pounded. His hunch was right. The man was headed straight for Luke's. He tied Rusty up to the hitching post, raced across the street, and crouched under Luke's office window.

"If we don't get that land for the Denver and Rio, we're dead men." He recognized Luke's voice.

Jesse moved over and stood by the side of the window where he was able to peer in unnoticed.

"You just thought you'd scare her? Make her think she had to do something you been trying to do for years?" The old man pointed his finger at Luke's face.

"I thought she'd keep Colburn occupied. Which she did."

"What the hell does that mean?"

"What does it matter? We were close to getting that land and now…damn it where is that money?"

"Figured I was holding out on you, that it?" the old man asked.

"What of it?"

"Why the hell did you think I stole the payroll from Clay?"

Clay. That must be the name of the train robber.

"Who else knew which train we were hitting and when?"

"Just Clay's whole gang." The son-of-a-bitch Tremain stood at least three inches taller than him, but the old-timer didn't back down.

Luke stormed around his wide desk toward the window. Jesse ducked.

"They're still here waiting for their cut." He'd heard that venom in Luke's voice before. He was on the verge of losing it.

"So am I."

How could two men dumb enough to be admitting their guilt and yelling about it get away with a train robbery?

"I know you're not stupid enough to rob us. 'Cause if you did, you'd have worse troubles than Colburn." Luke had lowered his voice.

"You're threatening the wrong man." The stranger answered clearly not intimidated.

A chair scraped the floorboards. Footsteps approached Jesse's hiding spot. He pressed his back up against the building, his face inches from the open window.

"Keep her out of it," the stranger said.

"It's just business."

"You made it personal."

"She came to me. I saw the way Colburn was looking at her. He'd give up a piece of land for a piece of that, so I used the opportunity to our advantage."

Luke used Sam. There was a scuffle, more yelling, and the noise of something breaking.

"Stay away from her."

"Fine. Get over to Georgia's and find out who's throwing cash around."

"I thought I was lying low?"

"We don't have time for that anymore. Somebody has to know something. Clay said the thief's in Aspen. All that money has got to be going somewhere."

A door swung open and shut with a bang.

"It's like a damn ghost came into town," Luke muttered.

"A ghost or a Yankee," a third voice said. It was the same voice as last night—the train robber, Clay.

"You talking about me?" the old man asked. He practically spat out each word.

"Thought crossed my mind." Clay sounded completely unaffected as if the old timer wasn't infuriating him.

The old man snorted. "First time for everything."

"Shut up both of you," Luke yelled. "Did you find the thief, Clay?"

"Getting close." Clay acted like nothing the other men said bothered him.

"Damn it. Find him." There was a bang. It sounded like a fist slamming wood.

Jesse peered in the window.

Clay sat on the desk picking wax off the mahogany. "Soon."

Luke fisted his hair. "We don't have time."

"Give 'em the collateral." Frustration evident in Clay's voice.

"What collateral?" the old man demanded.

"A knife," Luke said. "It's worth good money."

"You're going to give them a knife as collateral for all that money you lost?"

"I didn't lose it." He threw up his hands. "The son-of-a-bitch bushwhacked me like some blue belly."

"Why the hell didn't you shoot him?" The stranger narrowed his eyes and studied Clay.

They continued arguing while Luke's face turned a darker shade of red by the minute.

"He knocked me out." Clay shoved the other man in the chest. "When I came to, he stabbed me and took the money."

"What the hell you take me for?" the old man pushed him back. Luke stood up in between them men, but that didn't stop them.

"Why were you alone?" The old man was in Clay's face. "The plan was for you to split into two groups. Each man was to stay with his partner."

Clay calmed. "We got separated." He reached in his pocket and pulled out a tin of tobacco.

"Where did this robber come from?"

"Damned if I know," Clay said.

Luke started talking over both men and yelling at the old man. "You're acting like an old woman. Stop asking so many questions."

Ignoring Luke, the man stared at Clay. "Yeah, you

are damned if you know and I have a strong feeling you do know." He shoved Clay and swatted at his tin of tobacco knocking it to the floor. "You're lying, you son-of-a-bitch. Nobody knew about the hold-up except us."

Jesse ducked to the side of the window. Something began to itch in the back of his thoughts. He stole a quick glance into the room again. The two men were facing off, staring each other down. Clay raised himself up on the tips of his boots and leaned over the old man.

"You got anything to back up your theory?"

If his cattle hadn't just been slaughtered, he would've found their display of stupidity entertaining.

The old man raised himself up on his boots in response. "You got anything to back up your story?"

"Just a damn hole in my leg." He turned to Luke. "He's in town. I'm gonna get the payroll back."

"In town?" the older man snorted. "He's smart enough to ambush you, and yet he stays in town? Stabs you with a valuable knife and leaves it? Don't wash."

"Quit yer yappin'. Our necks are on the line, and we need to figure this out fast," Luke said.

Hard to believe Luke could be the most level-headed man in the room.

"Give 'em the knife, for now," Clay said.

"Let me see that knife," the other man demanded.

"What for?"

"I wanna see this valuable blade that's gonna save our necks."

There was a minute of silence. A drawer opened and shut.

"The thief stabbed you with this?" the older man asked. There was something strange about his voice. It was choked.

Jesse peered through the window just in time to see the old man push Clay up against the wall.

"What the hell?" Clay said. "Get off me."

"You saying the thief stabbed you with this after waiting for ya?" the old man said thrusting the knife's blade under Clay's chin.

"That's what I said." Clay looked at the man as if he knew something. Something neither one was spilling.

The old man released Clay, but he was deep in thought.

"Did you find out how much it's worth, Luke?" Clay said straightening his shirt.

"I'm working on it."

"I'll find the money," the old man said.

"What?" The train robber looked at him. "How you gonna find it. You don't even know what the son-of-a-bitch looks like."

"I'll go to Georgia's. One of the girls has got to know something."

"Good, get over there now," Luke said.

Jesse had to get to Georgia's first. He had a feeling the stranger knew more than he was telling. He sprinted down the boardwalk and hid in the shadows. But the old timer didn't head to Georgia's. He went straight for his horse. Jesse's heart pounded. The man lied to Luke and was veering from the plan. He knew something about the knife.

He ran across the road and leapt onto Rusty just in time to follow the man.

The moon was full and offered a lit path, but the crazy old coot was burning the breeze and likely to break his neck at this speed. Jesse gripped Rusty's reins, his body moving in tandem with the horse. The man was heading back the way he'd come, back toward Julia's—toward Sam.

****

The smack of a door kicked open, and a woman's scream pierced the quiet night. From his horse, Jesse saw the man barge through Julia's door, but he was too far away to do anything about it. Rusty pulled up in front of the cabin. Jesse leapt off and bolted through the door.

"How did Luke get this?" A thick blue vein bulged on the man's forehead.

Across the room, Sam, still dressed only in Jesse's shirt aimed a Winchester straight at the man's chest.

Not what Jesse was expecting but the woman was as predictable as fire.

At Luke's, this guy was raging on worried about Sam, but he comes storming in here? And Sam is holding him at gunpoint? A habit he admired and wished she'd break at the same time. Jesse wasn't getting answers; he was getting more confused.

And above all, it was damned hard to concentrate on the weapon when the butt of it was squished against partially exposed breasts. Then there were the long curvy legs spread apart in the proper shooting stance that practically stopped Jesse's heart, but had no effect on the other man.

"Jesse, what are you doing here?" Sam demanded.

"Been following your friend here."

The old guy gave him a look so cold it could freeze fire.

"Nobody invited you," the man said.

"Doesn't exactly look like you got an invite either, Old Timer."

"What do you want?" The man shook his fist in Jesse's face. "Can't you see we're in the middle of a discussion here?"

That statement would've surprised Jesse except that Sam did seem to have a lot of discussions while holding a gun. "I want to know why you told Luke and Clay…"

Suddenly the old guy puffed up his chest and stuck his nose in Jesse's face.

"How do you know Clay?" the old man asked.

Jesse pushed the man backward. He didn't use enough force to hurt him, but he sent him a message—he might scare Sam, but not Jesse.

"Why did you tell your partners you were going to Georgia's when you were planning on coming straight here?"

"None of your damn business."

Jesse tapped his mouth with his finger. "Does it have something to do with the bowie knife Luke has?"

Sam turned pale. "Bowie knife?"

"Put down the gun, Sam," the man said ignoring Jesse.

"What did you say to Luke?" Her voice sounded panicked.

"It's what Clay said to me that matters."

"Who's Clay?" she asked hesitantly as if she weren't sure she wanted to know the answer.

The old timer kicked at the floor and ran his hands through his gray hair. It was clear he didn't want to be having this discussion in front of Jesse. Didn't stop him though. "Clay is one of Luke's men. He had your knife and gave it to Luke."

"Your knife?" His stomach tightened. "The knife the robber gave to Luke was yours?" That's why she reacted so strangely last night at Luke's. Jesse's brain was scrambling to make sense of what he was hearing.

Sam's trigger finger trembled. She chewed her lip, narrowed her eyes and lowered the Winchester. "You know the man who robbed the train?"

This wasn't making sense. How could Sam know this guy and Luke but not Clay?

The man raised one hand slowly. "Put down the gun and tell me how Clay got your knife."

"I need…can we…" Sam said. She was recovering, but she still looked pale. "You said you were laying low." She came to life again and leveled her aim at the man's chest. "Were you there? Did you rob the train?"

"Forget about that." The man stepped forward. "I need to know about the knife."

"I said, were you there?"

"You ain't gonna shoot me." He walked toward her. She cocked the head.

"Jesse, please leave," Sam said.

"I'm not leaving." Jesse had no sympathy for this man, but still there was a code. "You can't shoot an unarmed man."

She scoffed. "He's always armed."

"Sam, why the hell are you acting like this? Clay's selling some story and Luke's buying it. He's saying some mystery gunman used your knife to stab him and…" He looked at him and quit talking. It didn't matter though; Jesse already knew what he was going to say: the mystery gunman took off with the payroll.

The man took small step forward. "That was all I

had of your mother." He spoke softly, so quiet the words were barely audible.

Of your mother?

Sam backed up but clicked the hammer. "At least you have memories. I have nothing."

The man pursed his lips and winced as if she'd slapped him.

Jesse didn't move. It felt like a puzzle picture was slowly emerging.

"Stay back," Sam said.

"How many times are you going to hold a gun on me?" the man asked. Guess Jesse wasn't the only one.

"This will be the last time, if you come any closer," she warned.

"Put it down." He moved slowly, intent on disarming her.

Jesse drew his pistol and aimed it straight at him. Two guns pointed at the old guy, and he didn't even blink.

"Stop," she ordered.

"Or what? You shoot me and you've got nothing, nobody." He took two quick steps and snatched the weapon. A bullet crashed into a small pile of dishes, as the smell and smoke of gunpowder exploded into the air.

"J.W.!" Sam screamed.

Nobody cared about the dishes, especially not Jesse. *J.W.?*

The old timer opened the gun's chamber. "You just wasted your last bullet on some damn dishes."

"J.W.?" Jesse said aloud.

The man turned to him. "Yeah, your pa tell you about me? John Ward."

"John Ward." Jesse stumbled backwards momentarily stunned. His eyes met Sam's with piercing intensity, "As in Sam Ward's father?"

He raised his chin in smug response. "So, you have heard of me."

"Jesse," Sam said edging closer.

It was as if he was in the Roaring Fork River and the rapids were tossing his body round and round. She spoke, but the words whooshed by like pounding water whizzing past his head.

"Sam, tell me how Clay got your knife."

"You said your father was kidnapped," Jesse interrupted.

She turned to J.W. "It's because of you that I lost it. Along with everything else."

"I gave you that knife more than a thousand miles from here. How the hell is it my fault?"

"Because you robbed that train," she screamed, "the train that I was on to save your lying hide!"

"You...you were on that train?" J.W. stumbled backward.

"Yes. Your plan to rob the payroll involved me getting robbed too."

"Clay stole the knife from you on the train?"

Jesse's heart pounded and sunk into his stomach at the same time. Sam was on the train. If Clay hurt her—no, he couldn't let his mind go there. But the thoughts wouldn't stop. The image of her cowering in her seat as Clay threatened her and took her mother's precious knife made him sick.

"Yes," she snapped.

"Why didn't you stab him with it instead of handing it over?"

Jesse felt his jaw drop. He expected her to stab a man? The robber, Clay, wouldn't have been alone, and there wouldn't have been anywhere for Sam to run.

"I taught you to fight for a reason." The man was shaking his head and pacing. "This wasn't supposed to happen."

"Oh, I wasn't supposed to get robbed?" she screamed.

"Where'd I leave that damn canteen?" He patted his pockets and pulled out his flask.

"The payroll was the only thing that was supposed to be taken." J.W. poured his tin's repulsive content down his throat. "They weren't even supposed to go near the passengers. Clean, in and out, that was the plan." He gulped more of the mahogany colored liquid.

He was talking to himself now. "That's how the son-of-a-bitch robbed Clay. It was a passenger. Someone who was already on the train." He searched her face for confirmation.

"I don't know," she answered. Figuring out how Clay got the knife was all that mattered to J.W. Her safety had never been a concern of his, ever.

He rambled on, "Someone jumped off and stole a horse in the commotion. He followed Clay. When the gang got separated, the son-of-a-bitch shot at Clay and stabbed him with your knife." He was shaking his head now, looking at her. "Of course, he took your knife from the loot Clay stole from the passengers."

"It makes sense. The thief wouldn't know the knife was valuable," J.W. said. He suddenly stopped pacing and said, "Explain it again."

"It makes sense?" Jesse roared stepping in between her and J.W. Standing over him, Jesse had three inches on her father. But J.W. didn't even notice the threat. He was too consumed with his greed.

"Did you hear what she said?" Jesse shoved him against the wall.

J.W. being lectured for mistreating Sam wasn't anything new. In fact, it was a regular occurrence at the front door of the Home for the Friendless. Jesse's outrage was due to the fact that he expected something more of J.W., something like compassion. The Sisters thought the most compassionate thing J.W. could do for Sam was to stay away from her.

She grabbed Jesse's elbow, yanking as hard as she could. She thought he would resist, but he didn't. His response was even worse. He looked down at her with pity and hurt in his eyes as if he were saying, "This is the good man with bad habits you lied about. His pity stung, filling her with regret and revealing the one thing she always carried with her: shame, shame of her father, shame of her upbringing.

J.W. drew his pistol. "You need to mind your own business, Colburn."

Jesse stepped around Sam and advanced on J.W. steeling his chest against the barrel of the gun. "My land, my cattle, and my horses are my business."

"And you lost them all."

"Thanks to you."

"You Colburns, you're a bunch of coffee boilers passing the buck and acting as if you're the ones gettin' it in the neck."

Jesse thrust his knee up into J.W.'s gut, knocking the gun loose. J.W. lunged for it but stumbled, tripping and falling to his knees.

"Passing the buck?" Jesse yelled, "You sent your

daughter on a thousand-mile train ride, alone. You show up and all you want to know is how she lost her knife? She tells you she was robbed, and you ask why she didn't stab the son-of-a-bitch? Maybe she was scared. Maybe she was afraid your partner was going to hurt her or kill her."

"He would never."

"Don't you dare say it." Jesse pulled J.W. to his feet and flung him across the room. "You said it was supposed to be clean in and out." Jesse stormed toward him. "But he didn't follow the plan, did he?" Jesse twisted his fingers in J.W.'s collar and shoved him against the wall. "So don't tell me what that son-of-a-bitch would never do."

"I'm gonna take care of Clay."

"When? After you sober up or after you stop demanding answers about the knife?"

"You damn Colburns," J.W. yelled leaning against the table to keep from sliding down the wall. "You're always putting yourselves in other people's business."

Jesse was trying to control his rage.

J.W. rallied on, "You would rather die than give up. Isn't that what your pa did?" he taunted. "Drove that ranch up the spout and left you with nothin' but debt."

Her stomach twisted. Jesse's fists clenched.

"You're nothing but a liar and a shoddy thief, J.W.," Jesse retorted.

J.W. lunged at Jesse. As if expecting it, Jesse dodged him, and J.W. slammed headfirst into the rocking chair.

"Do you even give a damn about her?"

"She can handle herself."

"That ain't what I asked."

"She'll be plenty happy when we're livin' on Enchantment." The old man smirked. "And you'll be enjoying them caves."

Jesse's eyes turned dark. She swallowed and shook her head. She hadn't told J.W. anything about the caves, but from the flush of his face and the drop of his chin, she knew he thought otherwise.

Her father never knew when to shut up. "You got everything that was supposed to be mine, and I got nothin'," he raged.

"You have a daughter who almost got killed trying to save your sorry hide. You just can't see what's right in front of your face. You came all the way out here for nothin'. You should've stayed in Boston where you had more than you deserved, Old Man."

J.W. lunged for his pistol and twisted around pointing it at Jesse.

The sound of her scream hadn't even registered in Sam's ears before she watched Jesse kick the gun out of J.W.'s hands. He hauled J.W. to his feet and wrapped his fingers around her father's neck.

Her heart pounded, a cry welled in her throat, "Jesse, let him go!" Using all her strength she tugged on Jesse's arm.

Jesse dropped J.W. and shook off Sam's grasp. "Was that all an act in the cave?" Jesse turned on her. She couldn't read the emotion in his eyes; was it anger or pain? He wasn't giving anything away.

"No, it was real," she said. "I swear."

"Real?" J.W. choked out.

"Yes, it was. Stop it. Get out of here. You don't know what you're talking about." Hatred boiled within her. He was poison. Arsenic seeping into her and sickening everything she cared about.

Jesse's glare molded her feet in place. "You're just like him. You can't see what's right in front of your face either, Sam. You're defending a man who doesn't care about anything but what he can't have, my land."

Jesse couldn't have been more wrong. She had always seen what was right in front of her. That was the problem. That was all she saw. Now, tonight, she could see more than that, but it was too late. The father she loved wasn't dormant or lost. He was gone. J.W. had orchestrated her leaving the convent. He was stealing land from an innocent man so he could get what he wanted without a lick of work. And now he was turning Jesse against her.

Coughing and gripping his throat, J.W. rolled over onto his knees. "Clay lied," he said. J.W. struggled to his feet. He raised his bony finger and pointed at her. "And so did you."

She never felt so broken, so lost and alone, so stupid for standing by J.W. Nothing Jesse had said meant anything to him. Instead, it was her story he cared about. It didn't hold water, so he was on her trail like a bloodhound. She had to throw him off the scent or get rid of him without Jesse putting the clues together.

"Jesse, this is between me and my father."

"Get out," J.W. hissed at him.

"If that's what you want," he said.

She swallowed hard. If he put the pieces together... Did it even matter anymore? There were too many lies.

"Consider me gone." Jesse tipped his hat. With his back to them, he stopped and tilted his head to the side.

"You can have your pa, and he can have his lies, but you're not getting Enchantment." He emptied J.W.'s pistol and tossed it across the cabin. Then he was gone.

J.W. scrambled to his gun and holstered the unloaded weapon. "Damn Colburns." He climbed onto the bed and took out his flask.

"Stop! Stop trying to justify stealing that land. It's his."

"No, it ain't." He chugged his drink.

She dropped into the rocking chair, closed her eyes, and massaged the headache forming in the back of her skull.

He rambled on. "Before I met your ma," he started, "I worked for Henry Tremain, Luke's granddaddy. I worked hard like all cowhands." Tilting his head toward the door, he said, "Every damn day I was out there sweating in the heat or freezing in the snow working sunup to sundown." He glanced at her. "And Henry promised me land when I settled down. He was a good man, a fair man." He pointed to the door with his flask. "Not many like him anymore. He cared about me more than his own son."

"Luke's grandfather cared about you more than his own son?" She asked opening her eyes and taking the leap of faith once again and listening to his story.

"Yup. Willy Tremain was the son-of-a-bitch's name. Luke's pa." He twirled his flask sloshing the liquid inside, "wasn't a good man. Got away with murder 'cause of who his pa was.

"If it weren't for Willy, I'd be working that land today with you and your ma," he wrinkled his nose, "if she were still with us."

Sam slid to the edge of the rocking chair, her spine

straight, taking in every word about her mother, wanting to believe her father was telling the truth.

"Your ma and me, we married and had you. Everything was right. That's what Henry wanted: a family man to pass the land on to. Except your ma got sick, and she made me promise to raise you back in Boston near her folks, proper and all." He sighed and gulped his Red Eye. "Henry told me to go Boston. Said it was the right thing to do. Said the land wasn't going anywhere." He smirked. "The man was like a pa to me. So, after your ma passed, you and me moved to Boston."

Sam edged her bottom back into the rocking chair quietly watching as he relived the past.

"Your ma's folks didn't want nothin' to do with us." He bit his lip. "I went there thinkin' they'd welcome us, or, at least, you. Wasn't much work in the old states for cowboys. Did my best. I didn't belong there though."

"What happened?" Sam asked.

He sighed. "Jack Colburn was murdered."

"Jack Colburn?"

He nodded. "Yup, Jessie's granddaddy."

"Jesse's granddaddy was murdered?"

"At Dirk's.

He must've read the confusion in her face.

"It's the mercantile in town. Jack Colburn and Henry Tremain were close as brothers. But Luke's daddy, Willy, was crazy. Henry couldn't do nothin' with him. He was bad from birth."

Sam started wringing her hands. She didn't know the story, but from the faraway look in J.W.'s eyes, she knew it ended badly.

"Luke's daddy shot Jesse's granddaddy in the back. Said he didn't like the smell of him." He took another swig. "If ya ask me, it was the smell of hard work he didn't like."

"Luke's pa murdered Jesse's grandfather?" She wiped the sweat of her hands on Jesse's shirt.

"In front of the whole damn camp, Willy didn't even flinch."

"That's what Henry said anyway in his letter to me. I was in Boston 'course. Jesse couldn't a been more than ten years old at the time." He took another long drink. "Henry said that Jesse knelt there cradling his granddaddy's head, blood all over the kid. Calling for help, crying out for his pa; no one helped. No one dared. Everybody was afraid of Willy Tremain."

"Jesse was there?" Sam shivered at the thought of Jesse witnessing his grandfather's murder a helpless child trying to save his grandfather. "Did Willy hang for it?"

J.W. smirked. "Nah, back then life was different. There were no honest lawmen." He gulped down his Red Eye. "That's what did it. I got that letter from Henry Tremain." He looked off in the distance. "Henry, like I said, was a good man. But he broke the cowboy code. Never thought I'd see it, but he did it. Went back on his word. He said he had to make amends, so he gave Jack Colburn's son, Jesse's pa, all his land, the land he had promised me." He pointed to his chest and raised his voice. "My land, the land I worked for."

He took another drink. "Luke never understood it either. He hated Colburn for it—felt that the land was his. But it wasn't, it was going to me."

"That's why Luke hates Jesse," Sam said.

J.W. let out a long and tired sigh. "He doesn't even know why he hates Jesse. He wants to destroy the land just to spit on his granddaddy's grave; stupid son-of-a-bitch."

"Does Jesse know?" Sam asked.

J.W. shrugged. "Henry never told anyone he was giving me the land. He knew Willy would try to kill me. After he gave it to Jesse's pa, I can't say what he told folks." He drained his flask. "Now do you understand?"

"I understand why Jesse and his pa would hold onto that ranch. His grandpa was murdered and in return he got land. Not much of a deal if you ask me. But Jesse's pa came close to losing it. Do you think Jesse's pa could live with himself if he lost it?"

"You don't understand."

"I—"

"Hush! You hear that?" J.W. clambered to his feet. He wavered from too much whiskey and fell back against the wall. "Someone's outside." His eyes drooped, and his head wobbled.

He was right. The horses whinnied. The sound of horseshoes against rock grew loud.

"J.W.! You in there?"

"Damn," J.W. mumbled. "Clay's back, and we're unarmed."

Chapter Seventeen

"Went to Georgia's. You weren't there, 'course. Thought you were looking for the payroll. Instead I hear you're with some new friend of Julia's." Clay called obviously drunk.

J.W. belched. Even after years of drinking, he still couldn't hold his whiskey. He dragged himself up, and bracing his weight against the wall, he headed toward the door.

Sam snatched a griddle from the pile of dishes and swung it at the back of J.W.'s head. With a thud he slumped to the floor blocking the doorway. If Clay came in the cabin, he would recognize her.

"J.W.," Clay was singing his name and coming closer. Still holding the frying pan, Sam dove behind the door.

Clay was just on the other side, only three inches of wood between them.

"Whaz sin da hell?" Clay fell into the door crushing her against the wall. Sam winced, not just from the pain of the door pressing into her, but also the nauseating odor of apple pomade and whiskey.

Between J.W.'s dead weight blocking the way, and Sam pushing back against it, Clay couldn't get through the door. "Eew yew. You pass out, you drunk son-of-a-bitch?" The idiot kept trying to push his way through the doorway.

J.W.'s prone body started sliding farther into the cabin. Clay was pushing his way through the doorway. Sam's hands grew slick as she gripped the griddle.

Suddenly, the weight against the door lifted. There was a groan and a rustling noise. She held her breath, and straining her neck, her heart pounding, she glimpsed out the door. There was nothing there. Clay was gone. With a long sigh, she expelled the breath she'd been holding. She jumped at the sound of a snort. J.W. had gone from a resentful drunk to snoring and snorting like a mud-happy hog in three minutes. He was still in the doorway. Until she moved him, she wouldn't be able to close the door.

Dusk had turned to nightfall casting the room into near darkness. Across the room a lamp sat on Julia's bedside table. She turned it up slightly in case Clay came back. Hopefully, he'd assume the cabin was empty if it was dark. Rolling up the cuffs of Jesse's shirt that she wore, she grabbed J.W.'s sleeves and tried to haul him out of the way so the door could close.

His drunken dead weight was heavier than she expected. Another two feet or so and his body would be clear of the door. The clopping of horse hooves approaching sent a shiver of panic up her spine. She glanced around the cabin. Julia's Winchester and J.W.'s pistol were out of ammunition. She grabbed the frying pan in one sweaty hand, leapt over J.W., and hid between the door and the wall again. If he got inside this time, she'd smack him over the head from behind.

The soft thud of footsteps sounded outside. Clay was trying to be very quiet. Killing him was her best chance. There were no other options, not this time. If she did, no one would know about the money. She wouldn't be in danger. But could she kill a man? Could she kill a man with a frying pan?

The door creaked. She pressed her back to the wall. He stepped into the cabin. She raised the griddle, ready to strike when a thump followed by a crash burst across the room.

"Damn it." A deep voice bellowed.

The darkened form strained to stand. Before he steadied himself, Sam kicked him in the back of his leg, lifted the frying pan, and brought it down hard. She had aimed for his head, but when he fell forward, his head moved and the brunt of the frying pan slammed into his shoulder.

Suddenly, pain shot through her wrist. He squeezed the pan from her grasp. With a bang, she heard it hit the far wall.

Sam started kicking and punching her assailant.

"Sweet Vinegar!" he yelled, and she was flipped onto her back on Julia's bed with her arms pinned out at her sides.

"It's me, Red. Stop kickin' me. I ain't gonna hurt you."

"Jesse?" Relief flooded her body.

"I wasn't sure what was going on in here. I didn't mean to scare you."

His heaving bare chest was right above her. His muscles bulging as he restrained her.

"What the heck did you hit me with?" he asked.

"A frying pan," she stammered.

"And I thought Mrs. Maples' biscuits were the worst thing a griddle could do." He lifted his weight off of her, yet still held her wrists out to her sides. The expression on his face turned serious when he noticed her body splayed out below him. He took in every inch of her from the crest of her breasts to the tip of her thighs. The shirt had gathered in the struggle and was bunched on her stomach barely covering her most personal area.

Breathless, she, too, feasted on the figure before her. Her eyes devoured each ridge and bulge of his muscles. A flat stretch of stomach met an indent that started like a shallow nook at the top of his pants and disappeared deep below.

She wanted to stroke his arms as she took in the size and strength of his muscles balancing his body above her.

"Are you going to let me go?" she said through staggered breaths. She trembled under him. She was vulnerable, exposed, and entirely his if he wanted.

"Sam." He looked at her with hurt in his eyes. "I would never do anything to you." He cleared his throat, "Unless you wanted me to."

He thought she was shaking out of fear. He couldn't have been more wrong.

"I know," she said softly. She couldn't look at him.

He lowered his head toward her. The area between her thighs tingled in anticipation of his kiss. He leaned to his side momentarily pressing his taut chest against her as he shifted his weight to his arm and released her hand. He repeated the movement on the other side. This time she felt his hardened form rub against her. Disappointment coursed through her when he released her completely.

He rolled onto his back and lowered his hat over his eyes. The rise and fall of his chest, the smooth muscular contour of his body caught her breath. She rolled onto her side away from him. He was done with her; he made that perfectly clear. She should have told him the truth before.

She pressed against the bed to stand and made her way to the bedside table and turned up the light.

She saw all of him now. His knuckles were red and traces of sweat trickled down the side of his face and glistened on his chest. He eased his hair out of his eyes and struggled to stand, wincing with each movement. Without speaking, she hurried to his side. Gripping his arm with all her strength, she did her best to lift him. He accepted her help wordlessly watching her with a seriousness she didn't expect from him.

"Is that what the frying pan was for?" He nodded toward J.W.'s sprawled body on the floor.

"It was better than shooting him," she said with a shrug.

He ran a hand through his hair. "I suppose."

"Besides I was out of bullets." Sam stepped in front of him to retrieve his hat in the corner.

"Guess I'm lucky." He nodded his thanks for the hat and pulled the brim low on his forehead.

Once he rose to his full height, his chin just above her head, he tipped his hat and headed for the door. "You're safe," he said.

She watched silently, saddened that he was leaving so suddenly and so solemnly. "What happened to you?"

He looked relieved that she said something. He turned toward her. "When you didn't answer Clay, I figured you weren't up for company, so I persuaded him to leave."

He smelled of sweat and leather. His fist was bloodied and bruised. "That was you? You made him leave?"

He nodded and caressed her cheek wiping her tears with his fingertips.

"He's gone?" she asked.

"Yes, you're safe."

"He doesn't know I'm here?"

"He doesn't know anything. He's tied up to his horse and taking a ride until he sobers up. I doubt he'll remember much."

She had no way of knowing what would've happened if Clay had made it through the door, but she was certain, with the speed Jesse had taken the frying pan from her, she wouldn't have had a prayer against Clay either.

She started shaking at the thought. In Boston there was a sense of invincibility living with the Sisters. The women seen coming and going from the convent were untouchable. There was no such invisible layer of protection here.

She wrapped her arms around herself. "Thank you," she managed to say in little more than a whisper. She attempted a smile. She was tired and drained.

"Sam?" He lowered his forehead to hers.

"I thought you were Clay." She put her hands to her face, trying to hide the tears desperate to escape. She'd held in her emotions too long and she was too tired to fight them anymore.

"No." His tender touch on her chin lifted her eyes to his, "I'm sorry I scared you."

He brushed the hair from her face, his eyes softening.

"Did he hurt you?"

She lowered her hands and studied him. Rubbing

her arms, she said, "No."

A look of relief spread across his features like a dam breaking. "You've been through a lot tonight. You should get some sleep." He tipped his hat.

"You're leaving?"

He turned to look at her, "Do you want me to stay?"

"It's just that…" she lowered her gaze. She didn't know how to say it.

He smiled, "I'm not leaving. I'm going to carry J.W. outside so he can sleep off his frying pan attack. You need to rest too."

She nodded absentmindedly. "Jesse!" she extended her arms out but pulled them back in quickly.

"Yes?"

"Thank you."

"You already thanked me, Sam."

"No," she said in a whisper, "I meant for coming back."

He stepped forward until he was right in front of her. He lifted her chin, "I never left, Red." The glint returned to his eyes.

"You didn't?"

"You've held a gun on me three times and attacked me with a frying pan. What makes you think you could get rid of me?"

She smiled. "It's just that." She nodded her head. Her cheeks warmed. "I'm sorry."

He cupped her shoulders. "You're alone, mixed up in something, and scared. You don't need to be sorry."

"It's not what it seems."

"I know."

She needed him to believe her. She needed an

anchor—something to hold onto or she would be whisked away, set adrift and swallowed by the venomous drink that was her father and his life.

"I'm not scheming with J.W. Until a few hours ago, I really thought he'd been kidnapped."

"I know."

"You do?"

"I overheard J.W. talking to Luke and Clay."

"What else did you hear?" her voice trembled.

"That you're seducing me to distract me."

"Is that what you think?"

"You are a hell of a distraction," he said tilting his head toward her bare legs.

"But you don't think I'm trying to seduce you?"

He sucked in the inner side of his cheek. "You're seducing me, but not for my land."

She sighed in relief. He believed her.

"Are you going to tell me what's going on?" he asked.

She didn't answer. But she owed him the truth.

"You're not afraid to be half dressed and alone with me, but you're afraid to tell me something?" he asked. "Like I said, you're not like anyone I've ever met."

"Jesse."

"You trust me with your body." He leaned closer his voice thick and deep. "But not with your secret."

Her fingers reached for the bottom of her shirt and started twisting it.

"I'm going to let J.W. have some fresh air. I'll be right back."

She looked at the window. "Hey," he said cupping her chin, "you don't have to be scared of Clay coming back tonight."

She nodded.

"Sam, this is between them. The only part that has to do with you is the knife. I'm sure J.W. never thought it would be stolen during the robbery. When he finds whoever has the money, you'll get your ma's knife back."

"And you will lose your ranch." Because of her. She took a deep breath. Her stomach lurched at her lies.

"One of us will be happy," he said with a wink.

"It's just a knife. The ranch is your home—all you have of your parents." The ranch was no doubt full of memories. He could look around his house and remember his folks. She only had mere stories of the knife.

He rubbed her shoulders. "My ranch is not family. I've been acting as if it is, but it isn't."

Sam looked down at J.W.'s sleeping figure wondering if she'd been making the same mistake.

"I'll move him outside." He released her and bent at the waist heaving J.W. over his shoulder. "You can sleep."

"I don't think I can." Her gaze lifted to meet his. Everything was a mess. She came out here to find her father and now she was the one in danger.

He closed the distance between them. "If it makes you feel safer, I'll stay out front for the night."

"You will?" Relief coupled with having him so close sent loosened the knot forming in her belly.

"Yes, I'll be right outside the door. No one, not J.W. or Clay, will be able to hurt you."

She held the door for him as he carried her father outside.

The glow of the full moon greeted her like a familiar face. A thousand miles from home and the soft pool of light she'd slept under, prayed to, and even whispered secrets to welcomed her with the warmth and comfort of an old friend. The forest was still and the night quiet. Carrying the lamp, Sam directed Jesse to an area a short distance away. J.W.'s slumped figure slid off his shoulder and landed in a pile of hay.

The yellow hue of light, barely more than a flicker, offered by the lone lamp crossed Jesse's rugged face showing late day stubble. Wind whipped the light linen shirt she wore. They took in the sight of each other. His body invited her eyes to feast on his chaps hugging every lean muscle it protected.

"Jesse, I know what you're thinking."

He stopped dead in his tracks. Red surfaced on his cheeks. "I hope you don't have any idea what I'm thinking." A twinkling glint sparkled in the warmth of his eyes.

He knew she was admiring his body and that made him grin. Looking at his body made her soft, made the area between her legs tender, but that smile, it was as if he knew what undergarments she was wearing and was never going to tell.

She shook her head, as if it could erase the blush from her face. She wanted to touch him and feel his hands roam her body. She'd never experienced a man, but saw the interchanges, the way it worked in the saloons, time and time again.

He stopped in front of the cabin door and tipped his hat. In silence he looked over her head and exhaled. She held her breath and rested her cheek against his chest.

"Get some rest." Jesse knew she was vulnerable

and all he could think of was kissing her. It wasn't the right time though.

"You are strong, Sam. I am sorry I said you weren't. You stood your ground with me and with J.W. tonight." He looked down at her and smiled.

"If you hadn't been here, I don't know what would've happened with Clay."

"You had your griddle. You handled yourself just fine. Besides, you traveled here alone, your train was robbed, and you somehow managed to find a horse," he winked, "and you do all kinds of unladylike things—anything to find your pa. I admire you for that. You got grit."

"Usually I am scolded for my unladylike behavior," she said with a smile of her own.

With a tilt of his head, his face fell and he repeated himself. You somehow managed to find a horse. "You were on a horse when I met you." He looked at her, his eyebrow raised, "How did you get a horse, if you were on the train?"

She stepped backward.

"No," he said, "not this time. Don't run from me or try to push me away." He gently held her shoulders. "I'm not going to let you."

Her jaw dropped slightly. And she took a few deep breaths. He leaned down, so they were eye to eye. "Whose horse was it?"

"Clay's," she said softly.

The rigidity of his body was instantaneous. His hands turned from soft to hard.

"Why did you have Clay's horse?"

She looked up at him and took in his full face. "Because he made me get on it when he forced me off the train."

"He…took you from the train?"

"Yes, I escaped with his horse and made my way to the river."

He stood very still. "How did you escape?"

"I stabbed him in the leg with my mother's knife. That's why I was so worried about Clay."

"That's why you jumped when you heard his voice."

She looked at his hands—he was clenching and unclenching his fists. "I don't know why you're so angry." Pain spilled from her. "I'm the one who was kidnapped. I'm the one who had to run for my life." As she spoke, her voice trembled but stood steadfast and stronger than she ever thought she could.

"Come here." Jesse reached for her trembling body. "I'm angry, but not at you." He held her tight against his chest.

"Did he…hurt you?"

"I stabbed him before he could do anything. He got the worst of it." She looked at him as tears began to stream down her face. "That's when I saw you by the river."

"That's why you wouldn't accept my help."

"Yes." She nodded. "Colorado hospitality was already wearing on me." She tried to laugh.

"Can we go inside now?"

Jesse held the door for her and they made their way into the cabin. Their fingers touched filling the cabin with unacknowledged tension.

"How did he get you off the train?"

"He and some other men boarded the train and demanded money from the passengers. Then he said he was greedy or something, I don't remember all of it. He pulled me down the aisle and threw me out onto the grass."

With one quick glance at him, she could see that he tried to remain calm, but his skin tightened at his jaw and his lips lost their color. He struggled to contain his emotions. Jesse, reminiscent of the stormy sky, was unpredictable. He'd listen; he'd also react.

"We rode for a while before we stopped. It's hard to remember," she lied. Every second of every minute was etched in her mind. She watched it unfold as if it were happening again. "He lunged at me. I was ready for him. I had my mother's dagger out, and I stabbed him in the leg. He was on the ground and reached for his gun. I think he got off a shot. I'm not sure. I took off. That's when I met you."

"So he didn't…"

"No." She shook her head.

"The thought that you went through all that and I was so close by. I could've…."

"I escaped. I told you, I took care of myself."

As he traced a tear on her cheek, his breath was soft on her face, "You're like the Roaring Fork River," he wiped away another tear. "You're gentle and persistent softening whatever you come across. Including me. Especially me." He put her hand on his heart. "That's how you're strong."

What she really wanted right now was to rely on his strength and his confidence. If this undeniably fearless man took her in his powerful arms and held her tight, she could stop pretending that she wasn't scared.

His shirt was smooth against her bare skin and his fingers swept to her cheeks gently stroking her face.

With a tilt of his head, he brought their faces together. A wave of his hair veiled his eyes and brushed her forehead. An intense relief settled her body. Only to be sparked again as an excitement grew between her legs as he cradled the nape of her neck. She sucked in her last bit of breath as he lowered his lips to hers. With a tender brush of his lips, his mouth covered hers. His grip tightened around her waist and she was encased in his strong yet fluid hold. It was unbreakable until his lips slowed.

"Why are you stopping?" She opened her eyes and peered up at him.

"With everything you've been through..." His body shifted and he pulled back.

"With everything I've been through, I want you to hold me and kiss me." Her body craved the comfort and security she felt with him.

"You need sleep, Sam." He sat up. "In the morning, I will take you to Enchantment. You'll be safe there."

The morning was too far away right now. The fears and tensions were gone for the first time. She wanted to be where she was and stay where she was right now. To feel him, and the emerging excitement coursing through her body, it appeared she was going to have to take matters into her own hands.

"I noticed you liked it earlier today when I told you I was wet," Sam said.

Jesse's eyes widened. He looked at the ceiling, closed his eyes and groaned.

"What else makes your groan, I wonder?"

"Sam, don't."

Sam reached for the buttons of her borrowed shirt.

She felt mischievous and light.

"I thought you were from a convent."

"Why do you think the good citizens sent me there?" She smiled up at him, "It wasn't for saying my prayers."

"No?" Jesse's said but his mouth fell and his eyes were concentrating solely on her shirt.

"I got more learning in the saloons than Sunday school." She unbuttoned the top of the shirt; it slid off her shoulders. "So, tell me what you want to do to me." Her fingers slid down the middle buttons, her breasts were almost fully exposed. "And I'll show you all the sinful things I want to do to you."

"Really? Now?"

"Now." She had no idea where this brazenness came from but she liked it.

"You don't seem like that kind of girl."

"I'm full of surprises."

"Yes, you are."

She finished unbuttoning the shirt and turned serious. "Touch me."

He looked at her, silently asking for permission again.

She looked at him deeper. He reached out his hand and cupped her breast. He pulled her into his naked chest.

She let out a little moan.

Grabbing the back of her thighs he lifted her up and lowered her onto the bed.

She smiled, closing her eyes and stretching her hands above her head. Relaxed and on fire, "Tell me, Jesse, tell me what you want."

His hands moved up her thigh to her soft belly. "I

want my shirt back." He spread the shirt open revealing her breasts. Her nipples tightened into small pink nubs. Wet heat spread in between her legs.

He slowly moved his hand coming closer to where she wanted his caresses: on her breasts. She lay beneath him as he drank her body in. She felt soft and wanted and powerful.

He leaned over and whispered in her ear, "I want you to spread your legs. Can you do that for me?"

"Like this?" She separated her legs and arched her back bringing his hands closer to where she was aching to be touched, where her body screamed for release.

"Yes, that's good. Now I want you to moan in my ear and cry for the sweetness I drive into you."

"Hmm," she murmured, rolling her head side to side as he licked and sucked her nipples.

"Can I wrap my legs around you like this?" She wrestled his hips.

He cupped her buttocks and pulled her taut against him. "I can't believe you talk like this—or let me talk to you like that."

"Don't stop, Jesse," she said taking his hand and cupping her breast with it. "Please." She opened her eyes.

"Sam," he groaned as he pulled her wetness to his waist. "I'm about to explode right now." He grasped her hands over her head. "I don't even want to know how you learned this."

"The nuns. Now stop talking."

"What?"

"Their racy books."

"Books!" He froze. "Have you ever been with a man before?"

Sam bit her bottom lip deciding if the truth was better than fiction here.

"Sam, the truth, are you…?"

She pulled herself up to her elbows. "The truth is you are my first kiss, my only everything."

Jesse groaned again and rolled off her. "Then I can't be having this conversation with you."

"Were we having a conversation?" She nudged his legs with her foot. There was no way to stop the smile that broke out across her face.

One large hand halted the advances of her foot. "This is no way for me to be acting with a virgin."

"How do you think women become non-virgins?" Crouching forward she kneeled next to him pressing her chest against his arm.

"Sam." He gave her a disapproving sidelong glance.

She nestled her head against his shoulder. "Jesse."

He kissed her forehead. "The only thing I want you sleeping with tonight is your frying pan."

He stood and headed for the door looking rather uncomfortable.

"Jesse!"

"Go to sleep."

"Are you sure you're okay, you look a little swollen." She bit back a laugh.

"I'll be right outside, just say the word if you need me."

She stood and walked toward him. "I thought you said you could never leave a lady stranded?"

He shook his head and walked out the door.

Chapter Eighteen

The sun rose in a cloudless Rocky Mountain sky, adding more heat to one of the hottest mornings in years. Hours earlier, Jesse awoke with a crick in his neck from sleeping on Julia's front porch. He wasn't about to leave Sam behind until Julia showed him her Colt .45 and swore on her granny's grave that no one was getting past her.

Jesse's pacing practically wore out the wool rug in his bedroom long before the sun came up. He waited for the first sign of dawn with his boots on. One person kept his head off his pillow all night, and it wasn't Sam Ward. It was the son-of-a-bitch who kidnapped her.

It was easier to think about the pain Jesse would inflict on him than the possible hurt the bastard caused Sam. She was tough and formidable when he met her in the woods, but she was also vulnerable and scared. And that, besides Sam's thorough study of the nuns' books, made sleep elusive.

Sam had him going last night. The brush of her breasts against his chest, the softness of her neck, and the taste of those supple lips heated his blood. Beauty and mystery weren't rare in Aspen except when it came to women. He wanted her, wanted her more than anything, and that was sitting a little off kilter for him—not because he didn't want it to, but because he did. Someday soon he was going to make her feel love from the inside out.

"I'm going to town to pick up supplies," Jesse said to his housekeeper, Mrs. Maple as she reported to the kitchen.

"Of course, you are," she responded with a smile that said she wanted to pinch his cheeks.

"Say what's on your mind, Mrs. Maple," Andy said from the corner.

"What are you going on about?" Jesse groaned with a glance at his longtime housekeeper.

"Just noticed you came in later than usual and proceeded to practically pace a hole through the ceiling."

Andy just shook his head. Jesse could think of nothing to say, not in mixed company anyway, so he headed for the door.

Never thought going to town would be the relief of the day, but the long ride was a welcome distraction. Finding a woman at the same time he was losing his ranch wasn't right, 'course it wasn't a coincidence either. Jesse wanted to punch a hole in the sky. Instead, he gritted his teeth and rode on toward Aspen and whatever awaited him. Like Andy said, after six months of chasing his parents' death, it was time to find something else and Sam Ward was just that—something else.

It wasn't even mid-morning and the townsfolk already appeared sluggish and exceptionally grumpy. He didn't need to feel the heat to know the weather. The stench of Aspen's miners on a hot day was a dead giveaway.

Jesse meandered through the streets wondering why someone smart enough to outwit Clay would stay in town. If J.W. was right, and it was a passenger, didn't he know Clay and his gang would find him?

Clay had to be holding out on J.W. and Luke. Nothing else made sense. How would Clay know the thief was in town? And why hadn't he found him yet? It wouldn't be that hard to find someone in a town with more talk than sense.

"Drink up." He tied Rusty next to a full trough outside Johnson's Mercantile. Jesse shoved the shop's swinging doors open, welcoming the shove back. It had been a while since he bought supplies. Since he was leaving the ranch, he really didn't need them. Today, he wasn't buying, he was proposing to barter with the proprietor, Dirk Johnson; his ranch furniture for supplies.

"Quit yer moping," Dirk Johnson called from behind a counter.

"What?" Jesse said turning around.

"Colburn, the sun's a shinin' and the wind ain't whistlin'. What more could you ask fer?"

Everybody knew Dirk Johnson didn't accept frowns or self-pity in his shop. The feud between Jesse and Luke was legend. Most folks knew Jesse had been through hell in the past six months. Dirk made it clear he thought Jesse should be moving past it all. Dirk, as usual, was right.

"I got the point," Jesse said.

"Morning, Sheriff," Dirk called.

Jesse turned toward the door as Sheriff Brown strolled into the mercantile.

"Morning," the sheriff said with a warning glare for Jesse.

"Something you want to say, Colburn?" the

lawman asked.

"Tremain walking around a free man makes me want to say plenty."

"Already talked to Andy. Luke had an alibi yesterday when your cattle was supposedly poisoned."

"'Course he did." J.W. killed the cattle while Luke was in town getting an alibi.

"Ever hear of a J.W.?"

"J.W.?" the sheriff let out a long whistle. "Ain't heard that name in two decades. Why? He come back to steal your ranch?" He laughed.

"As a matter of fact, he did."

"You're getting crazier every damn day."

Jesse had to agree with that and decided that conversation would go nowhere with Sheriff Brown.

"Catch the train robbers?"

"Marshals are looking into it."

"Don't need to look far. He's right over there." Jesse titled his head toward Luke's and ignored the sheriff's pair of squinty eyes. He didn't care how lazy the man was, the train robbers took more than payroll. They took Sam and that poor young man's wife.

"Leave it alone." The sheriff's philosophy had been the same all his life: use no more words than necessary and save your breath for breathing.

"Just another reason to hang Tremain, if you ask me," Jesse replied.

"Nobody did." Sheriff Brown narrowed his gaze. That man's eyes were so sharp they could bore a hole through a brick wall.

Jesse returned the glare and placed his order, "Pound of coffee, Dirk."

Dirk measured the coffee as Jesse glanced around

the store. It had been a long time since he noticed much. The shelves were lined with candy jars and tins of tobacco. Yards of fabrics and ribbons created a garden of colors. It was the same as it was two decades ago when he came in with his mama. Only back then he noticed everything.

"Anything else, Colburn?" the store owner asked.

"Maybe."

"Never seen you put so much effort into picking out a few provisions."

Johnson was right. "It's the heat."

But it wasn't the weather, and he knew it. It was Sam Ward. With her dark hair and meadow green eyes, those same eyes that glistened when she laughed and scorched when her temper flared. But it was her resolve while she was crying and scared that really got him. She had it all: looks, grit, and guts; and she had him by a mile. There was a lot to that woman and he was all in.

Her choice of relatives was a problem. Once he cared about someone, life dealt him a blow. Why did she have to be related to that scheming dog? What kind of future could there be with that hand at play? Even though she had her own mind, J.W. was family and Jesse knew the strength of that bond.

"That's all, Dirk." The furniture would have to wait. He wasn't about to barter in front of the sheriff. He paid and walked back out the swinging door.

Enchantment Ranch was all he had left, for now. Memories of his family were deeply imbedded in the walls, but that's all they were. Pa hammered every nail. Ma hung every painting, every photograph. Their presence surrounded him, but they could never hug him or pat him on the back. Memories were just photographs in one's mind, fading with time.

The only purpose he had in his life was keeping Enchantment and feeding Mrs. Maple and Andy. It had been the only thing he cared about, until Sam Ward rode into town—on his horse. All the energy he spent on Luke was wasted time. Sam was more than a relief or a distraction from his obsession with revenge. She was a reason to live again.

There weren't many folks about. It was still early, but with this heat, town would be busy soon enough. Julia was walking his way. She wasn't alone. Her companion caught his eye. She had a bandana covering her face and a hat covering her head. It looked good on her. The way she wore something of his warmed him. It was as if they had a secret, a special connection. The thought made him smile, but the bandit could still recognize her. It wasn't enough of a disguise.

"Morning," he said.

"Morning," Sam said. "Did you sleep okay?"

Jesse tipped his hat. "Sweetest dreams in years." He tilted his head, trying to see her face.

"I'm sending a telegram to the Sisters to tell them I got here safely."

He chomped down on the inside of his cheek. She didn't get here safely, but she was safe now. "I'll wait for you. When you're ready I'll take you to Enchantment," Jesse said.

She looked at Julia. "I have to do something first."

"I'll go with her to Enchantment in a bit," Julia said.

"All right." That was odd and made him feel uneasy. There were still secrets. He was trying to make peace with it. Secrets he could handle. Lies—that was a different story.

Did it have something to do with the Sisters? It was safer back in Boston. He couldn't exactly blame her for going back there.

While the women went into Dirk's to send the telegram, he meandered toward Luke's, checking to see if Clay or J.W. were about. Tightening his fists, he wished they were. Thinking about Sam going back to Boston put him in the mood for a fight.

"Colburn!" a deep voice broke his concentration.

"Sheriff," he nodded.

"Meant what I said, leave Tremain alone."

Just then another deep voice called from behind him, "Sheriff Brown, Mr. Colburn!"

Wade Rush approached them out of breath and dusting off his pants. A pair of spectacles stuck out of a wrinkled vest pocket. The young man's eyes were red; he was exhausted.

"Doing all we can to find the missus." The lawman patted the desperate husband on the back.

"Thank you. She's in a whole heap of trouble. That train robber was pure evil." Wade wrung his fingers as he spoke.

"Your wife is still missing?" Jessed asked looking from the young husband to the sheriff. "Pure evil," Wade's words rang in his ears.

"Mr. Rush, I know you're familiar with the law, being an attorney and all, but you leave this to me. That goes for you both." He glared at Jesse.

"I know who kidnapped Mrs. Rush," Jessie said.

"That's enough, Colburn."

"No, they kidnapped another woman, too." He promised Sam he wouldn't say anything, but she would understand if another woman's life was at stake.

"Shut your mouth, Colburn, before you start a damn panic." The sheriff shook his head and muttered, "What in the hell is going on with all these Yankee women all of a sudden?"

He'd be no help. Jesse decided he needed to help Wade on his own. But he needed to get rid of the lawman first.

"You're a lawyer?" Jesse asked.

"That's right."

"Ever deal with land disputes?" Jesse said enjoying the red face Sheriff Brown suddenly wore.

"Ah, a little."

Jesse wasn't so insensitive to discuss his problems right now. He was hoping to lure the man from Sheriff Brown.

Questions about his land and someone sabotaging it weren't that important. Sometimes he confused Enchantment for family. One look at Wade's eager reddened face reminded him of the difference.

"I'd be happy to talk with you. Maybe it would keep my mind off things while the sheriff investigates."

The Yankee was naïve. Was he really going to sit back and let the sheriff handle his wife's disappearance? Easterners trusted their law. Here, it was still every man for himself.

"I can help you find your wife," he said quietly.

"You can?"

Jesse studied the earnest newcomer. He twisted his fingers and shuffled his feet.

"I am sure our good sheriff here is doing all he can," Jesse said, nodding to the ever-crimson Sheriff Brown.

"She can handle herself well. She may come through it," Wade said.

What was it with this morning? Jesse was getting all these odd feelings. That sure as hell was a strange statement for a husband to make. The man was worried, preoccupied and all, but just the same, it sounded like he was describing childbirth or something. Sure as hell wasn't the way he would phrase his wife's kidnapping.

"My ranch is close. We can head out there and talk about land disputes," Jesse offered. Jesse gave Sheriff Brown his own pointed look.

The sheriff leaned closer. "I've got every available man looking for her."

Wade turned to face the sheriff. "Thank you. I appreciate your—oh, my goodness!" Wade shouted, "Thank goodness!" Wade's shoulders butted against the sheriff's as the young husband darted past them.

"What in the hell?" Sheriff Brown muttered.

"My wife!" Two skirted legs rocked back and forth hidden behind Wade's frame as he embraced someone in his arms. "Thank God you're safe."

"You didn't go to California? But I thought…what about your nephew?"

"I couldn't just let you be taken. You needed help," Wade answered, his voice wavering.

"I'm sorry to worry you." Her voice was sweet and familiar.

Sorry to worry you? Is that what you say after being kidnapped? This couple mystified him.

"I am relieved to find you safe. Let me introduce you to the men who were going to help me find you."

Wade twisted around to face them. "Gentlemen, let me introduce you to my wife," he stepped aside. "Mrs.

Samantha—Sam…Rush."

As her head tilted toward the sky, Sam's lips parted in surprise.

"Sam?" Jesse gasped.

"This is the missus?" Sheriff Brown's eyebrows reached the top of his face as he flashed his smug grin.

"Wife?" Jesse managed. "She is your wife?"

"Mr. Colburn, have you met…?"

"Your wife? Yes, we've met," he said through a clenched jaw.

"You didn't mention you had a husband," the sheriff said clearly amused by Jesse's reaction.

"You know her, too?" Jesse asked. "Why the hell am I surprised?"

Sam reached for him. He raised his hands in defeat and stalked away.

"Wife?" he repeated under his breath. She was confusing as hell, unpredictable and somewhat intolerable, even prone to giving innocent men, women, and children headaches, but married? That, he didn't see coming.

"Jesse, wait, please!" He felt a tug on his shirtsleeve. "Please, Jesse, I can explain."

He spun around catching her waist as she bumped right into him. Stepping backward, he held her an arm's length away.

"Of course you can, Sam or Mrs. Rush or whoever you are."

She crossed her arms and sighed. "It's Sam."

"Sam what?" Why was he even asking? It was supposed to be the more you got to know someone, the more you knew about them. But not with her. Suddenly thirsty and craving a drink, he turned away from her.

"Jesse, please listen." He felt the tug on his sleeve again only this time he didn't stop. "Wait, where are you going?"

"I need a drink," he yelled over his shoulder.

From the clap of her boots behind him he could tell she was keeping up with him. "But it's morning." The confusion in her voice made him even angrier.

"You have that effect on me." Turning around and holding her, listening to her latest story would be easy. For now. But then what? He needed one thing from her, honesty, and she couldn't give it to him.

The hat he'd given to her, or the one she'd stolen at gunpoint, depending on how you look at it, whizzed by his head and landed a few feet away.

"After everything we've been through, can't you give me a minute?" she cried.

He heard the pain in her voice. It may have sounded like a simple plea, but it wasn't. It was much more. That was just it, after everything they'd been through he wanted more than a minute. He wanted a lifetime.

His feet were telling him to run, but he walked away instead. One boot in front of the other as Pa used to say. He was a fool. He was no lawyer; he wasn't an educated man. As of tomorrow, he'd have no land, no house, nothing. He was nothing. Why had he even kidded himself? He could never have a woman like her.

Suddenly something smacked his shoulder. And again, this time it was harder, more of a wallop.

The hat again? He was being pounded in the back and shoulders with the hat. Small, yet strong, determination in her eyes, Sam stood there wielding the hat like a whip lashing him in the middle of the street.

"Don't walk away from me." Usually she was demanding, this time she was pleading.

"I know. I know. There is some logical explanation." His shoulders went rigid and he stopped. "Except that I am done with explanations and excuses. You worried your husband." He gestured toward Wade. "Didn't you think he would come looking for you?" He wrestled the hat from her grip and met her glare. "If I were your husband," his voice cracked. He swallowed trying to hide his hurt. "I would die before I stopped trying to find you."

The scent of her hair filled him as he leaned over her, his mouth brushed her ear. "You need this hat to disguise yourself from Clay." He rubbed the hat against his leg, knocking the dirt off it and placed it on her head. "Don't take it off again," he said harshly.

Wade approached them. He didn't want to care what her husband thought, but he did. None of this was the young man's fault. He liked him, and besides, the poor guy was doing the best he could. Sam was a handful, to say the least.

"It's not the way it looks," she protested.

Jesse shook her off. "It's your husband's job to protect you. And I'm not going to disrespect the man."

He tipped his hat at Wade. Then, loud enough for Wade to hear, he said, "Your husband has been searching for you for days. Do you have any idea how worried he's been? He thought you were kidnapped."

Her face went white. She looked around, fear frozen on her face.

A pit of regret jabbed his gut. "Sam?"

She looked as if she was about to faint.

Instinctually, he reached forward supporting her

light frame. She looked up at him, and with a trembling finger at her lips, she motioned for him to be quiet.

Damn it. He didn't know what was real and what wasn't anymore. It was as if he were looking through binoculars. The object was there but where it stood was unclear.

With a quick glance behind her, she put her small hands on Jesse's shoulders and stretched to reach his ear. Her body pressed into his chest. Her soft and gentle figure fit perfectly into the fold of his arms.

Even though her husband stood right next to her, she whispered, "Please, don't tell anyone about the kidnapping."

He studied her expression. The fear in her eyes made him uneasy. "I told you I wouldn't tell anyone," he whispered, taking her arm. But then a bitterness he couldn't fight took hold of his tongue and he said, "But your husband just announced it to the whole town."

"Sam?" Wade called.

Blood seeped from Jesse's lip as he bit down hard fighting to suppress the pain wrenching his guts from his body.

"Thank you," she said. She reached up on her toes and brushed her feather-soft lips against his cheek. Her delicate fingers against his chest remained motionless for a moment before the faint push of her hands against his chest separated them and she walked away.

He felt the void in his heart as soon as he felt it in his arms.

Julia and Wade hovered around her. They were her protection from J.W. and Clay now. Her husband claimed her, and she didn't deny it. She didn't scream or struggle to fight him off. She willingly went to

Wade.

There was nothing he could do except visit the only woman he trusted in Aspen. The only person he wanted to see right now: Georgia.

Chapter Nineteen

Sam turned around to find Julia watching her. Her eyebrows raised and her eyes wide. Her new friend took her by the elbow and hauled her up the walkway. "What was that all about?" Julia asked her.

"I have to get back to the cabin right away."

"Excuse me, ladies," Wade interrupted. She felt his gaze on her as her cheeks burned with embarrassment.

Wade studied Julia for a moment and introduced himself. "Hello, Wade Rush, Sam's husband." There was a flush to his cheeks reminding her that he was lying for her and lying made most people uncomfortable. Even so, he reached for Julia's hand. "It's a pleasure to make your acquaintance."

Julia's eyes, blazing with comprehension, met her gaze. Fighting her darn corset for more air, her bosom rose sharply as she took a deep breath. Who had the patience for a corset especially in the West? Why wear something traditional in a camp that was anything but?

When Sam finished taking her anger out on her corset she watched Julia look her "fake" husband up and down. He was handsome with his golden red curls shooting out from under his hat at all angles. He had the look of a man attacked by nerves, rumpled, yet kind. A feeling of genuine relief and joy shone through his smile. Which made Sam feel sick. She never thought he would search for her. Now here he was when he should be on his way to California.

Wade stood a few inches taller than they and he laced his hands behind his back. Sam surmised the tension was obvious. But, she thought, perhaps the source of that tension was not obvious to him.

She lowered her voice to Julia, "Wade told the sheriff I was kidnapped. If the bandit finds out where I am…"

"Right." Julia nodded understanding the situation.

Turning to Wade, Sam said, "I apologize, but I have to go. I am not feeling well." Heaven help her she was lying to the man who already sacrificed too much for her.

"I will escort you," Wade offered.

"No, you said you had to get to California quickly for some kind of family situation." He had explained it on the train, but she only listened to half of what he had said. "I'll be fine. Julia will look after you and make arrangements for you to get on the next coach to Leadville."

"It was very kind of you to come for her." Julia stepped in front of her.

Julia whispered in Sam's ear, "Jesse will cool off. Take Pearl and head back to the cabin and get out the Winchester in my granny's old chest. I'll take care of Wade."

"Come with me, Mr. Rush." Her new friend pulled Wade by the elbow and drew his attention away from Sam.

Her feet were slow and heavy like the lead from the mountains, but she had to get out of sight fast.

****

Town was beginning to buzz with miners and

drunkards as Jesse made his way up the boardwalk. Rusty was content as he drank from the trough, so Jesse headed to Georgia's.

"Mr. Colburn!"

Jesse cringed. Nobody had called him that since School Mistress Hanson scolded him in grade school.

"Sweet Vinegar." Jesse grunted as Wade strode up next to him.

"Jesse," a female voice rang out in a tone reminiscent of the old broad Hanson again.

"Damn it," Jesse muttered under his breath as he stole a quick glance toward his intended destination. Whiskey was the only company he wanted. "Not now." He grunted to Julia. He quickly checked the area for Luke.

"You know Wade Rush?" Julia asked, ignoring his rudeness.

"We've met." He couldn't meet Julia's eyes. He knew damn well he was acting like child. If only he could hate Wade, but he didn't. Something about his appearance and anxious eyes made him feel sympathy for the guy. Which angered him even more. Feeling sorry for the man married to the woman he was having intensely strong feelings for was just a pain in the ass.

"Jesse." A solid grip on his arm halted him to a stop. "Hold on a minute."

He looked over Julia's head at Georgia's Saloon wishing he was inside the cool bar with a shot in his hand.

She waved her hand in his face. "Georgia ain't gonna run out of whiskey at ten o'clock in the morning so let the man say his piece." The woman was no Sunday school teacher, but she demanded respect all the same.

"Mr. Colburn." Wade tipped his hat. "I—"

"Out here we go by first names," Jesse cut him off. He stole a glance at Julia, whose frown turned into an all out scowl.

Wade gestured toward Georgia's. "Jesse, can I buy you a drink?"

Jesse was taken aback by the thought of this kid drinking anything stronger than water. "No." He picked a piece a straw from his pants pocket and stuck it in his mouth. Usually the feel of it on his tongue relaxed him.

Julia frowned with obvious disappointment. "Quit being a stubborn fool."

Jesse kicked the boardwalk with his boots and studied the dirt before addressing Wade, "Where's the missus?"

Julia snorted. "Jesse, just listen to the man."

"Don't like being lied to." He spoke to Julia but was staring at Wade.

She sighed and snapped her fingers demanding his attention. "Nobody does. But folks gotta do what's necessary."

Damn, this woman would've made a hell of a school teacher. "Got to be who you are, Julia." He leaned against the storefront and kept his eyes trained on Luke's place.

Julia snorted and crossed her arms. "Never met a man who cared who I was only cared about what I could do."

"That's different." The conversation was going nowhere. Suddenly he wasn't craving a drink as much as a fight. He couldn't hit Wade though. It was hard to believe a man as refined as Wade was a lawyer.

"No, it ain't. Women bury who they are every day—ain't nobody complain 'bout it."

Jesse didn't meet her eyes—he looked away—toward Luke's. She was right, damn it. He needed to quit feeling sorry for himself.

"I got a meeting with Luke," Jessie said.

"Thought you were getting a drink?" Julia called after him.

Forget the damn drink. He was angry and ready to take it out on Luke. Why was he so damn gullible when it came to Sam Ward or Sam Rush or whatever the hell her name was?

"Just what are ya intending with Luke?" Julia asked catching up to him as he headed toward the land office.

"Revenge."

"Doing something stupid isn't going to make anything better."

"Putting an end to Luke Tremain and the Tremain family will." He took a wide step around her. Why couldn't people just leave him alone? Life was easier when he pretended no one else existed.

"Why?" Wade pressed.

Damn he was following him too? "Why?" Jesse said. "What the hell kinda question is that?"

Julia shot Jesse a look. "You best not do nothin' rash, or you'll end up sharin' ya grandpa's fate." Almost a full foot shorter, she could still make him come to a standstill.

Julia caught her breath and kept on talking. "Your grandpa died 'cause Luke's pa rushed to judgment. His gun was an extension of his heart. Thought with one and killed with the other. If a man uses his brain as his weapon and his gun as a shield, he'll never regret what he does."

"You weren't even there," he retorted.

"Didn't need to be; whole town talks about it. Heard it so many times I could've been there."

"Who said anything about regret? Didn't see Luke's pa regretting anything, and neither will I." Lectures—he was sick of them.

Julia looked at Wade. "Jesse's grandpa died standing up for him, his only grandchild. He told Luke's father to keep his no-good son away from Jesse. Willy Tremain didn't take kindly to the remarks folks were making about his boy. Jesse's grandpa was the last man to stand up to him. Even long after Willy Tremain died, folks still remembered that Old Jack Colburn got shot in the back."

Jesse heard the words and saw the story unfold before his eyes, as he did just about every day for the past fourteen years. Gramps spoke his last words to protect him. Lying on that dirty floor, blood red as basalt rock streaming out his mouth and trickling down his jaw. Jesse cradled his bleeding head, begging for help, pleading for Gramps not to leave him. No one moved. No one came. He was ten years old the day his childhood ended. The death of his pa's hero, his hero, etched in his mind forever. Pa never said it, but Jesse knew he blamed him for Gramp's death. Pa's grief lined his face like the Roaring Fork; his sunken eyes never looked at him the same again. Jesse was left with nothing but guilt and a vicious craving for revenge.

This morning it wasn't Gramp's red blood that woke him. He had dreamed about Sam and her kidnapper. The image of her green eyes slowly roused him from his fitful slumber. That was how he wanted to wake up from now on, looking at Sam's eyes. Only he wanted them looking back at him.

"Forget it." He pivoted hoping they'd finally take the hint, and he headed toward Georgia's.

"Good advice," Julia answered. "Now listen to Wade."

"Mr.—ah, Jesse, Sam isn't my wife." Wade practically stepped on the heel of his boot. "I agreed to pretend to be her husband."

Jesse turned. "Why did she ask you to do that?"

"Keep things proper."

"That's proper?"

"Ah, Sam, ah, I'm not sure how to…"

"Actually, that explains her perfectly." Damn it, Wade wasn't the only man at a loss for words when it came to Sam Ward. Jesse had fallen for her, fallen hard. It was as if she were a steam train barreling toward him. All he had to do was step out of the way before impact, he just wasn't sure he could.

Wade was still trying to explain. "I was supposed to keep her safe. I failed though." The younger man's eyes wouldn't meet his.

Failed didn't even come close. He could blame Wade, but Jesse was no better at protecting his loved ones.

Was this her big secret? Jesse kept sensing there was something more she wasn't telling him. He'd been teetering close to whatever it was.

"When she boarded the train, she sat next to me and started talking about the Sisters…"

"Wade," Julia interrupted.

"Right, ah, Sam asked if I would act like we were

ah, married. She knew me from the convent. She said it would make the Sisters feel better."

"But…" Jesse waited for more of an explanation.

"But I don't think the Sisters knew she was leaving. She's brave, but still, I think she was scared of coming all this way alone."

Scared of coming all this way alone. A pit the size of Snowmass Mountain churned in his stomach. That's how he found her—scared and alone.

"I didn't do her much good." Wade continued, "The robber hit me in the head with his gun and knocked me out. When I woke up, I ran to the doorway of the coach." Wade sighed. "I jumped from the train. I thought I could get to her in time because the robber was tying the saddlebag with the payroll onto his horse. She didn't even see me." Wade stopped again; he was looking out toward Aspen Mountain. "The robber forced her onto his horse and tied her hands. I tried to call out to her, but I got punched in the stomach. I fell to my knees." In a quieter voice he said, "By the time I got up, they were gone; they were all gone." He sighed again and looked at Jesse. "She was counting on me to protect her. I'm sorry I let her down."

"Are you listenin' to the man, Jesse?" Julia was yelling at him. Yes, he was listening. He heard every word, every shred of regret in Wade's voice.

"I thought you should know. I can tell you care about her."

"Where is she now?" Jesse asked.

Julia answered, "You cool off and give her some time. She's got something she's gotta do. I'll bring her to Enchantment."

"Something to do?"

"Yup." Julia nodded to Wade and the two of them walked away leaving Jesse alone. The world became a distant rumble, like something being said under water. Connections were being made, but one detail was still escaping him.

She wasn't married. This called for a celebration. He eyed the bar again. A few drinks and he'd hopefully forget this morning even happened. Why not, Sam had something to do so he might as well use the time he had before he'd see her again. A group of children bumped into him. He muttered an apology and continued on his way to Georgia's through the fog of his thoughts.

Wade wasn't the only one who let her down. So did he. He acted like an ass when she tried to explain. He even accused her of lying about the kidnapping. Cringing at the thought, he needed to inflict some pain, and he knew just who to treat to that hurt: Luke Tremain. Sam had lied to him so many times—that's why he didn't believe her and that was Luke's fault.

In Georgia's, Jesse signaled to the barmaid for a whiskey. He threw back the liquid burn and waited for the warmth to soothe him.

When it did, he went to the door and looked out at the scene before him. The sun was making her daily climb. So much beauty in the sky, so much deceit on earth, he wondered where the two truly met.

Reading people was a necessary skill. It saved his life more than once, but he was losing his touch. Sam was affecting him like no one else ever had. He needed to refocus on saving his parents' legacy. He needed to put their dreams before his own and redeem his father's name and move on.

"Another whiskey." He raised his glass like he was

making a toast. Georgia was easy to read. Her scowl said it all.

"You don't want people drinking this early, don't open," he said.

He reached into his pocket and pulled out the yellowed deed to Enchantment. It was creased and ragged from folding and unfolding it for six months. Tomorrow he would turn it over to some banker in Leadville. No one had even heard of Leadville Bank until a year ago when Pa brought the mortgage papers home. Probably not even a real bank. Just one of those soul-sucking places lined up after the big find in Leadville years ago. Just waiting on suckers like Pa.

Another shot of whiskey only made his mood worse. He had to think. He shouldn't be drinking; he should be figuring out his move to keep his ranch.

But all he could do was think about Sam. She was like that ray of sun that finds you and warms you just where you're standing. Its depth barely wide enough to cross your body, but you stand there in its glow, waiting with dread, knowing it's got to move. You realize its comfort won't last and at some point, when the earth moves just enough, you'll be standing in the cold shadows again. But, for that moment, when you raise your face to the sky and the orange and yellow shine is so bright, it's like a message from the heavens.

Damn it. He fingered a sweaty glass as it smacked against the mahogany. "Another shot, Georgia."

Disapproval registered on the barmaid's face again. "Since when do ya drink before noon?"

Jesse tossed more than enough money onto the bar to cover the whiskey. "Since morning."

"What's gotten into ya?"

"Not enough whiskey." He smirked as she poured him another.

He downed the drink and wandered out the swinging saloon doors with an eye toward Tremain's building. He recognized Luke's horse. There was another one there he didn't recognize.

Mumbling from the bar beckoned him back inside. He signaled Georgia for another drink, gulped down the whiskey, and savored the bite sliding down the back of his throat.

Town was quiet. The heat muted the usual sounds.

"What's the matter with ya?" Georgia asked again.

Something was nagging at him. "My wife was taken from the train." Wade's words echoed in his ears.

She wasn't his wife. Sam had pretended to be someone else, no surprise there. How many more lies or disguises would he catch her in? He couldn't figure the little horse thief out.

The whiskey flooded his mind. Anger had lured him here, now regret and liquor held him. He needed to think straight. The only thing worse than the whiskey was that Wade apologized. That was the last thing Jesse wanted.

Jealousy circled his heart and began to squeeze. Sam trusted Wade to keep her safe. But she never fully trusted Jesse. There was still something she was holding back.

A sick feeling crept through every inch of his body. He was missing something. He tried to focus on it, but the whiskey was making his mind murky.

"You see who's leaving Luke's?" Georgia asked.

"What?" Jesse looked up. Georgia's brown eyes were watching him. The barmaid barely spoke a word in the past ten years, and suddenly she's holding an inquisition?

Jesse put his glass down on the bar and lifted his hat off his face.

Nothing happened in the vicinity of Georgia she didn't know about. Folks said, before she shot him, she could smell her husband one hundred yards away. Same was true for outsiders and outlaws. They never got within sight of the place without Georgia first cocking her Winchester.

The booze was warming his mind, just like Sam Ward did his body.

Georgia was looking out her window. Men said she did it on occasion in case her senses let her down. Jesse didn't believe that. She did it to make a point—to get the man in need of that point to look out the window.

"One of his regulars lately. Seen a lot of him in the past couple of weeks," Georgia answered her own question. Even Sheriff Brown shared more words than Georgia. Yet today, she talked like a drunk on payday.

"One of his regulars, so what?" He closed his eyes and tried to comprehend what Georgia was going on about.

"New horse. Don't recognize it."

Damn it, why don't women just say what's on their minds?

"Got a limp now," she continued.

"So?"

"Guy got a limp in the past few days and a new horse."

Jesse nodded. "He's got a limp and a new horse. I'll go tell the *Rocky Mountain Sun*. It'll be in the paper tomorrow."

He laughed at his joke. But then something about what he said made his brain start swimming.

"Somebody got the bastard's leg real good." She clicked her tongue as if the noise represented something he was supposed to understand.

Like a man who got stabbed in the leg. Clay was at Luke's. That son-of-a-bitch kidnapped Sam, but she got away on her horse. No, wait, it wasn't her horse. It ran away from her and never came back. What did Wade say? "He put her on his horse and tied her hands."

Damn it, she must've been so scared. Wade thought he could catch her—thought he had time while the robber was tying the payroll to the horse. Tying the payroll to his horse. Jesse knocked over his drink. Georgia looked at him, but she didn't say anything, she just strode down the bar.

Sam took the robber's horse. Clay told Luke and J.W. that the thief took his horse and the payroll with it.

Sam, the little thief, was the thief. She had the money. Luke, Clay, even J.W. were looking for her, but none of them realized it, not yet. Wade was telling everybody, including the sheriff, that his wife was kidnapped. There was only one woman kidnapped. Clay knew that. Once he put the pieces together all he would have to do would be to figure out where she was. One conversation with J.W. or Luke and Clay would know. Jesse had to get to Clay first.

He threw a coin on the bar, headed for the swinging doors, and braced for the full light of day. He stumbled onto the boardwalk swaying and knocking into people before his eyes adjusted. He shook his head clearing the whiskey haze from his eyes and ran toward Luke's.

He shoved his shoulder against Luke's office door, but the hard wood knocked him back. He should feel pain, but he didn't. He felt his gut wrench and his mouth run dry. He rounded the corner. The horses were gone. Last night Clay said he was closing in on the thief. Damn. His heart pounded, pumping panic through his veins as he raced toward Rusty praying he wasn't too late.

For too long his thirst for revenge had choked him. It was his only way of making amends to Pa. He couldn't save his folks or Gramps, so he needed to save Enchantment. Now, he didn't even care about Enchantment.

The bitter taste of fear was on his lips. How many times would he try saving someone and fail? He couldn't allow himself to feel fear now. Fear was like snow. Once it starts to fall, once one little bit crashes down the side of the mountain, it starts to take everything with it. And that's what kills.

Chapter Twenty

Sam shuddered as she replayed the shock on Jesse's face when Wade introduced her as his wife. Jesse had slept on the ground right here in front of the cabin to make her feel safe. And now, God knows what he thought of her.

Julia risked her life housing Sam. Clay would kill Julia in a heartbeat to get the money. And Wade, he needed to get to California to help his nephew, but instead he was here looking after her.

That was it. She was done hiding and asking more of others than of herself. She tugged her boots on, the only things she actually owned anymore, pulled Jesse's borrowed hat down low, and headed out the door.

"You ready for another ride, Pearl?" She holstered Julia's Winchester to the saddle and grabbed the reins. With one foot in the stirrup, she grabbed the saddle horn and kicked her other leg off the ground.

Before she could mount, someone grabbed her around the waist, knocking the air out of her. She was hauled off the horse. Forceful arms put her in an inescapable hold. Helpless and taut against what felt like a brick wall, fear rose like bile in her throat. A large hand clamped over her mouth, and the odor of alcohol invaded her nostrils and told her one thing: Clay had found her.

"Where do you think you're going?"

She barely registered the words. His breath was thick with whiskey and his voice husky. One arm pinned her against his solid chest, but her legs were free. She smashed his foot with the heel of her boot. Then she seized the rough skin of his palm in her clenched teeth and bit him.

"For the love of God…"

That rugged voice; the unmistakable twang of a cowboy—Jesse?

"Are you going to stop kicking and biting and listen?"

She nodded and muffled yes through his clamped hand.

The heavy arm around her waist released. "You promise you're going to be quiet," he whispered in her ear before unclamping her mouth. She twirled around.

"Jesse?" She threw her arms around him. "What are you doing here?" She stepped back and scrunched up her nose. "You smell like whiskey."

"I thought you said you were going to listen and be quiet. And, I told you before I was getting a drink." Taking hold of her wrist, he locked her in his grasp and pulled her toward the cabin.

He was here with her. Her stomach felt as if it would drop to her knees.

"I know you're angry about Wade. I can…"

He threw open the cabin door. "Again, you said you were going to listen and be quiet."

He kicked the door shut behind them and slid the table in front of it.

"What are you—?"

"Where were you going?" he demanded cutting her off.

"I was going to…"

"Alone," he interrupted again. He looked around the cabin his voice barely controlled. "Clay's after you." He glanced out the window. "Isn't he?"

"You mean…Wade?"

"No, Sam, I mean Clay." He lifted the frying pan off the wall and walked toward her.

"Jesse, it's not what you think." Her heart raced. She was confused and a little nervous by his behavior. "You have to trust me."

"Trust you? I have to trust you? Is that what you just said?" He slammed the frying pan against the table.

"Jesse, you're—"

"Here. I'm here, aren't I? I'm here through the charades and the half-truths. I've been the one trusting."

"I trust you," she snapped.

"No, you don't. You're still keeping secrets."

She swallowed the words she wanted to say. Her secret was that she was going to save his ranch.

"It doesn't matter. Get your clothes. I am taking you to Enchantment now."

"No."

"No clothes, fine. Take the frying pan, we're leaving."

"Julia's Winchester is on Pearl."

"I know. You need both. Use the frying pan if Clay takes the gun from you. Trust me; he'll never suspect the frying pan." He knocked the table aside.

"Jesse, wait!"

"No," he yelled over his shoulder, "you're not safe here."

"What's going on? Why are you acting this way?"

He stopped short and spun around, his eyes blazing

in anger. "Why didn't you tell me that you had the money?"

She stepped back. Her hands flew to her face, covering her mouth. He was staring at her. His eyebrows raised waiting for an answer.

"Because I was going to use it against you."

"You are a part of this."

"No, no, I never was."

"What were you going to do with the money?"

She inhaled deeply and studied the ceiling as if the words she needed were up there. "Luke demanded I get the deed to Enchantment in order to get J.W. back. But since that was impossible—"

"You planned to give him the money instead," he finished her thought.

"Yes."

"So, in order to save your pa, you were going to hand over the stolen money to Luke so he could use it to get my ranch?"

She crossed her arms. "Yes." She looked at him, owning what she had planned to do.

"Why didn't you?"

"Why didn't I?"

Two steps forward and he stood over her. "You wouldn't be in danger if you had. Clay's not stupid. He's going to figure this out, and when he does, he will come for you." His rugged voice melted into a pained softness. "You should have given the money to Luke."

Her head was spinning. Confusion and nerves made her grab her temples. He was angrier than she'd ever seen him—all because she didn't give the money to the man who would use it against him?

"Where is it?"

"I don't have it."

He let out a loud sigh. "What?" He ran a hand through his hair.

"When I took off on Clay's horse, I didn't realize I had the money until I stopped. Then you came and the horse ran off."

"The money is on the horse?"

"No, I buried it."

"And that's where you were going? Into the woods? Alone with a half dozen men looking for you."

"Only Clay knows I have it."

"Isn't that enough?"

She blinked and looked away; his words were an invisible prick on her skin.

"I wasn't going to get the money for me. I was going to give it to you."

"To me?"

"Yes. It's J.W.'s fault that you are losing your ranch. He poisoned your cattle. I don't know if he burned your barn. If those horses hadn't been killed, you would've been able to sell them to that buyer and save your home."

He shook his head. "I'm not using stolen money to save my skin."

"Turn it in for the reward."

"How can you think that I care about my ranch when Clay is looking for you? He's desperate. Do you understand that? The railroad men will kill him and..." He swallowed hard and wouldn't meet her eyes.

"And?"

"And...he's already tried to force himself on you once."

"No, I—"

247

"Don't lie to me. Don't tell me he didn't try."

Words, where were the words? She couldn't speak, couldn't breathe. His words were harsh and his eyes were...cold, but softening.

"You're smart. You would've known the best time to stab him would've been when he was preoccupied. That's how I know."

Her arms were shaking. He had known what she was thinking from the look on her face.

He took a deep breath and straightened his hat. "What if he found you in the woods? Nothing would stop him from doing whatever he wanted."

"I..."

"Stop!" He kneaded his palms. He twisted and turned away from her as if he wanted to pummel something.

"Don't say you would have. Goddamn it, Sam." He took a deep breath and straightened his hat. He lowered his face until he was eye level with her and gently held her arms. "You have the will of a warrior, I know that, but you have the strength of a woman." He bit the inside of his cheek. "I'm sorry to say that, but that is the truth."

She shuttered at his conviction. "I know I'm a woman, but..." She bit down on her lip.

"Do you?"

"Yes, and I can do this. I can get the money and save your ranch."

"J.W. is going to figure this out, too."

"He won't hurt me."

"Are you so sure?"

"Yes, the others maybe, but not him."

He backed away. "How can you say that? How can

you think like that? One man is more than enough."

"Last night you said I was strong and today I'm…"

"In danger, just like you were last night." He sighed. "In danger from a man intent on getting that money and silencing you." Jesse leaned lower, skimming his lips over her forehead. "I won't let that happen."

He wrapped his arms around her and lowered his face to hers.

"I can't protect you if you keep running around as if you're not in danger. Clay was at Luke's this morning. J.W. will be talking to them soon. It shreds me from the inside out to think what would've happened if they had figured this out first."

"In case you have forgotten, I escaped from Clay, got the money, and have managed to keep myself safe. I am not some helpless woman."

"Why aren't you more careful? Why do you care more about me and my ranch than you do about yourself?"

Because that's what she did, always did, risked her life to rescue J.W. time and time again. He was all she had in the world. He showed her love only after she'd rescued him. Then he'd laugh about it and tell her how she was his little savior. That feeling, those times, were the only strings she had to love, all she could pull to get J.W.'s attention.

She said softly, "Maybe it's because no one ever…"

"Loved you…before?"

"Before?"

"Before now." He caressed her cheek.

"Now?"

"Sam, I'm no expert. But what I do know is that love is not about needing someone or wanting someone, it's about putting another person first. I'm not going to let you risk your life to save Enchantment."

Tears streamed down her face. "I can't let you lose your home; it's all you have."

"Haven't you heard anything I've said? I would spend the rest of my life in a cave if it meant you were safe."

"But you can save your ranch, your parents' dream."

"I won't take stolen money to save myself, my ranch or my parents' dream."

"Okay, we'll give the money to the sheriff. If Luke can't get it, then he won't be able to buy the ranch," Sam said.

"Get the frying pan. I'm taking you to Andy."

"Then you'll give the money to the sheriff?"

Jesse didn't reply.

"Jesse, you'll give the payroll to Sheriff Brown?"

"No, I am going to give the money to Luke."

"Luke! If you give Luke the money then—"

"Then you will be safe."

"No, I can do this, Jesse," Sam said gripping his arms. "I'm getting that money. You deserve it after what they have put you through, after what they have taken from you."

"You're killing me, Sam." Jesse threw his arms up in the air. "They haven't taken anything from me I can't replace."

"But what would your parents want you to do?"

"I don't know what my folks would have done, how far they would go to save it. All I know is what I will and won't do."

"I will give the money to the sheriff," Sam said. She started pacing.

"You're not giving it to anyone. Clay is going to figure it out and come for you or track you. He just needs to talk to J.W. to put the pieces together. You're going to Enchantment." He opened the door, but she didn't move. "Sam, are you coming...willingly?"

Sam turned pale.

"Sweet Vinegar, I'm not going to hurt you."

"No, that's not it. It's J.W. He left for Luke's just before you got here."

"I didn't see him."

Her fingers were sweaty and that knot, that twisted pit in her gut that J.W. controlled, started to ravel and twist tighter and tighter.

"Sam." Jesse took her elbow and led her out the door. "I will take you to Enchantment and then go to Luke's and deal with J.W."

"There's no time. You're right. J.W. will figure it out."

"You'll be safe at Enchantment." He opened her clenched fist and rubbed her fingers. "Let's go."

"No, J.W. can't know that I had the money. If he figures it out—he'll never forgive me."

"Forgive you?"

"I'm sorry. I know." She wanted to bury her head in shame. "He has a hold on me—I can't disappoint him. I can't stand up to him."

"You are one of the bravest people I have ever met. You can stand up to anyone including him, Sam."

He cupped her chin, "But if it's that important to you, I will get to J.W. before he gets to Luke's."

"I'm sorry." She shook her head. "Thank you."

A good man with bad habits. That's how she characterized J.W., but she was the one with the bad habit of believing in him. Few people understood how she felt about her father, not the sisters, not the prostitutes, no one except the orphans. She didn't need to explain it to them. They too would've done anything to get their parents back. To be loved again. Not just fed or cared for, but truly loved, embraced. To be wanted, not out of pity, or charity, or duty, but for no reason at all.

"Stay here, Sam. Take your gun and your frying pan and sit in the back corner."

She nodded.

"And Sam, shoot anyone who walks through the door."

Chapter Twenty-One

Luke, J.W.—it didn't matter who his enemy was; all that mattered was Sam. He'd given both men enough chances and they had taken every one and spit them right back in his face.

The thought of her sitting in the corner, alone and scared holding a gun and a frying pan, made him sick.

She could take care of herself for a while, for now, but not forever. They would hunt for the thief until they found her and the money.

As he and Rusty headed for Luke's, he fingered the worn paper in his pocket. It'd been in one pocket or another for months as a reminder of his duty for justice. Now the deed held a different meaning, a new purpose.

In town, he tied Rusty to the hitching post with a full trough below it. He'd ridden his horse hard, and Rusty needed to be ready to ride again, soon.

Raised voices bellowed from Luke's open window. Yelling could be heard from the boardwalk, but no one took notice. On hot days like this no one paid attention to much. The heat had that effect on people. Tempers ignited faster than flint, but indifference was always simmering. Folks breathed in its fumes and lived with it for so long that callousness was just another citizen of Aspen.

Once he knew the three men were in Luke's office, Jesse took a deep breath. He leaned against the wall directly beneath the window.

"I said where'd you get this knife?" It was J.W.'s voice, loud and angry. How the hell was he going to get to J.W. before the three of them figured out Sam was the thief?

"I already told you, the thief stabbed me."

"You lied. You got this knife because you thought you'd get a little extra money on the side."

"I'm done here," Clay responded. "I need to get out there and find the thief."

"You're lying."

"What the hell, Luke, shut this old coot up, or I will." Jesse bent low and entered the outer office. The men were too busy yelling to notice.

"Your lies are gonna tie you up like a lasso 'round a bull."

"Call me liar once more, old timer—"

"And what?"

Jesse shook his head. They rob trains, murder horses and cattle, but God forbid you call one of them a liar.

J.W. wouldn't let it go. "You robbed Sam on the train and stabbed yourself to make it look you were bushwhacked."

"Who the hell is Sam?" Clay demanded.

Damn it. Jesse's fists tightened. If only he could wrap his fingers around J.W.'s throat and choke the stupidity out of him.

A woman's voice drifted through the open door. It was Julia. He inched over to the outside door and signaled to her.

"Go get Sheriff Brown. These idiots are admitting to the train robbery," he instructed her. If the sheriff overheard the conversation, the men would be done in.

"I'll find him." Her eyes widened in understanding. She lifted her skirts and headed out the door.

Jesse crept back toward the office door.

"His daughter?" Clay's voice was rising.

"Yeah," Luke answered, "she showed up a few days ago wondering where J.W. was."

"You never said nothin' about no daughter."

"Why the hell would I?"

"Where'd she come from?"

"Boston, by train," J.W. answered. "The one you robbed."

Jesse wiped the sweat from his eyes. Damn, he just gave up his own daughter. It was happening too fast; the sheriff wouldn't be here in time.

"She's your partner," Clay said.

That smug son-of-a-bitch knew Sam wasn't involved. He was baiting J.W.

"She's not a part of this, and you know it. You took the payroll. Where is it?"

"Why would I still be here if I took the money?"

"'Cause you're stupid and greedy."

"Where's your daughter? I'll talk to her myself," Clay asked.

Jesse glanced out the door. He had to do something to get their attention and keep J.W. from talking until the sheriff arrived.

"Don't go anywhere near Sam, you stupid son-of-a-bitch."

"You calling me stupid?"

"Yeah. No thief would waste an expensive blade on your leg," J.W. said. "Only you would, knowing you'd get it back. You stole it from Sam. Then you took off with the payroll and hid it along the path to Aspen. Then you limped in here as pathetic as your story."

"Shut up," Clay yelled.

J.W. ignored him. "Nobody knew that train was being robbed except you and your men. So who the hell could've robbed you?"

Luke rose from his chair and edged his way toward Clay. "He has a point."

Jesse fetched the deed from his pocket.

"Obviously he tipped off his daughter about the plan. Where is she?"

Luke pursed his lips. "Good idea, let's talk to her."

Jesse had to act now.

Luke continued, "She's—"

Splintered wood flew through the air as Jesse's boot slammed against the door. He burst into the room. "Meeting of the mindless, I see."

"Get out of here, Colburn," Luke demanded.

"I don't think you want me to leave."

"I'm sure I do," Luke said coming toward him.

Out of the corner of his eye, Jesse saw Clay's fingers twitch and slide toward his holster.

"You don't want to do that," Jesse said to him.

"Quit telling us what we want to do," Luke said.

"Who the hell is he?" Clay asked, his hands still idling by his gun.

"Aw, you don't remember me?" Jesse said. "I helped you onto your horse last night."

Clay's eyes narrowed, and his hand glided across his ribs. "That was you, you son-of-a-bitch?"

"Whoa." Luke stepped in between them extending his arms to keep the men apart. "Colburn probably knows where Sam is," Luke smirked. "Probably knows a lot about her."

"That so?" Clay said. "Why's that?"

"They've been getting acquainted from what I hear."

"I know where she is," J.W. said. Anger painted red on his face, "I'll go to Julia's and get her."

Damn it. He just gave up her location.

"I have the payroll," Jesse blurted before J.W. could do any more damage.

The three men stared at him. Each had a very different set of emotions on his face.

Clay's mouth hung open as he tried to make sense out of what he was hearing.

"I knew it. It was you—you stole the money," Luke said.

"Yeah, I have the money."

"This is a trick," J.W. said. He spun around. "The sheriff must be here."

"No, it's just you thieves and me."

Luke sat on the edge of his desk with his arms folded. "You've got the money, and you thought you'd come here and announce it?"

It was working. Luke was curious. They wouldn't try to kill him or go after Sam if they thought he had the money.

"What do you want?" Luke coiled his fingers and rubbed his fingertips together. He was anticipating getting his hands on the money. Jesse smiled; Luke was practically counting the money in his mind.

"Nothing from you."

"Why are you here? Gloating that you're gonna pay off your incompetent Pa's debts?" Clay circled him looking him up and down. The limping half-wit tried to intimidate him. If these fools made him even remotely nervous, he wouldn't have barged right into the room.

"And watch you get hunted down by the railroad. That would be fun, but that's not why I'm here either."

The floor shook as Clay lunged at Jesse. "What do you want?" He cocked his gun and shoved it under Jesse's chin.

Jesse raised his head and swallowed hard. "I want you three outta town."

Luke laughed. "Even if you could get rid of us, the railroad will never leave you alone. They're coming, through Independence Pass—through you—whether or not you cooperate."

"You mean they'll sabotage my land like this here saddle bum," Jesse said eyeing Clay.

Jesse didn't care about his land right now, and while taunting these men was sweet, he was more interested in Sam's safety than his revenge. He stole a glance at the floor clock. What the hell was taking Julia so long?

It was true the railroad wouldn't give up, even if the sheriff came and arrested these three. There were more, there would always be more.

"If you leave town," he said slowly, "I will give you the payroll."

J.W. snorted and dismissed him with a wave of his hand. "It's a trap."

Luke fiddled with the cup on his desk. "What do you want, Colburn?"

They had to be caught with the money. It was a long shot and not well thought-out, but the only plan he had at the moment.

"I will tell you where the payroll is if you agree to

leave town." Jesse forced himself to look Luke in the eye.

"He's setting us up," J.W. said.

Luke huffed and rose to his feet.

Jesse fingered the deed again. If he gave it to them, they might believe him. They would get what they wanted, and Sam would be safe.

He slowly lifted his hand and opened his palm. "This is the deed to Enchantment." The fragile yellowed paper shook in his trembling hand.

"Take my deed, take the money. Sell it to the railroads and get out of town and never come back."

"And?" Clay asked.

Jesse looked at Clay. He tilted his head. There was something very familiar about him.

Clay smiled. "Aw, you don't remember me?" he threw Jesse's own words back at him.

It came back to him then. He'd worked on the Ranch a ways back. He disappeared after Enchantment started failing and the work dried up.

"I want the bowie knife," Jesse said.

"The bowie knife?" Clay laughed.

"Yeah."

"What's so important about that damn knife?" Clay asked.

"You wouldn't understand."

Clay sneered. "You're no better a businessman than your pa. You're giving up everything for a knife?"

"Do we have a deal?" His fists ached to punch the smugness off Clay's face.

"Your pa's luck ran out, poor soul. Just couldn't manage the business." Clay was baiting him now.

It sunk in like all bad news. The first stab of pain

was in his heart then it flowed out his chest and rippled through his body when the words registered completely.

Jesse sized Clay up and spoke slowly, "You sabotaged Enchantment while you were working on it, didn't you?"

Clay laughed and straightened his shoulders.

"You made sure my pa couldn't pay back the debt," Jesse said, finally putting all the pieces together.

Luke started to roll up his sleeves. "You're saying you stole the payroll from Clay and didn't pay off your debt?" Luke narrowed his eyes. "Now you're giving us the money and your deed." He stepped forward and poked Jesse in the chest. "And all you want in return is the bowie knife?"

"And all you outta town."

"It don't wash," J.W. mumbled.

Jesse ignored J.W., and Luke and spoke directly to Clay. This message was for him alone. "I won't tell anybody the details of the robbery. We will keep that between us. Now you can stop looking for the thief. Leave Aspen and never come back."

"Yeah," Luke said shaking his head, "feels like a trap."

"It's not a trap. My pa borrowed money from Leadville Bank. Time is up tomorrow to pay them back. You can go there with the deed and pay it off."

Jesse bit his lip. All his restraint lay in not killing the men. For the past year, folks had been calling him crazy when he was right the whole time. Guilt swished around in his head. His father wasn't a terrible businessman. He trusted his cowhands and fell victim to the evil of other men's greed. All this time, Jesse had doubted him.

"What are you up to, Colburn? You got Sheriff Brown out there waiting to hear some kind of confession or something?" Luke pressed.

"No more questions." He looked at Clay again, "I'm your thief. Stop hunting me all over town and give me the knife."

Luke sighed. "I—"

"I believe him," Clay interrupted. "Give him the knife." He waved his hand impatiently at Luke gesturing for him to give it over.

"No," J.W. said pushing his way through the men.

Clay sucked in a breath and acted as if J.W. wasn't even there. "Tell us where the money is."

"You're taking the deal?" Jesse stepped back from the circle of thieves. He eyed Clay who had taken over the leadership role of the greedy group.

Clay shoved a heap of tobacco his mouth. "Yeah, I don't care how you got the money."

"Well I do." J.W. shoved a finger into Jesse's chest. "And you're not givin' him the bowie knife."

Jesse grabbed J.W.'s wrist and twisted his arm until J.W. yelped in pain.

Clay fisted J.W.'s shirt and shoved him against the desk. "Shut up, J.W. Nobody cares about the damn knife."

"It's a scheme." J.W. shouted ready to charge again, but Luke held out his arm holding him off.

The men were partners—in on the robbery together—but in the end they were each as crooked as a dog's hind legs and didn't trust each other. That made them unpredictable and therefore extremely dangerous.

Boots bounding up the boardwalk and the rumblings of hushed voices caught Jesse's attention. He fought the urge to look out the window. The sheriff must be here. Now was the time to set them up. "The payroll is by the cut in the Roaring Fork, buried in the bed on the west side."

Luke cocked an eyebrow. "The deal was we paid off the lien and deliver a portion of the land to the Denver and Rio." Looking at J.W. he continued, "We take the money from the sale and you get the rest of the land. We got the deed and the money—"

"So we ain't got any need for the knife," Clay finished.

"Right." Luke walked around to the front of his desk.

Pretending to look at Luke, Jesse gazed over the man's shoulder and out the window behind him. Julia was back. She was out of breath and red in the face. She was craning her neck back toward Georgia's.

The rough sound of wood scraping against wood signaled the sound of a drawer being yanked open.

"How are you so sure that's Sam's knife, J.W.?" Clay asked.

Jesse clenched his fists. Clay didn't need to know that.

"The ruby in the hilt. Made it just for her mama."

Clay blew out a breath. "Suppose I owe the girl an apology."

Jesse swung around staring at Clay. "Thought we had a deal." He had to get them heading toward the money immediately. He said to Luke, "Give me the knife and go get the money before I change my mind."

Luke pulled out the knife and extended it toward Jesse. J.W. stepped forward and shoved him off balance and tried to swipe the knife.

Jesse recovered and pulled the old man until they were eye to eye. "Get out of here," he whispered. "I know why you want the knife." He slid it under his belt. "I want it for the same reason."

The old timer wasn't listening. He came back at him and slammed his shoulder into Jesse nearly knocking him over.

Clay took the opportunity to punch J.W. in the gut and shove him to the floor.

Jesse waved his arm toward the door. "If you want that money, get going."

"Let's go." Luke crossed the room.

Jesse looked out the window for the sheriff praying he was close. The lawman was in front of Georgia's and making his way slower than a pregnant heifer.

"Way ahead of ya," Clay said.

The hair on the back of his neck prickled. He heard a grunt behind him. Turning at the sound, pain seared his face as Clay's fist smashed into Jesse's nose.

The back of his legs collided with the desk knocking him off balance. Clay walloped him in the nose again and struck the side of his head with the butt of his gun. Darkness engulfed him. Blood smeared the mahogany as Jesse slid down the side of the desk onto the floor.

"Don't move." Clay warned him and kicked him in the gut. The weight of the bowie knife was lifted from his belt. Clay twisted his fingers around Jesse's collar and whispered in his ear, "I'm gonna get her and finish what I started." He smacked Jesse's head against the floorboard.

J.W. was across the room rolled in a ball and moaning on the floor.

"What the hell you doing, Clay?" Luke demanded, the pitch of his voice rising with each word.

Jesse twisted his pounding head and rolled onto his side. A groan escaped the back of his throat. Luke's shadowy form bent over Sam's father. A crash. A blur of colors and a chorus of grunts erupted where Luke knelt. He needed to get over there to make sure J.W. wasn't hurt. He rose to his knees. A shot of pain surged through his skull. He struggled to focus. When his eyes cleared and the throb in his head subsided, he saw Clay hovering over Luke, the hilt of the knife tight in his hand, the blade buried in Luke's back. He gritted his teeth. He'd promised Sam he would keep J.W. safe. Anger propelled him to his feet just as Clay released the knife and dropped Luke's limp frame onto J.W. who lay in a heap below.

Standing over both men, Clay said, "Sorry boys, I ain't aiming to share." He glanced back at Jesse and with a grin twisted as rope he said, "'Course, I'll be sharing a little someone with you."

Jesse's heart pounded, and his fists balled ready for a fight. He had had enough of this man. The pain and fear Clay inflicted on Sam was about to be revisited on him.

Jesse reached for his revolver, but Clay was already aiming at him and let off a shot.

Jesse lunged to his left behind the desk just in time.

"I knew you would double cross us," J.W. choked out.

Clay spit in J.W.'s direction, "Yeah, 'cause you're so smart, Old Man. You stupid fool; your daughter had the money this whole time."

Jesse's ribs burned; it stung just to open his eyes.

264

He calmed himself by trying to keep his breathing steady. Where the hell was the sheriff?

"You were never meant to have that land, were you?" Clay taunted J.W.

The old man wouldn't give up. He slid on his belly toward Luke. Wrapping his fingers around the hilt of the knife, he wrenched the blade from his dying partner's back.

Luke whimpered a weak cry of protest. He gasped for breath as his blood sprang from his wound. His tongue swept over his lips wiping the red liquid seeping from his mouth. His head fell with a jerk, and his wide-open eyes stared blankly before him.

Shaky on his feet, J.W. limped toward the wall and he leaned against it for support. He looked at Clay, "What did you say?"

Crouched behind the desk, Jesse began to move quietly toward Clay.

"You heard me. Your daughter robbed me. She stabbed me with that knife and took off with the money. She didn't mention that to you, did she? She's a better thief than you are," Clay taunted. "And she gave it to Colburn. Now I'm going to get that money and her."

Keep talking; Jesse maneuvered his way close enough to strike. He lunged at Clay knocking him back against the floor clock. He punched Clay in the nose, slammed the son-of-a-bitch's arm against the glass releasing the gun from his grip.

Jesse sensed J.W. coming up behind him. He elbowed J.W. in the gut, swung around, and hooked his cowboy boot into the old man's face. J.W. stumbled and dropped the knife.

"You think you're going to kill me?" Not needing

an answer, Jesse knocked J.W. against the desk and then into Clay and the clock.

For some reason, Sam cared about J.W., so Jesse wouldn't kill him even though every muscle in his body ached to do it.

Jesse put the bloodied knife in his belt loop.

"You ain't getting' the knife," J.W. said to him.

"It's not for me," Jesse said, heading for the door. He had to get out of here before the sheriff came in and found him with Luke's dead body and the knife. "I'm not wasting my time on you J.W. I am going to save your daughter, you worthless son-of-a-bitch."

"She doesn't need you. I raised my daughter to take care of herself."

"You abandoned your daughter to take care of herself," Jesse spat back.

He heard movement behind him. He turned to see Clay take off out the door. Damn. Suddenly, a searing pain coursed through his head. Before he registered what happened, he saw J.W. holding the candlestick from Luke's desk.

Jesse fell to his knees. "No, Sam—" Jesse said panting.

"Like I said, you lost it all." J.W. took the knife from Jesse's belt. Jesse shoved J.W. away, but the knife sliced Jesse's arm. J.W. cut Jesse's skin again. Blood flowed from his arm like May's snowmelt.

Coldness enveloped him. Jesse dropped to the floor. He tried to keep the pain and shock at bay, but it was no use. His head jerked backward as J.W. wrenched his shirt in his hand momentarily lifting Jesse's shoulders off the floor. Helplessly, he could only watch as Sam's father wiped the blood from the blade onto his shirt and put the knife in his boot.

J.W. knocked off Jesse's hat and grabbed the hair at the back of his head. Whiskey-laden breath and spit hit his face. "I'll let her know how you tried to take off with the money, but I caught up to you." He dropped Jesse's head and climbed onto the desk and propelled himself out the window.

Capturing the bandana is his mouth and biting the material, he loosened it from his neck and quickly wrapped it around his wounded arm. He bit his lip to stifle a howl of pain.

Sam was in more danger than ever. He needed to get the hell out of Luke's before the sheriff showed up. He raised his arm to slow the bleeding and stumbled over Luke's body on his way to the door.

The world was growing dark. He leaned into the desk, begging his legs to move, but his limbs wouldn't comply.

Suddenly he heard his name; a female voice was calling him.

"Sam?" Jesse whispered. But it wasn't Sam. She was waiting at the cabin about to be ambushed by Clay and J.W.

"Jesse?" Julia said.

He wanted to shout to her to run and get Sam, but the darkness threatened him again. Pressing his bloodied hand against the wall, he lifted his body. When he could, he staggered toward Julia. She hurried toward him and braced his weight against her side. Jesse stood covered in his and Luke's blood.

Sheriff Brown, out of breath and red-faced, walked in. He took in the room. Luke lie crumpled on the floor, blood seeping from his back and a stream of red forming a pool around him.

"I told you to leave it alone, Colburn," the sheriff said shaking his head. "You did it this time—stabbed a man in the back."

"Jesse?" Julia said.

"You're gonna hang for this, Colburn," the sheriff said leaning over Luke's body.

"No!" Julia gripped Jesse. She helped him to the couch, threw off his soaked bandana, and replaced it with hers.

"It's not serious," he said brushing her hand away. "Get Sam. She's in danger."

"Folks get restless in the heat," Sheriff Brown said. He tilted his head at the deputy. "Ready the noose, before all hell breaks loose."

Julia sprang to her feet. "You can't hang a man without a trial."

"You might want to get Father for last rites." Sheriff Brown patted her on the shoulder.

"No." Julia glared at the lawman. "I'll be gettin' his lawyer."

"Lawyer?" the sheriff frowned. "What lawyer?" He glanced at the deputy like the man was holding out on him.

Julia folded her arms. "Wade Rush. He's a Boston lawyer."

The sheriff turned a darker shade of purplish red. "You mean that young'un gettin' cuckolded by him?" he said with a loud laugh.

"Julia," Jesse yelled. "Forget about me and forget about Wade. Go get Sam."

"He's your only chance." She rushed back over to him and checked the blood spilling down his arm.

He grabbed the red-stained bandana from her hold. He stood up and pointed to the door. "Go save Sam." Why wasn't anyone listening? He didn't care if died today or tomorrow. As long as Sam was safe, he didn't care what happened to him at all.

"Sam can take care of herself. You need help," Julia said and dashed out the door.

Chapter Twenty-Two

Sam sat in the corner with the gun pulled tight to her chest and the frying pan next to her leg. Jesse took off to stop J.W. from going to Luke's. He never even asked her about Wade.

Following instructions was never a strength; following her instincts was. The same could be said about waiting; she rarely did it. The nuns called it impetuous; she called it guts. Jesse had told her to stay put, but she was done waiting on people and doing what she was told.

It was time to make up her mind and stop being caught between the two places she always lived: the space between independence and dependence, between truth and deception, between New England and Aspen, between a girl and the woman she wanted to be.

The money was buried by the river, so why was she still crouched in a corner waiting to shoot someone or to be rescued? The warm handle of Julia's gun was slick with sweat. She stretched her fingers, cramped from clenching the weapon far too long and far too tight. She searched for a rag to wipe the Winchester clean. Instead she found Jesse's shirt. Leather and lilac wafted through the cabin. It was the smell of her and Jesse together.

Ever since she'd met Jesse, her mind ran to thoughts of him. Her body ached to be touched and to feel the definition and form of his muscles. He was so strong and yet so gentle.

He asked her just a little while ago why she wasn't careful. Was it because she had never been loved before, he asked? He said that he loved her. She hadn't even explained about J.W. or Wade and he raced off to find J.W. because she was too afraid to confront her own father.

She loved Jesse. He had taken care of her ever since he laid eyes on her. Now it was her turn to return the favor.

He wouldn't take the money, so what could she do? She could do what was right, what she should have done days ago: return the money to the railroad. Then Jesse wouldn't be able to give the money to Luke. And Luke wouldn't be able to pay off the lien.

With the frying pan in one hand and the Winchester in the other, she raced out the door.

"Going somewhere?" A wave of relief swept through her until the familiar voice registered in her ears. It didn't belong to Jesse. It was J.W.

He emerged from the side of the cabin, alone. Jesse should be with him. "What are you doing here?" The fear in her voice betrayed her.

"You've been holding out on me. You had the money this whole time."

"How did you...?"

"Clay told me," he said through gritted teeth.

She swallowed. One shaky hand covered her heart as it began to pound. "Clay knows?"

"Why didn't you tell me?" His eyes narrowed.

She shook her head violently. No, he wasn't going to accuse her of lying when all he did was lie. And

Clay…didn't J.W. know she was in danger? She risked her life for J.W., her home, her security all for him and he only thought of himself. "I thought I needed it to rescue you."

"I didn't need rescuing." His voice grew loud. Red splotches crept across his discolored and bruised face.

"I thought you were kidnapped." The calm in her voice didn't reflect the dread coursing through her body. She dropped the frying pan and gripped the Winchester's full of weight of steel in her slick fingers.

"You knew yesterday I wasn't." Brown fluid, a mixture of whiskey and tobacco no doubt seeped from his lips. He wiped the stream of gook from his chin and spit the concoction toward her boot.

She shook her head and leveled the gun at him. He was disrespecting her. Spitting on her boots was breaking the cowboy code.

"It's stolen money." They were in Aspen, a thousand miles from home, and they were having the same conversation they'd had for years.

"You held onto that money after you knew I wasn't kidnapped." He was calm, too calm. "You even gave me your high and mighty nun speech."

"If I gave you the money, you would've lost it at cards before morning."

He stepped closer. His nose flared and his eye twitched. "No, I would've gotten us a ranch."

"It's Jesse's ranch. You think I want to live with you after you swindled it from him?" This fight was a long time coming.

"I earned that ranch." His hands turned white as he clenched his fists.

"You've got everything you've earned," she said.

"And then some."

"You don't know nothin'." He sprang forward standing so close she saw the vein throb in his neck.

The muscles in her shoulders ached, but she kept the gun steady. She dug her boots into the dirt anchoring her stance. She wasn't a casualty of his delusions any longer. "Yes, I do. You hop a train for Aspen, you plot to steal land from Jesse, an innocent man. You work with Luke, a man you've despised for years. I thought more of you than I thought of myself. Now I know better."

"I did all this for us, Sam." His voice was gentle again. "The real me is the man I am out here, but you've never known that man. Give me a chance to show you."

"No, whether you like it or not, whether you believe it or not, I already know the real you."

He shook his head. "I need to be here, Sam."

"Then be here…without me."

He edged forward. "I can't. Being here with you is all I ever wanted."

"You haven't been with me in ten years." Unease waved through her making her doubt herself again. He deserved every ounce of her harsh tone, but he was still her father.

"I want to be. Why you can't see that?" His fingers steepled together as if in prayer begging her to see reason.

Her teeth ground into her lower lip. The pain would keep her from drifting off into the lies he was spewing. "Because you've had twenty years to show it. You can live wherever you want, but it won't be with me." Her resolve was dissolving she had to walk away before she was lulled into believing him. She lowered the gun and without a word or glance turned away from him.

"Where are you going?" His voice grew loud and desperate behind her.

Pearl was within view. Determined to get to Jesse before she could be swayed, she marched toward the horse. "To Enchantment." She flung the words over her shoulder.

A firm grip on her shoulder spun her around. "Jesse ain't there." The venom in his tone forced her back.

She paused for a moment deliberating what to do. "I'll wait there for him." She shrugged her shoulder and resumed her walk toward Pearl.

"He won't be going back there," he called the taunting in his voice obvious.

The distance to Pearl seemed endless. Her feet came to halt bracing for what was coming next she asked, "Why not?"

He let out an exasperated sigh. The sound of him gathering tobacco and spit in his mouth sent a chill up her back. "Tell me where the money is," he demanded.

"No." The butterflies in her stomach started fluttering deeper and faster.

His footsteps pounded the ground behind her. "Jesse said it's by the cut in the river. I'm beginning to think that's true."

She swung around to face him. "Why would Jesse tell you where the money is?" A cold chill forced its way up her back causing her to shudder.

He shrugged his shoulders. Looking her up and down circled around her clearly strategizing his next move.

The anger simmering for a decade erupted. "Where is Jesse?" She raised the gun to his face.

His eyes fixed on hers. "About to hang for Luke's murder."

Her knees buckled. "He wouldn't do that. He wouldn't give up everything for revenge. Unless he was trying to protect me."

He closed his eyes and took a deep breath before rocking back on his heels and stalking toward her. "He didn't do anything for you."

Drops of sweat slid down her cheekbone. She wiped them away with her shoulder. "What do you know?"

"Where's the money?" He lunged forward attempting to grab the gun.

Swiveling to avoid his grasp, she pulled back. He lost his balance, and she kicked his knee. Taking a deep breath to clear the haze from her mind, she leaned over his hunched body. "What do you know about Luke's murder?"

He rubbed his knee and smirked. "I know that Jesse didn't do it."

"How?" She lowered the gun. They both knew she wouldn't shoot him.

"'Cause I saw who murdered him." Straining, he rose to his feet. He leaned on one foot to keep weight off the leg she kicked.

He was the opposite of everything the nuns taught. Everything that common sense and human decency dictated. "And you're just going to let Jesse hang?"

He shrugged his shoulders again. He was waiting for the truth to sink and then strike a deal.

"It was Clay, wasn't it?" She challenged his silence. "You have to tell the sheriff."

"Give me the money and I will." And there it was. The truth.

At least he didn't pretend he was being charitable this time. "You selfish son-of-a-bitch."

"Wahoo." J.W. grinned. "You've become the child I always hoped for." He smirked. "Now, let's go. And ah, you best leave the gun and the frying pan in the cabin."

Chapter Twenty-Three

The putrid stew of coffee, cigar, and a lax inclination to practice good hygiene lapped at Jesse's face.

"I've seen a man die by fire, by hanging, and by firing squad. It ain't a pleasant sight, Colburn."

Sheriff Brown spat on the floor and squished his molasses colored saliva with his boot. "It ain't gonna be pleasant." He repeated shaking his head and leaning closer to his prey.

"Come clean now, and we'll show you some mercy."

Jesse's blood pounded through his head. His fists clenched so hard his fingernails gouged his palms, sprouting blood.

He glared at the fleshy man squinting back at him, "I would take pride in killing a man like Luke Tremain."

"Then admit it; be proud of what you done," the sheriff goaded.

"I didn't kill him."

Sheriff Brown sniffed and looked toward the jail's barred windows, hands deep in his pockets.

They thought they had him good. Caught him standing right next to Luke with blood on his shirt. The sheriff enjoyed taunting him. Like a vulture circling his prey, Sheriff Brown baited him, ready to trounce and declare victory. There was no time for games, though. After his granddaddy's death, helplessness was a feeling he swore he'd never feel again, but he felt it now. If he didn't get out of here soon he would be too late, again.

"I gotta admit you're pretty smart. Stabbing him—not using your revolver. A lesser man would've fallen for it—would've been thrown off the trail."

Jesse didn't flinch. A lesser man? Luke's dead body was mere feet from Jesse when the sheriff walked in. Didn't take much to put it all together.

"You used a pretty substantial dagger." The sheriff sniffed again.

"I didn't use it. That's why you can't find it."

"We'll find it."

Jesse slammed his fists onto the wooden table. The deputy's fist slammed into his face subduing the ragged pain in his hand.

Blood trickled down the side of his mouth and seeped into his late afternoon stubble. He swallowed his blood and glared at his antagonist.

"I told you I didn't kill him." With a quick toss of his head, his wavy curls fell away from his eyes only to be replaced by sweat gliding down his forehead and into his eyes blurring his vision. His head ached from countless, useless questions.

Sheriff Brown sucked on his lush cheeks and snarled, "You ain't gonna make a fool of me, Colburn." He proceeded to chew the side of his twisted mouth. In all the years Jesse had been acquainted with him, it seemed Sheriff Brown cared about nothing and did nothing about it. Now, suddenly the man cared?

"Lock him up," he ordered his deputy.

"Sheriff!"

Jesse heard a man's voice over the sound of horse hooves.

"Sheriff!" the man called again.

Without even looking, Jesse knew it was Wade.

"Your lawyer's here." The sheriff smirked looking out the window.

The door flung open filling the room with odious sunlight. Wade gulped in the dirty air, dusted off his vest and coughed. "Sheriff Brown, I implore you to listen to me. I have new information."

"You implore?" Sheriff Brown scoffed.

"Wade, what are you doing here?" Jesse said signaling him over.

"Julia told me you needed help," he said earnestly

A minute ago, he wouldn't have thought his stomach could twist any tighter. "You're my help?"

"Yes."

"I thought you worked for nuns?"

"Yes, that's true."

"Ever get one of them off a murder charge?"

Wade winced. "Can't say as I have. Just trust me."

Words he had said a dozen times to Sam in the past few days. Suddenly the hollowness of the request echoed in his ears.

"Do you have any idea how to get me out of here?"

"Not yet." Wade turned to the sheriff, "I am Mr. Colburn's attorney."

"Is that right?" Sheriff Brown's rumpled face expanded as a smile burst through his massive cheeks. The lawman welcomed Jesse's young lawyer. "Did you hear that deputy? Young Mr. Rush here is representing our killer."

The deputy laughed.

"Word was Mr. Colburn was romancing your wife, Counselor. You're an awfully forgiving man."

"Wade, get out of here before you make this worse," Jesse ordered.

"Worse? Jesse, you're set to hang."

With a raise of his eyebrows, Jesse watched Wade appeal to the lawman. Wade's eyes were steady, but he wrung his hands restlessly.

A grimace surfaced on the stout lawman's purple lips. "I don't know about you, Deputy, but something about a Yankee charging into my jail and yelling demands puts me in a bad mood."

"Sure does, Sheriff," the deputy replied.

"Damn it!" Frustration pricked at Jesse's skin. Helplessness taunted him, encircled him like a snake strangling his meal. It wasn't the late afternoon sun that made the sheriff narrow his marble eyes. Everyone knew that the sheriff considered Aspen his house. And in a house where mud's the foundation and walls are rock thousands of feet high, anything new, anything not as solid as its leaden citizens shined too bright for the sheriff to tolerate. Like the miners after ancient silver, visitors were temporary and therefore a nuisance.

Wade was clearly caught by surprise with the last comment.

A mixture of annoyance, curiosity and pleasure framed the sheriff's face as Wade regained his composure.

"I can prove that Jesse Colburn is innocent." This rather bold statement managed to gain the full attention of the room.

Sheriff Brown studied the man before him with the

same intensity a child gives to an insect while he decides whether to play with it or squash it.

"Rush."

"Yes."

"Don't waste my time."

"I told you I can prove he is innocent," Wade insisted.

Jesse swore under his breath. Souring the sheriff's milk was only going to get him to the gallows faster.

The pit in his stomach grew watching his so-called lawyer gather the courage to speak. Wade swallowed and cleared his throat. "Where's the murder weapon?"

"I ain't showing you the murder weapon." The lawman slurped his coffee while studying Wade from head to toe. He was licking his lips like he couldn't wait to share his story at the saloon about the Yankee lawyer he outsmarted.

"Because you don't have it." Wade stated evenly with a confidence Jesse didn't expect.

Brown beady eyes bulged from the sheriff's red face. "Because this ain't a trial, Mr. Rush."

"Exactly. You're going to take it upon yourself to hang a man without a murder weapon at the scene of the crime. If he killed Luke, it would have been in there. There's nowhere for it to go. But it wasn't there because it was taken by the real killer."

"I may not be a fancy old state's attorney and all, but I know proof and that ain't it."

"You're going to hang a man, with no proof, no murder weapon, and no witnesses? A man who had you summoned to the scene? I'm just a Yankee, but I know a hanging without proof is against the law—even in Colorado."

"If you don't have any proof he's innocent, then you ain't got any reason to be talking to me."

"I was just about to get to my proof."

"So get on with it." The sheriff called his bluff.

Chapter Twenty-Four

Sam gritted her teeth and clung to Pearl's neck as they narrowly missed clusters of thin white trees blanketing the mountainside. Jesse was set to hang because he went to town to find J.W. for her. Now she was more afraid of losing Jesse than her father.

J.W. had witnessed Luke's murder and would only tell the sheriff the truth if he got the money first. The son-of-a-bitch hadn't changed: bills before blood.

As they rode toward the money, it wasn't just the terrain that threatened her. Jagged rocks and trees were the least of her concern. Her biggest worry was J.W. backing out of their deal. Shuddering at the thought of Jesse being hanged, she tightened her grip on the horse, pressing her body lower and the horse faster.

Jesse's hat protected her head from low-lying branches. J.W. was cursing behind her as she wound her way through the forest. He was seated behind her yelling in her ear about getting scratched and cut from the tree limbs, which was fine by her.

Once she came across Independence Pass, she knew they were close. She wove her way through the dense forest listening for the thunder of the Roaring Fork River. Her lungs burned in her chest. Preoccupied and distracted, Sam hadn't realized she'd been holding her breath.

"Come on girl," she whispered to the horse. Pearl's

neck was slick from sweat, but Sam held tight.

White rapids and a clear current racing toward Aspen came into view. The horse surged ahead bursting with intensity as if she were aware of the stakes.

The wave of the treetops and howl of the wind whisked Sam forward against a week's worth of self-doubt.

They came upon a spot that looked familiar. She pulled on Pearl's reins to slow her down. "How do I know you will keep your word?" She gritted her teeth. He wouldn't keep his word.

"Because I want to see Clay's boots swinging."

It didn't matter what he said, she'd never trust him again. She leapt from the horse and ran to the riverbed. Throwing off the rocks that provided cover for the saddlebag, she soon found the buried treasure.

Sam's fingers dug into the ground before finally hitting leather. Tracing the outline of the dark bag, she scraped handfuls of earth. Her fingernails filled with dirt. Soon she clutched the bag and yanked it from its hiding space and ripped it open.

J.W. took a step forward. He fanned his fingers gesturing impatiently. "Throw me the bag."

She ignored the trickle of sweat dripping down her face as she tried to think of what to do next. Then she remembered she had put the bandit's second gun into the saddlebag. J.W. was going to go to the sheriff's even if she had to hold a gun on him the whole way.

"We had a deal," J.W. said.

Suddenly a gunshot rang out.

"Hate to interrupt a family quarrel, but we had a deal too didn't we, J.W.?"

"Clay," J.W. said, "what are you doing here?"

"Taking care of unfinished business." The robber's eyes brightened as he looked at Sam. "Throw me the bag."

Instead, she thrust her hand into the bag frantically searching for the gun.

"I said, throw me the bag."

The thought of shooting him with his own gun made her search even faster.

"Do you want me to kill your father?"

"No." She let out a faint cry, but she wasn't talking to Clay. There was no gun. She had taken the gun out of the bag yesterday. Jesse tossed it off to the side of the riverbed. She swiveled around searching the grass for it.

"Throw me the bag, or I'll put a bullet in your daddy's head."

"Sam, throw him the money," J.W. yelled.

"Okay, don't shoot him." As the bag hurled through the air, she sprang forward remembering the soft thud of the gun landing in the tall grass off to her side yesterday.

The payroll landed at the bandit's feet. "I see the brains and the beauty lie solely with your daughter, J.W."

"Leave her out of this," J.W. demanded.

"Out of it? She's the center of it." Looking at her, Clay said, "You're a damn better thief than your old man. You took off with the money—even met with the sheriff and never mentioned it."

The men didn't realize she was searching the grass. They probably thought she was trying to escape. Finally, she felt the heat of steel warmed by the sun.

Days ago, Clay threw her to the ground and accosted her. Today that fear turned to anger. She stood still and silent clutching the gun behind her back.

Clay aimed his revolver directly at J.W.

J.W. was shaking his head. "Thought a blue belly like you would've left town after killing Tremain."

"Didn't you hear? Colburn's taking my place at the noose."

"I was there, remember?"

I remember, you're the only witness to Luke's murder." Clay laughed. "What do you think my unfinished business is? And thank you for bringing me directly to the money."

Sam studied J.W. He was planning something; she'd seen that look a hundred times before.

Her fingers tightened their grip, and she slowly brought the weapon forward until she heard a pop and another pop.

She almost fell from the shock. J.W. cried out. He was on his knees. A pistol dropped from his hand to the ground. He had taken a shot at Clay, but missed. Clay hit his target: J.W.'s thigh.

J.W. slumped to the ground clutching his leg. A red stream of blood seeped through his fingers. His mouth hung open and his eyes bulged as he tried to catch his breath.

She ran to him. He lifted his bloody palm to her face. "I'm sorry. Don't worry about me. I'll make it, I promise." He balled his fists and grimaced.

"What about Jesse?" Frustration raged. "You have to get to the sheriff."

She heard laughing behind her. "Get to the sheriff? You really think he was going to help you?"

A week ago, J.W. was all she had, so she risked her security with the nuns and set out to find him. Now she needed him to do something novel: risk his neck for someone else.

"Nobody's coming to help you. Luke is dead. J.W. is soon to be dead. Jesse's swinging south of here right now. You see a pattern here?" Clay said to Sam.

"Yes, you'll be dead soon."

He laughed. "You're amusing today. Not so funny the other day," he said nodding toward his leg.

"Wasn't much fun for me either."

"Then you should've gone back to Boston."

"I will."

He smirked. "The Roaring Fork don't go nowhere near Boston." He stepped forward. "J.W., let's end this." He winked at Sam, forcing her to choke down the bile in her belly. "Then you and me are gonna finish what we started, luv."

Clay drove his boot into J.W.'s wounded leg. J.W. wailed and clutched his thigh. His head fell back, and he panted in pain. His eyes blinked a few times, and he passed out.

"Looks like your pa has left you to fend for yourself, again."

The bandit approached with a sneer. He tossed his gun off to the side. "Won't be needin' that, and I don't exactly trust ya, luv."

He took another step forward and reached for her shoulders. That's when she pulled out her gun and shoved it into his ribs.

"You're right. You shouldn't trust me." She smiled. "Now back up and keep your hands in the air."

His face fell, but he quickly recovered. "You're not going to shoot an unarmed man."

"I don't give a damn about the cowboy code. Can't

shoot an unarmed man, but you can kidnap and attack an unarmed woman?"

"As I recall you were armed." He scowled and reached for the gun. She squeezed the trigger. The gun didn't fire. It must've been too wet from yesterday's storm.

He laughed and shoved her to the ground. "Now, where were we the other day when I was so rudely interrupted by your knife in my leg?"

****

"You're wasting my time, Mr. Rush. You don't have any proof," Sheriff Brown said, anger coloring his face.

"The proof is your burden, not mine."

"Funny, I don't feel burdened." The sheriff and the deputy started laughing.

"Luke's partner killed him. He stabbed Luke and framed Jesse," Wade said for the tenth time.

"It don't wash," Sheriff Brown balked, looking sharply from one man to another.

"Wade, get over here," Jesse ordered from the jail cell. "What are you doing?"

"You said it was the train robber."

"Yes," he said as patiently as possible. "And he is on his way to get Sam. You need to make sure Sam is safe." He closed his eyes praying someone would listen to him.

"Why wouldn't she be safe?" Wade asked.

"Because she has the money."

"What money?"

"The stolen payroll. If I don't get to her, J.W. or Clay will."

"Sam has the money stolen from the train? How

did she do that? Where is she?"

Jesse wondered if there was a breath in there somewhere.

He grabbed Wade by his lapel and held him an inch from the bars. "Did you hear me? She's in danger!"

Wade nodded his understanding.

The sheriff interrupted them. "Your proof is accusing Luke of the train robbery. I've been through this; he had an alibi."

"Luke's accomplice stole the money and killed him."

"I've been telling him that, and he ain't buying it." Jesse tightened his hold and pushed Wade away. He needed to punch something. His knuckles connected with his cell's steel bars. The release of anger felt better.

"Did Sam take the money from the robber?" Wade's eyes went wide.

Jesse wasn't listening. Images of his grandfather lying on the floor flooded his mind. If he didn't get to Sam…

"Where's this proof that Colburn's innocent?" Sheriff Brown tapped the toe of his boot against the floorboard.

Jesse's hands throbbed. With a calm he didn't feel leveled his gaze at the earnest lawyer. "Get out of here. Save her."

"I will," Wade promised. He held up his hand to Jesse gesturing for one more minute.

"No." He slammed his palms against the wall. "Go, go to Julia's."

"Quit wasting my time." The sheriff lifted his belt

over his protruding gut. "I've got work to do."

"You have nothing to keep him." Wade spoke as if that mere fact mattered to Sheriff Brown.

"Is that right?"

Jesse kicked at the bars. All this time, all he cared about was his ranch. As soon as he started to care about his life again, it fell just beyond his fingertips, just out of reach.

Wade sighed. "I'll try another tactic."

"No, go to Julia's. You said you would save her."

"That's what I'm doing." He turned to the sheriff, "You say you have witnesses? Where are they?"

"That's a different tactic?" Jesse asked.

"Right." Wade nodded. "When will the District Attorney be arriving?"

Light, the color of copper, suddenly boiled in the sheriff's eyes. Jesse stood mesmerized, astonished as life finally penetrated the brick soul of Sheriff Brown.

"Just what are you gettin' at?" The frown on the old lawman's face rippled down his features.

"Huh?" Wade looked up with that innocent expression he used so well. "I am merely asking when I may speak with the prosecutor."

"You got no jurisdiction here." Pressing his sausage like fingers against the rim of his desk he pushed himself to a stand. "Get outta here, now."

"Are you suggesting I solicit a Colorado attorney? Hmm, from Denver, perhaps; I have no objection. That may be a more prudent idea anyhow... Someone who is familiar with how the law here properly works." Wade turned toward the cell and winked at Jesse. He nearly fell back from shock. Was Wade's naiveté all an act?

Jesse felt a small smile creep across his face as the

light in Sheriff Brown's eyes dimmed. Jesse could have sworn he saw the sheriff's arrogance seep from the man's hefty body. For a moment hope was restored as he beheld a force between the sheriff and Wade. The release of confidence deflated one man and inflated the other.

"He stays here until the judge says different," Sheriff Brown stated. He was wavering, but still stubborn.

"You hear that? You won't be hanged until you've had a trail." Wade was practically jumping with joy.

"Get out of here, Wade, before you get me hanged and shot. Go bring Sam to Enchantment."

Wade wiped a trickle of sweat from his brow. "I'm not done." He sighed and reluctantly said, "I'll pay his bond when the judge gets here." He coaxed a gold watch from his pocket and continued, "Or," he paused for effect, "I could give it to you, now."

The building's door flew open. Julia and the murmur of restless spectators itching for a hanging burst into the office.

"What are you doing here? You're supposed to be with Sam," Jesse yelled at Julia. Damn it why wouldn't anyone listen?

"Sam's gone." Julia was out of breath and panting. "I don't know where she is, and there is no sign of J.W. either."

Jesse's stomach sank. The fury of helplessness gripped him. He couldn't fail at saving someone he cared about again. He tugged uselessly on the cell bars.

"You know he didn't kill Luke." Julia's voice was thick with contempt.

"He was covered in blood."

"His own blood."

"And he didn't have the murder weapon," Wade interjected. "You're holding the wrong man and losing the opportunity to secure this fine watch. It's very rare and expensive."

Sheriff Brown's pudgy hand gripped the watch. The heat of his stubby finger formed an imprint on the gold.

"Pure gold." Wade said relieving the sheriff of the watch.

"I know gold, Mr. Rush, and diamonds."

"Ah, you noticed, very perceptive of you. Of course, a lawman would be. Yes, there are twelve diamonds circling the face." He twisted the watch catching the soft light dancing over the gems. "It's worth a fortune." He handed it back to the sheriff.

Sweat streaked down the side of Jesse's face. His stomach turned with each agonizing twist of the sheriff's hand as he inspected the watch.

Sheriff Brown coughed lightly, his lump of a tongue circled his prune lips, and to no one's surprise, he liberated the watch from Wade's loosening grip.

"Perhaps we need to look into this further. I'll be sure this watch gets to the proper person." He cleared his throat. "Release him."

Chapter Twenty-Five

Sam's fingers fastened around a jagged rock. When Clay got close enough, she hurled it at him hitting him in the eye. She pulled up her skirts and ran for the rock ledge. He was fast upon her. His ragged breath sounded in her ears.

Pain seized her as he squeezed her arm. She screamed as he flung her to the ground. She landed on her stomach. He grabbed her boot. She kicked him off and slowly managed to pull herself to her knees and crawl to where he'd tossed his gun. He was upon her quickly, though. He wrenched her arm behind her, twisting it until she rolled over. He smiled revealing his lack of teeth, raised his arm and punched her firmly in the thigh. She screamed and crumpled into a ball protecting herself from his next blow.

Kneeling over her, he separated her arms and straddled her. The force of his legs tight against her thighs nearly choked the air from her lungs. He crouched above her, and using one hand, he held her two hands over her head against the ground.

"No!" She choked out a sob.

Spit slid from his lips onto her chin, "I've been looking forward to this." His scaly hand greedily ripped the neck of her dress. "This seems familiar, don't it?" He shoved the torn piece of her dress into her mouth.

She twisted and squirmed. No matter how hard she

flailed or kicked, she couldn't get him off her. She eyed him. If he were going to accost her again, then he was going to have to do it with her glaring at him.

"Watchin' how it's done, are ya? Good, you can tell Colburn all about, if he's still alive." He laughed. "I like an audience anyway."

He leaned his weight forward, pressing his chest against her, sandwiching her into the ground. He started to unfasten his pants.

She braced for the inevitable, but the inevitable never came. Instead a flash of white and brown whipped through the air above her, taking Clay with it. Instantly, her hands were released.

Did J.W. just save her? She lifted her head. A bloodied fist pounded Clay's face, but it wasn't J.W.'s fist. It was Jessie's. He veered to the right and landed another blow square in Clay's leg. The bandit tried to fight back, but he clearly was no match for Jesse.

Catching her breath, Sam got to her feet and hobbled toward the river, stumbling through the grass in search of Clay's gun. She reached it, cocked it, turned, and aimed.

They were moving too fast for her to take a shot. She hurried closer. But Jesse stopped. With finality, he rolled the bloodied man over leaving him lying unconscious in the green grass now speckled red.

There he was, safe, kneeling just feet from her. His chest heaved from exertion. Sweat slid down his cheeks. He shook his hair from his face and wiped his hand across his mouth.

A sob bubbled from inside. The shock and relief released a cry buried so deep she couldn't fight it.

"Sam!" Jesse leapt to her side, studying her

intently. "Did he hurt you?" For the first time she saw real fear in his eyes.

She shook her head violently. "You're free?"

His touch, tender as water trickling down stream, reassured her. He caressed her cheek and smiled. "I'm here." Concern lingered on his face.

He looked over her body for a sign that she was injured.

"I'm okay." She looked up at him. "Thanks to you."

He eased the gun from her clutches. Releasing a deep breath, he uncocked it and laid it next to him. Gently, he brushed the hair from her face and softly traced the stream of tears from her cheeks. He searched her eyes, as she searched his. He pressed his forehead to hers and drew in a deep breath to steady his pounding heart. Safe. She was safe and in his arms where she belonged. He threaded his fingers through her hair and lowered his mouth to hers. The taste of her lips calmed the fear and fury racing through his veins.

She lifted her arms around his neck and slid her body into the spot made just for her. Answering her unspoken reply, his mouth became harder. His tongue parted her lips and delved in with determination. She nestled her chest against his becoming as close as possible. He kissed her with an intensity unleashing a fierce passion within her she never knew existed.

Something stirred from where J.W. had fallen.

"Wait," Jesse said breathlessly, lifting his head. "I heard something."

"It's J.W."

"J.W. is here?" Jesse jumped to his feet. "Where?"

The rustling of boots scraping rocks and someone

muttering came from a dozen or so feet away. J.W. was struggling to move. He picked up the saddlebag and stumbled toward the river.

Jesse's fist was clenched as he headed after him.

"J.W.! Where are you going?" Sam ran in front of Jesse.

J.W. glanced back his dark eyes conveyed no emotion, just nothingness. He shrugged his shoulders. Clutching the saddlebag, he moved toward the river's edge.

"J.W., don't."

Jesse caught her arm and held her back. "Let him go."

Shocked, she swung around and looked up at Jesse, "He has the saddlebag. You need the money." She tried to wrestle her arm free.

"No, I don't." He folded her into him.

J.W. limped to the edge of the river. He slipped the bag's strap over his head. With one last look at them, he took a deep breath and plunged into the rapids. For just a moment, the whitewater became red carrying him down river like a log.

"J.W.!" Sam cried.

J.W.'s head bobbed. He stretched an arm toward a fallen tree limb, but it slipped from his grasp. Within seconds, he drifted out of sight.

Sam stood motionless. He survived the shot, but then, without a word, he left again, and with the money. He never cleared Jesse's name with the sheriff.

"Your last hope just got swept downriver," Sam said.

"J.W. is not my last hope." He lifted her chin and looked into her eyes.

"What about Luke's murder?"

Jesse nodded his head toward Clay. "We just captured Luke's killer. Anyway, Wade got me out."

"But your ranch…"

"Sam, listen to me." The calmness in his voice soothed her nerves. "Clay and the rest of his gang, even the railroad men, would be after you. Your life would always be in danger. There would've been no end until the money was found."

"We both lost what we tried to protect," Sam said solemnly.

"And found something even better," Jesse said.

She looked up to spy the twinkle in his eye she knew would be there, and it was.

Jesse leaned down and kissed her.

His dungarees were snug against his thighs. A flurry of excitement swirled within her.

"I love you, too." Sam looked up at him and smiled.

Jesse looked at her puzzled, as she knew he would.

"You said you loved me at the cabin. I didn't tell you how I felt."

He smiled and cleared his throat. "You have no idea how happy I am to hear you say that."

"Yes, I do. Kiss me again, please."

"I was right," he said and nuzzled a feather kiss on her neck.

She arched her eyebrows in surprise. "Right about what?"

"I recall saying something about you drooling on this very mountain." He laughed.

"You were talking about cows." She pushed him down and rolled on top of him. "For the love of God, man. Kiss me again."

"Mrs. Rush!" Jesse laughed in feigned surprise.

Sam gasped. "I have to tell you about Wade."

Jesse was kissing her neck. "Do we have to talk about your husband right now?"

"Wait," she said pushing against his chest and lifting her head up. "Wade is not my husband. I asked him to pretend to be so that I wouldn't raise eyebrows traveling alone."

"You, raise eyebrows?"

"Jesse, you came to get me...not even knowing..."

"I knew."

The warmth of his eyes singed hers. She felt the heat course throughout her body as he spoke. "From the moment I first saw you, I knew you were for me."

Her heart was beating fast. She bit down on her lip, not sure of the words to say. "Really?"

"I was all in. I bet Rusty, my gun, my shirt... I knew I'd win it all back."

"Don't tell me you're a gambler."

"Only when it comes to you," he said. "You may enjoy disguising yourself every chance you get," he put his hat on her head and wrapped his arms around her, "but you can't hide who you are from me." He was silent for a minute. She listened to the breeze gently caressing her hair.

She leaned in to kiss him.

"Sam?" He pulled back studying her expression. "I don't think—"

"Jesse," she said running her hand through his hair. "Please stop thinking."

He laughed. "Clay is still over there, remember?"

Sam nodded. "Guess we better take him to town.

He won't be passed out much longer."

"Before we go, I want to ask you something," Jesse said.

She squinted her eyes. "Okay."

"Will you spend my last night at Enchantment with me? I want you to know what a special place it is."

Sam pursed her lips.

"Just for supper," Jesse pleaded. "I won't tell the Sisters."

"It's okay if they know."

His eyebrows arched in astonishment. "What?"

She shook her head and scrunched her nose. "I don't think that life is for me."

"No?"

"Not after that kiss."

Jesse laughed. "So you will come?"

Kissing Jesse was wonderful. Last night she acted as if she knew what she was doing with him, but she really didn't.

"Will you think about it?"

"I don't need to think about it. I'll come."

"Good and remember, I'm all in. Now it's your call."

Chapter Twenty -Six

"What have you got against my rug? You're wearing it out again," Julia said, back at the cabin.

"Jesse asked me to go to Enchantment tonight for supper." She twisted her fingers in the front of her dress.

Julia clicked her tongue. "Supper, huh?"

"It's his last night at Enchantment, and he wants to spend it with me."

"And he wants to spend it eatin' supper? Don't think so." Julia laughed with a snort. She headed over to where she kept the brandy. "Another special occasion," she said raising the jug.

Taking a deep breath and biting down on her lip, "I've never…"

"Had supper?" Julia winked and poured them each a shot a brandy.

"Been with a man." Sam felt the flush of warmth across her face. She dropped her head back and emptied the glass in one swig.

Julia arched her eyebrows in surprise as she held out her glass for more. "Aspen's rubbing off on you." She refilled her glass. "You're nervous about your first time, it's natural."

"What will Mrs. Maple think?" She was biting her lip and wringing her hands again.

Julia coughed up her tea concoction. "Mrs.

Maple?"

Reaching across the table, Sam grabbed a rag and handed it to Julia. "Jesse's housekeeper."

Julia snorted. Guess I was wrong; you're still being influenced by others. Or…" She twisted her lips deep in thought. "That's not what you're scared of."

She shook her head in confusion. "What do you mean?" When was she going to learn that brandy wasn't good for her brain?

With a smile and a click of her tongue, Julia pointed her finger at her. "You're afraid he's goin' ask if you are staying here or going back to Boston."

Butterflies fluttered in her stomach. "I'm not sure what I should do."

"Then tonight will help you decide." Julia lifted her teacup. "To supper," she said with a wink and emptied her drink.

A laugh escaped the back of her throat before she turned serious. "I just hope he doesn't have any expectations."

Julia snorted again. "He sure as hell has hopes."

She sprung to her feet shaking her head and rubbing the nausea churning in her stomach. "About me staying out here?"

Julia stood. "'Course." She poured water into her tin tub. "If you're going to Jesse's, we need to fix you up real nice."

Sam fidgeted.

"Don't be scrunching up your nose at me. Why wouldn't you want to live out here anyway?"

"I don't know because I have been kidnapped, accosted twice…" She kicked off her boots. A bath was a perfect way to settle her nerves.

"The time you were dressed in Ned's clothes doesn't count." Julia reached for the laces on Sam's dress and untied them.

"I wasn't counting it. Chased by outlaws…" When the laces were undone, she pulled the dress over her head. Her mouth practically watered at the idea of soaking in a warm bath.

"Outwitted some bad guys and fell in love…" Her new friend was singing the words. Why Julia was this giddy, Sam didn't know. Maybe it was the brandy.

She sunk her toe into the bath water. It was perfect. "I don't know anything about men."

Julia pulled out her soap and started crushing up flower petals. "There are two types of men who visit Georgia's. The first comes in with empty eyes. He can't stand himself. He's got no plans for the future 'cause he don't think he's got one. He lives for that day and that day only, and that means dangerously. When they look at me, they see twenty minutes that they don't have to think about their miserable selves. Their women are up at night waiting for the sheriff to knock on the door and tell them their man's time ran out."

She sprinkled the crushed petals in the bath water.

"Then there are the ones who play cards. They look at us girls with pity in their eyes. They go home to their wives every night. Those women sleep at night. That's Jesse. He'll be home at night."

Sam smiled. "You have a good way of putting things."

"I hope you stay. Your being here has brought me back to life. I've been saving coin for years waiting for the day I can walk out of Georgia's and go where no one knows me."

"What will you do?"

"Someday I'm goin' to work my own piece of land. I ain't never goin' to look in hopeless eyes again."

Sam hugged her. "I know you'll do it."

"You don't have to go back to Boston, Sam."

"I know. I also know J.W. will climb out of that river and claim Jesse's ranch."

Julia waved her hand. "Ah, so your pa stole his family home and plans to live in it. You've overcome worse. You can't rescue Jesse anymore than you could J.W. You need to stop looking for problems." Julia pursed her lips and looked down at the worn rug covering her dirt floor.

"You've had a lonesome upbringing, left on your own and taken in by nuns. Being with Jesse, a man who cares about you is going to be one hell of an adventure."

She smiled. Julia had made her feel better already.

"But you have to follow your own mind, Sam. You can't consult with the nuns this time."

"I won't even read their telegram," she promised, "if they send one back to me."

Julia shook her head. "You come all the way out here, fight off bandits, steal horses, and you're afraid of a bunch of nuns? I gotta meet these women."

Sam laughed. "I never looked at it that way."

"Livin' life by others' expectations is a coward's way of livin', and you ain't no coward. Don't you forget those Sisters have faith. You have it too, in yourself."

"Did you always have it?"

"I found it. The low life I followed here had a whole different idea of how we were goin' to live. I left

303

the bastard soon as I could and started making it on my own."

The fear of going back to a life with no risks was scarier than living a life with no rules. The nuns drilled order and community. Her own way, her own mind, was a weakness. In Aspen, it made her strong. Back in Boston, the days ran by a schedule. Everything was predictable right down to fish on Friday. The Sisters wore black and white for a reason—there was no gray.

"Let's treat Jesse to a little something special," Julia said interrupting her thoughts.

"It's just supper, Julia."

"Ah-huh."

Chapter Twenty-Seven

With eyes fixed and lips pursed, Sam gave Jesse's front door a determined knock.

An older gentleman answered the door. A pair of squinty blue eyes looked down at her. It had to be Andy, the foreman.

After working up the courage to see Jesse, seeing Andy was even worse. He made her even more nervous.

She introduced herself, which made his squinty eyes squint even harder.

"Ward, huh?"

"Yes, I can come back later if this is a bad time," Sam blurted, turning to leave.

"There ain't no 'later'," he grumbled, "so you might as well stay."

"Don't be hazing the tenderfoot, Andy." A warm female voice drifted through the doorway. "Come in, dear, Jesse's out by the lake. You can wait for him in here." The owner of the voice, a plump woman with flour in her hair and carrying a rolling pin appeared in the doorway. Her hair, bound high atop her head, coupled with two very red chins, gave her the appearance of a pleasant rooster.

Sam's eyes drifted to the distant mountains. The sun would be setting soon. The beauty and serenity were not just impressive; it was unmatched. "Thank you," Sam said, hoping Jesse was on his way back.

The woman's warm hands grasped hers and pulled her into the hall. Her skin was soft and her eyes bright. It felt as if a long-lost relative was reaching for her, drawing her in.

"Now, have a seat, miss," she said directing her into a side room kind of like a parlor back in Boston. "I'll fetch you a cool drink of lemon water."

"Thank you," Sam said, but the woman had already slipped from the room.

Her surroundings were tidy and comfortable. It had the look of a room well cared for, but not often used.

The cheery housekeeper, she surmised to be Mrs. Maple, returned with a glass of hazy water.

"As promised," she said setting the glass on a small oak table adjacent to Sam's cushioned chair and wiped her hands on her apron.

"We haven't gotten to this room yet." A faded smile flashed in her eyes. "The rest of the place is just about done." Sam followed her glance to a larger room off to the side.

"Thank you for the water." Sam took a sip, puckered her lips, and coughed at the sour taste.

"Here, dear," the woman said handing Sam a napkin. "That's my family recipe."

"Thank you. I don't think I ever had a drink like this before."

The woman smiled proudly. "Well now, my name is Mrs. Maple. I have been the Colburn's housekeeper for oh, since Jesse was this high," she said holding her hand parallel to the ground at her waist.

Mrs. Maple's eyes filled with pride as she glanced at the far wall where a portrait adorned a large mantel.

She peered at the entryway while stretching her neck toward Sam. She leaned close and whispered, "So, now, miss, what brings you to see our Jesse?"

"Mrs. Maple, the biscuits are done, and it's time for us to be heading to our rooms," the man said from the doorway. He hunched over slightly.

"Don't worry. I won't be burning yer supper," she called back.

"Quit jawin' her to death. I'm hungry and don't want crispy biscuits on my last day in this house."

With a grimace, Mrs. Maple waved her hand dismissively and continued, "Now…"

"Mrs. Maple—the kitchen," the man yelled louder. "I won't be starving."

With an exasperated sigh, she excused herself and headed toward the hall.

Sam's mouth ran dry from nerves and the fact that she didn't want to drink anymore of Mrs. Maple's family recipe lemon water.

A loud bang accompanied by hushed voices and an occasional shrill escaped from down the hall. Sam stood and began to pace. The lone picture on the mantle was of a young boy surrounded by a kind-looking couple. His parents she assumed. The boy looked to be the heart of the grouping. The parents gathered around the child as if he gave off heat to warm their hands.

She peered in the adjacent room. It was barren except where white empty blocks of space checkered the walls. Portraits had once hung there. Now, a film of dust outlining their existence was all that remained.

Mrs. Maple raced back into the parlor with surprising speed. Andy sauntered in behind her.

"I see you haven't finished your drink, dear," Mrs.

Maple said.

"No, not yet. Jesse's by the lake, did you say?"

"Yes, indeed," Mrs. Maple replied nodding her head. "That is what I said."

"Jesse said he wanted to show me the lake."

Mrs. Maple's eyes widened, and her ear jerked liked a hunting dog sensing prey.

"Andy, Jesse is going to show her the lake."

"My hearing is in working order, Mrs. Maple," Andy answered sharply. He stared intently at Sam.

She felt herself blush as the housekeeper eyed her.

"He will be back soon enough," Andy replied.

"I could ride out to meet him. I don't want to be a bother."

Sam glanced at Mrs. Maple whose head was bobbing up and down approvingly. "Did you hear that? She wants to ride out to meet him."

"Did you hear me? I said my ears still work."

"Miss Ward, you must have important business to discuss with Jesse," her conspirator said with a wink. "Andy can point you in the right direction."

"I don't need her ridin' around gettin' lost."

"I'll be fine," Sam assured him.

"I think Jesse would like to fetch you himself."

"Jesse might like the surprise too," said Mrs. Maple with a wink to Andy.

Andy scowled at the housekeeper. "Never hear the end of it anyway." The foreman shook his head, gave Sam explicit directions, and headed into the kitchen muttering something about salvaging biscuits.

Chapter Twenty-Eight

A row of lanterns lit a path to a serene lake. By the water, kindling was set up for a fire. Sam looked around for Jesse. He wasn't about, so she decided to enjoy the secluded spot for a few minutes rather than call out for him. The setting sun's yellow rays seemed to reach for her, so she tilted her head back and savored the warmth on her face.

The whip of the breeze returned to rustle her skirts and echo in her ears. No ballroom or hall could ever be decorated to equal the beauty of the Colorado sky. Blue faded to black and dancing stars peeked from the heavens illuminating the twilight sky. The scent of pine floated around her, contested only by a meadow of fragrant and unfamiliar flowers.

The sparkle of the emerging starlight glimmering in the lake glowed like fire. Sam longed to abide by the will of nature. She stared at the moon, the only thing reminding her she remained on earth. Out here, surrounded by the scenery, she yearned to ride through the night with only the sky to guide her.

She spied a smooth rock, played with it, and hurled it into the water. The plop of the stone breaking the surface rattled the quiet.

"You came." Jesse's tall, formidable figure stepped from the shadows. His white shirt pulled tight across his chest accentuating his taut muscles. He embodied strength and courage yet, he approached her tentatively. "I never know what you're going to be wearing when I see you. Tonight, I must say you are breathtaking."

Julia had dressed her in an emerald green dress that matched her eyes and apparently accentuated her bosom. Her hair was partly up and also cascaded around her neck. Julia said Jesse wouldn't be able to stop staring and, so far, she was right.

Suddenly she was grateful for the shadow the woods provided so he couldn't see her blush. A rush of excitement warmed her body.

"I wanted to see you." Her voice sounded like a whisper.

"I missed you." He stood still. Only the light playing in his hair moved.

She could see his features only slightly, but she knew he was grinning.

Her stomach was full of flutters, and her mouth couldn't stop forming a smile. She moved closer to him into the full glow of the moon, and her suspicions were confirmed: he was smiling down at her.

The white embroidered linen shirt he wore with its sleeves rolled up to his elbows showed off his tan and strong hands. She swallowed as she thought of his fingers on her body. His open collar exposed wisps of dark hair. Standing near him made her feel small and wanting, wanting his caress.

He cleared his throat and stepped closer stopping an eyelash's length from her. "I'm so happy you're here... with me."

She put her hand lightly on the front of his shirt. "Thank you for saving my life today."

The gentle caress of his finger brushed her cheek.

"Thank you for saving me." The bright pools of light in his eyes conveyed the depth of his feelings.

"That was Wade," she said lightly. The weight of her emotions in her chest and head made her dizzy.

"No, Sam, killing Luke was all I thought about for months, that and saving this ranch. I'm about to lose it, and I have never been happier. I owe that to you; you saved my life."

Forcing his eyes from her, Jesse gazed at the sky, and the millions of stars that decorated the night. He learned the constellations on the trail. He guessed she learned them in a proper school. It seemed as if he'd known her for so long, yet he really didn't know that much about her.

The real question was whether she was going to stay or return to Boston? He cleared his throat. "Dirk told me you have a telegram waiting for you at the Mercantile from the Sisters of St. Joseph."

"That was quick. I just sent them a telegram this morning."

"What are you going to do if the nuns tell you to return to Boston?"

She talked of independence, but he worried that her obligation to the nuns overshadowed her will.

"This lake is beautiful."

She was changing the subject, and for the sake of the moment he complied. "I can't think of a better memory to leave with than this one." He wrapped his arms around her waist pulling her taut against his chest.

"So what happens tomorrow?" she asked.

"I'll head to Leadville, to the bank; although, I don't have the deed anymore. I wonder if J.W. grabbed it from Luke. With the deed and the money, he could pay off the lien in the morning. He'll have everything he wanted."

"Not everything. He wanted me to live with him, but I won't."

Jesse regretted mentioning J.W. He didn't want him to be a part of tonight. She had to make peace with who her father is or was.

"Andy sold most of the furniture to Dirk today. He offered me a nice sum. I'll be set for a while and so will Mrs. Maple and hopefully Andy."

"Why hopefully Andy?"

"This land is in his blood as much as it's in mine."

She nodded her head in understanding. "I've never seen any place like it."

His heart pounded in his chest. The question he needed answered he feared would ruin the night. "What about you?" He took a deep breath, "Have you decided to stay in Aspen?"

"I haven't made up my mind yet." Her sparkling green eyes danced from the dim light.

"Competing against a bunch of nuns really isn't fair."

"I'm willing to hear your argument." She tilted her head to the side and looked up at him with her eyes shining.

"Who said anything about talking?" He gently lifted her chin and pressed her lips to his.

Sam returned his kiss. The warmth of her mouth sent every inch of his body soaring. He pulled her closer.

He had no answer tonight, but he had her, all of her. His lips found the soft skin below her ear and slowly eased his way toward the nape of her neck. Her fingertips kneaded the muscles of his shoulders.

"Sam," Jesse whispered breathlessly, drawing back. "This is not why I invited you here. I wanted you to see my home because it is—was—an important part of me."

"I want to see all your important parts," she said with a grin.

He shook his head, "Just how many of the nuns' books did you read?"

"Lots."

"Seriously, Sam, I want your first time to be special."

"What could be more special than this?" She gestured toward the lanterns and the lake. "You're a man who loves his land. I want to be on that land when you make me moan in your ear," she giggled, quoting him from last night.

Placing his hand at the small of her back, he pulled her into him. Bringing her mouth to his, he kissed her gently.

Sam hungered for him in unfamiliar anticipation. She saw the same demand in his eyes and she craved for that lust to fill her.

Lifting the white linen shirt out of his belt, she slid her fingers up his chest. Firm muscles and his low groan kept her fingers roaming.

"For the love of God, Woman."

With her eyes closed, she felt the contours of his hard muscles beneath her fingertips.

"Now this is the Sam I want—the real you—naked from any disguises."

"Did you say naked?"

"I did." He unbuttoned the neck of her dress and

313

reached around the back and unhooked the rest. Warmth flooded her body as the cool evening air met her skin and her dress fell to her feet.

Together they pulled off her chemise dropping it to the ground. Jesse's eyes filled with want as he took in her nakedness.

She lifted his shirt from his shoulders and slid it down his back revealing his broad shoulders. His tight muscles were warm to the touch.

She undid his pants and laid them on the ground next to the blanket for soft cover. A warm breeze blew the grasses caressing their skin.

Without breaking their gaze, he led her to the middle of the blanket and pulled her down with him.

She lay on her back watching him for guidance. On his side, he caressed her face and softly kissed her lips. Drawing his fingers from her face, down her arm and to her belly, his touch sent shivers through her body. They laughed at the goose bumps covering her flesh.

He became serious. She knew what he was looking for—a sign of uncertainty. She wouldn't give him one. Instead she smiled gingerly and took a deep breath, savoring his smell and the sweet anticipation of their lovemaking.

Tenderly, he encircled her breasts with his fingertips. Her back arched eager for more. The feel of his fingers fondling her and massaging her made it nearly impossible to concentrate on kissing him. Her lips slowed at the exquisite pull of need. She relaxed, surrendering to his touch.

Lying on her back, she reveled in the feel of his mouth making a path from her throat to her breasts. One hand cupped her buttocks lifting her off the blanket. She arched her back, rising, thrusting her body to his lips.

She ran her hands through his hair wiping stray curls from his face. He smiled and his eyes conveyed a devious grin as powerful as his hands exploring her.

A breeze whistled through the pine needles around them filling the air with its sweet fragrance. Jesse's curls waved in the wind covering his eyes again.

He moved his hand to her hip, his tongue mercilessly licking and sucking her breasts.

She moaned as sweetness flowed to her most personal area. An ache began to grow and spread. While still kissing her belly and breasts, Jesse's hands descended to the soft innermost area of her thighs where she needed him, where the tug of desire yearned for release.

A vexation was building. She was so close to it yet didn't know what it was.

She arched her back, opening her legs wider as her body begged. She wanted his hands lower, his fingers probing; she pressed his hands down to where she could no longer bear his absence.

He raised his head watching her. He smiled at the torture he put her through.

"Jesse?"

But he continued to suck her breasts. His hands made circles on her inner thighs.

"Jesse, please," she asked.

"Please?"

His fingers entered her and caressed the softness within. She rolled her head back and forth side to side.

With a raised eyebrow, a smile formed ever so slowly on his face. His eyes dazzled with light and fire as his fingers moved methodically.

The slight warmth of the setting sun on her face and the warm probe of his finger inside her was perfection.

She was free, naked in the Colorado grass amidst the breeze of the Aspen trees. The river roared beside her as she moaned at the pleasure that roused within her.

"What do you want me to do to you?" he whispered.

He rubbed her breasts and sought their softness with his mouth, sucking. She responded by grabbing his buttocks and pulling the taut flesh.

"Please" was all she could say.

"Because you begged." He grinned. He entered her thrusting his hips gently and slowly. Watching her, he asked in a husky whisper, "Do you like it?"

She rolled her head from side to side and moaned in pleasure, "Yes."

He wiped the hair from her face. "Do you like it hard?"

"Yes, harder, please." She dug her fingernails into his back urging him on.

"Do you want it?" His hand slid down her waist, inside her thigh to where he entered her.

She raised her hips to his, opening her legs wide. "Yes."

"Say it, say you want it." His voice was rough and husky.

Matching his thrusts, she cupped his chin and kissed him." I want you." Then she dropped her hands and her head fell back. She closed her eyes. "Please, Jesse, I want you."

He complied hungrily.

It was upon her, the release, the sweet, sweet relief her body yearned for.

The feel of his solid hardened flesh encapsulated her, engulfed her as he rhythmically moved his hips. Her eyes flew open as a surprising pain surfaced. He kissed her neck softly and whispered, "It'll hurt for a moment. Do you want me to stop?"

She was on the verge of saying yes when the pain turned to intense pleasure. She moaned involuntarily and her fingernails clenched the blanket.

Her breasts were his for the taking, her legs spread for his pleasure; she had never been so open so vulnerable to anyone before.

She closed her eyes again, pressing her body against his rigidness, unable, unwilling to stop her body from answering each thrust of his hips with her own. The ache grew in her breasts. Her back arched needing his mouth on her breasts more and more. He licked and sucked her as he thrust harder and faster. She opened her legs wider. He groaned in response.

She gripped his muscular arms, moaning.

"Your legs are nice and wide for me," he said. Sliding in and out faster, deeper.

"Oh," she moaned. Her lips trembled and her breath shook as her body writhed beneath him.

"That's good. I like that." His chest crashed against breasts.

With each pulse of his drive, the pleasure intensified building and spreading throughout her body. "Please don't stop."

"I won't." His legs pumped, igniting her core.

Clenching her teeth, she tried to suppress the

whimpers and moans growing louder within her. "It feels so good."

"Like this?" he asked his eyes ablaze with heat.

"Yes."

He gripped her inner thigh raising her leg slightly and driving into her deeper.

"You're so wet."

Her legs spread wide, his mouth took her swollen breasts deeper into his mouth, with his hardness solidified and one more thrust from his muscular body, she cried releasing her torment. He thrust his way through the dam of sweetness flooding her, coursing through her until her entire body was light and satiated.

He moaned in release of his own pleasant agony. She wrapped her arms around his neck and cradled his descent to the grass.

He sighed. "You're so beautiful, Sam. I can't stop watching you." He smiled, his eyes sparkling of amber melting in the swirl of brown warmth.

"Jesse?" She bit his lip. "Can we do that again?"

"For the lov—"

Before his protest was complete, Sam's lips were making their way down his chest.

Chapter Twenty-Nine

"Good morning," Sam said as she nestled against him under the blanket. Her soft warm breasts pressed against his chest.

She put her hand on his arm and her head in the crook of his neck. She smelled like fresh air. He was right where he was meant to be; with her, in the open Aspen countryside.

"Good morning," he groaned in response.

"I should sleep outside more often. That was the best night's sleep I've ever had," she said.

It probably had more to do with their love making than the fresh air, but he kept that to himself. She would find that out soon enough. "I always loved going on the trail herding the cattle and sleeping out under the stars. Waking up to the birds chirping was nice, but waking up to you is incredible."

"Have you been awake long?"

"A bit, I like watching you sleep." He caressed the smooth skin on her cheek. The trust and innocence in her eyes warmed him.

She blushed and tried to cover her face, but he took her hands away so he could see her.

"What have you been thinking about?" Soft fingers rubbed along the length of his chest. She was teasing him again.

"Ah." He shook his head. "Are you sure you were

raised in a convent?"

"Only the last few years." She laughed.

"Oh, right, it was those books you were reading, wasn't it?"

Her cheeks turned crimson. "Are you going to tell me what you were thinking?"

"No," he said. "I don't want to raise eyebrows."

She pushed him gently in the stomach and let her fingers linger there.

"Well," he started, "I can tell you that I think I figured out what my ma meant by the secret of Enchantment."

The green eyes he looked forward to sparkled as he knew they would. "You did?"

"Yeah." He kissed her on the nose. "I held onto Enchantment waiting for it to bring me happiness like Ma told me." He grinned sheepishly. "Thing is, I think she meant us; my folks and me. We were the ones who made it special. We were the secret of Enchantment."

He sighed. "I miss my folks. I've been angry for so long about losing them that I forgot what I missed most about them: the times we had at Enchantment. After Ma died, I knew Pa was dying, not because he didn't have Ma's love anymore, but because he couldn't love me the way he did before she died. That killed him slowly. Now I understand that kind of love." He looked at Sam. With a sigh, he looked away, out at the sky. "So now I know what she meant. And what it's like to face losing it.

"Anyway, I think the secret of Enchantment is like the secret of life. A home is meant to be shared to be appreciated. It's not about the house; it's about the family in it."

She bit her lip and smiled up at him with those green eyes watching him.

"I love you, Jesse."

"I love you, too, Sam." He kissed her lips.

"Are you hungry or thirsty?"

"Hmm, do you have any of Mrs. Maple's delicious lemon water?" she teased and raised herself up to kiss him. Her breasts spilled into his hands. The strain of not touching her all morning was killing him.

"I'm hungry for what you did to me last night. I want you to do that again."

He wanted to be all over her, touching her, rubbing her. He cupped her breast and whispered, "Say it. Say what you want me to do to you."

"Spread my legs and fill me. I want you in me."

Jesse was practically spilling his sweetness already. Her desire and naïveté hardened him instantly. "I'm going to watch you when I give you what you want."

"Will you suck on my breasts?"

He started kissing her everywhere, everywhere except there.

"Why do you want me to suck you?"

She closed her eyes and moaned into his chest.

"Is it to make you wet?"

"Yes."

He used his arms to prop himself up and slid along her body suckling each breast until her hips were writhing.

He unleashed his tongue endlessly caressing as his lips sucked and fingers fondled her flesh.

"Jesse, please." He cupped her buttocks and made her wait a little longer. Her moans of protest grew louder. She spread her legs inviting him in. Complying, he slid into her delicious softness losing himself in her velvety wet heat. Her cries increased until she begged for release and her head rolled side to side as she cried out in ecstasy. Jesse released his own agony and let the bliss take him.

He rewrapped her in the blankets and folded her into his arms where she was snug and warm. He smiled as she cuddled in his arms. He kissed her forehead and she closed her eyes and fell back asleep.

Chapter Thirty

"Ah, I see the glow of a woman on your face," Julia said as Sam opened the door to the cabin.

She felt the flush of heat color her cheeks but didn't give in to the bait.

"You don't need to say nothin'." Julia laughed. "Your eyes say it all. So, this mean you're stayin'?"

"Yes." She didn't even try to suppress the smiles breaking out across her face.

Julia snorted and sunk into her rocking chair. "Bet Jesse was happier than a pup with two tails."

"I didn't tell him." Sam looked over at her with her nose crinkled. She never been aware of her little habits like that until Jesse pointed them out to her.

"What are you waitin' fer?" Julia folded her hands over her chest shaking her head in disapproval.

She threw up her hands. "I don't know where I am going to live or how I am going to live, yet."

"You'll live with me until you figure it out." She stood and started pulling out the water and the coffee mugs. "Now don't make that man wait any longer."

"I have to send word to the Sisters. I'm going to miss them. But this is what I want. I can't give it up because I'm a little scared, right?" She wrestled the flint from its tin above the fireplace and sparked the flame. Who would have thought she'd feel so comfortable living in a saloon girl's cabin a thousand miles from

323

Boston?

Julia slid the iron kettle above the fire. "Nope. Hold onto your dreams. For most girls that's all they have to get them through the night."

"You're right," Sam said nibbling on a warm biscuit Julia handed her.

"I know. You have to live your dreams, not the nuns' or Jesse's. Everybody gets one future. We're all equal in that way."

Sam nodded. "I spent my time waiting for J.W. to change."

"You can't put your life on hold and pick it up later. Life ain't like the Montgomery Ward catalog. It don't show up at your doorstep for you to be pickin' out what you want. You're living on the dash."

"Living on the dash?" Sam choked out.

"Yeah, you know." Julia looked at her like she was crazy not to know what she was talking about. "From the gravestone, the marker, its engraving."

Sam shook her head still having no idea what she was talking about.

"Born eighteen-hundred and sixty-eight, died nineteen-hundred and thirty whatever." Julia got up and took a photograph off her mantel. She handed to her. "All you got is the mark carved between the dates on your tombstone. That's what my ol' granny said anyway: 'Living on the dash.' You best make the most of it. And don't worry 'bout it. Nobody writes down nothin' about your life except the beginning and the end of it. Only detail they get is a dash."

Sam sank into the rocking chair. "I've never even been around a married couple, Julia."

Julia smiled again. "My grandpops, when he came

home at night, he'd look at my granny like she was a treasure. My brother and I were presents, gifts he unwrapped every night like it was Christmas. There are good men out there, and Jesse Colburn is one of them."

"I need to start making my own rules and living the way I'm comfortable without following anyone's conventions."

"Now you're thinkin' like a Westerner."

"You're right. Can I have the trousers back of that low-down son-of-a-bitch you followed out here?" Sam said with a laugh. "Think I'll put some pants on and take another look at the river before it belongs to J.W."

"Now, you're talkin' like a Westerner," Julia laughed.

"I'm gonna start living the way I want and doing what feels right without caring what anybody thinks. Then I'll find myself some work. I can sew pretty well."

"As I said, you're welcome here as long as you need."

"Thank you." Sam hugged Julia.

"Here are your pants," Julia said handing them to her. "I'll wear the other pair."

There was a sudden banging on the door.

"Open up, ladies."

Julia grabbed her pistol and aimed it at the door. She signaled to Sam to open it.

Sheriff Brown stood red-faced with sweat dripping off his chin.

"What can I do fer ya, Sheriff?" Julia asked with a slight grin across her features.

He stepped in and walked over to Sam. "Where's that man of yours?"

"J.W.?" She closed her eyes and waited for the nerves to bundle and knot in her belly, but they didn't. He wasn't her responsibility anymore. "I don't know."

"Not J.W.," the sheriff muttered wiping his forehead with his sweaty palm.

"Jesse?" She heard the pitch in her voice rise. What happened now?

"No." The sheriff let out a growl and held his head like it hurt just to talk to her.

Sam stared at the man. She only knew two men in Aspen.

"I'm talking about Wade Rush."

"He was heading out this morning, Sheriff. Why?" Julia intervened.

"Just got a telegram from Boston. Seems Miss Ward and Mr. Rush took off after a burglary."

"A burglary?" Sam gasped.

He watched her measuring her answer. "That's right. A Father Ryan's diamond and gold watch was stolen the morning you two left Boston."

"I told the nuns that Wade was with me." She turned to Julia and back to the sheriff. "I had nothing to do with the robbery."

"Yeah, the Sisters said he was acting out of character by running off. You leaving didn't surprise them, though."

Sam ignored his comment. "I haven't seen Wade since yesterday morning. He said there was a family situation."

"I liked the fella, but he's in a heap of trouble. Where was he headed?"

"California."

"Not much I can do about that. I'll have to be

returning the watch though. Good thing Colburn is innocent." He tipped his hat to leave.

"Wait, Sheriff, what happened to Luke's murderer?" Sam asked.

"Confessed—seems he's mixed up with some railroaders. Without Enchantment, his life ain't worth a dime."

He walked slowly toward the door, looking around the interior of the cabin before stepping out into the bright sun.

"I hope Wade's all right. He seemed really agitated on the train about getting to California."

"Yet the man stopped here to find you and make sure you were okay," Julia said. "Then he saved Jesse."

"Well, sometimes people are forced to steal in order to save someone they care about."

Julia laughed. "True."

"Think I'll head to the river now." Sam changed into the trousers.

"You look like a real cowboy. Where's your hat?"

"You mean Jesse's?"

"He wants you to keep it."

"I know," she said feeling a grin spread across her face.

"Good. Everythin' will work out for the best. There will come a day when the swish of a horse's tail behind you is all you'll need."

Chapter Thirty-One

Jesse unbridled Rusty and watched him run as the sun began its descent behind Aspen Mountain. This land was no longer his, but it would always be a part of him.

The heat of the sun's final rays warmed his back as he made his way to where he first met Sam. For a second he thought the sun was playing tricks on him. But then he realized Sam was there at the river pacing back and forth across the grass. She was wearing his shirt again and a man's trousers and his hat. He smiled. No matter where she ended up or where he found himself living, knowing that she wore his hat made him feel he was still a part of her life.

She had a big decision to make that was weighing on both of them.

"Sam?" A glint of sunlight reflected off a piece of metal in her hand. It was her mother's bowie knife.

"You found your knife?" A pit formed in his stomach. J.W. jumped into the river with it yesterday, and now Sam clenched it in her fingers.

She let out a loud sigh. Her eyebrows creased. He knew that look of apprehension well. Could she be thinking of returning to Boston? After last night, he thought he'd given her plenty of reasons to stay.

"I just found it here. J.W. left it for me. He knew I'd come back here." There was a flicker of longing in her voice.

He picked up a piece of straw and stuck it in his mouth twisting it around with his teeth. It was a bad habit he picked up years ago. "You should have it. It means so much to you." He sighed in relief. She was just nervous about telling him J.W. was alive.

She held out two pieces of paper. "These were attached to it." There was a hesitation in her voice.

A hole pierced each paper from the knife's blade. Jesse didn't need to read the top paper to know what it said. It was crinkled and worn, soft and yellowed. He'd read and reread that paper a hundred times. It was the deed to Enchantment.

The second paper, a letter, shook in her hands as she handed it to him.

Samantha,

I realize now that we can't live here as a family. The lien has been paid on the mortgage. Enchantment is free of debt. I want you to have it. Discover what I love about this land. Your mother feared the West. She wasn't cut out for this life. You are like her in countless ways except one. You're not afraid of anything or anyone. You are meant to be here.

~Your Father

An array of emotions twisted Jesse's gut: relief, anger, jealousy, and happiness mixed together in an instant.

Sam was watching him intently. "Say something."

"You own Enchantment Ranch."

"I can't take it."

"J.W.'s right, Sam. You do belong here."

Jesse never felt so sure of what he wanted so in control of his intentions, yet his stomach clenched at the uncertainty of what Sam was going to do.

"Jesse, I want you to have it."

"It's getting late. You need to get home before it gets too dark."

"Is that all you have to say?"

He studied his favorite time of day: dusk. Why did the sun seem the brightest when it was about to set? How could he explain that the ranch didn't even matter without her? He shifted uncomfortably and felt the heat of uncertainty spreading through his body. He cleared his throat and watched the long shadows of the trees disappear into nothingness.

"Come on, Sam, let me walk you home." He took Rusty's reins and handed her Pearl's.

"I don't think that's a good idea."

"Why not?"

"As I recall, someone said a few days ago, in this very spot, that it was a three mile walk over the most treacherous mountains you'll ever climb."

"You are impossible!" He laughed.

Sam studied the river. Its winding rocky path reminded her of her life. What did Jesse say? She was like the river softening everything in its path, especially him.

"I'm not impossible, Jesse." She dropped Pearl's reins and took his hands. "But I might be a challenge."

"I've never strayed from a challenge, Sam."

"Are you sure? I really don't think I'm going to be easy to live with," she said putting his hands to her face.

"Live with?" He shook his head. "I'm listening."

"Enchantment belongs in your family, and it needs to stay that way."

"You can't give me the ranch."

"I didn't say I was giving it to you. I said I wanted it to stay in your family," she said smiling at him.

"I want to separate one piece of land from the ranch."

"You want land?" He smiled.

"Yes." She answered carefully and arched an eyebrow.

There was something about her answer that nagged him. But he asked the question burning in his mind anyway. "Is this the piece of land you want?" He gestured toward the river.

"No, the land isn't for me."

"Who…who is it for? Not J.W.?" He sucked in a breath. The anticipation of losing her was replaced with an even worse fear: her trusting J.W. again.

She bit her lip and reached for his forearm. "No. Julia."

He nearly choked on the straw still twirling in his mouth. "Julia wants land?"

"Yes." Sam took in a deep breath. "But she can't have this piece." A smile broadened across her face. "This is our spot."

"Actually, we haven't christened this spot, yet." He took a step closer and cupped her shoulders. "I'm willing to, though. Just say the word."

She smiled and started rubbing her hands up and down her arms.

"Are you cold?" He began to rub her arms too, only faster. Intent on warming her up because he didn't want this moment to end.

"A little. The sun seems to run for cover a little quicker out here."

"You're beginning to sound like a real cowboy." He held her chin and tilted her gaze toward him. "I'll build a fire." Thankfully he always carried flint in his pocket. "But we won't make it back to Enchantment before it's too dark."

"Actually, I'm only cold because I'm nervous."

"Why are you nervous?" His voice was husky and thick.

She took a step back. "I have an idea, but I'm afraid to say it."

He regarded her with confusion. "I can't believe you're afraid of anything." He stepped forward not allowing any space between them.

Her cheeks turned rosy and her eyes twinkled with mischief and apprehension. "I want Enchantment to stay in your family."

"Sam," he cut her off, "I am not going to just take Enchantment. I want you to stay." His voice cracked, "But if you leave, I want you to know..." He glanced down at her. "Well, just say the word, and I will come and get you."

He tipped his hat and studied his leather boots. He hesitated, watching to make sure she understood him.

"What's the word?"

The surprise in his eyes made her smile.

"What did you say?" he asked.

Her heart pounded. She cupped her hands to her mouth and yelled, "I said, what's the—"

Before she could finish, Jesse pulled her close crushing her to him and smothered her mouth with his.

She pulled back and extended her arms, her fingers taut against his chest. "I will only stay if Enchantment stays in the Colburn family.

"Sam—"

She clapped her hand over his mouth commanding him to stop talking. "Will you marry me, Jesse?"

His eyes grew wide. He grasped her arms in his hands and leaned his forehead against hers. "You're asking me to marry you?"

The blush of her cheeks spread to a sheen in her eyes. "Yes."

"Didn't those books teach you about propriety?" He rubbed his forehead against hers.

She pulled back. "You're expecting propriety?"

"No, I want you." He smiled.

"Okay, because those books did say something about no love making before marriage."

"You're right," he said. "You aren't going to be easy to live with."

She laughed.

"Are you sure?" He held her at an arm's distance studying her face. "Are you sure you want to get married?"

"I never felt at home anywhere until now. Here, in Aspen. Here, with you."

He reached for her with a look as if he were standing on the edge of a cliff. He slowly cupped her chin. He was reading her eyes, silently searching for a sign of regret, but it wasn't there. She had no regrets, no fears, only hope and happiness.

"Yes, I'm sure." She grabbed his collar and twisted it as she pulled him in for kiss. "Now I decide where to hang my hat."

"Your hat?" he said with a wink.

A word about the author...

Kathryn E. Crawford lives in Massachusetts with her loving and very patient husband and their three wonderful children. She enjoys reading and writing romance novels while sipping red wine and devouring chocolate.

Kathryn writes historical western and new adult romance novels.

After her brother's wedding in Aspen, Colorado, she immediately fell in love with the landscape and mystery of the Rocky Mountains. She knew she had to write a novel capturing the beauty of Aspen and it's romantic yet ruthless legendary history.

CPSIA information can be obtained
at www.ICGtesting.com
Printed in the USA
BVHW040218070520
579347BV00015B/657